DIXIE GHOSTS

D1279767

Volumes in the American Ghosts series:

DIXIE GHOSTS

Haunting, Spine-chilling Stories
from the American South

Edited by
Frank D. McSherry, Jr., Charles G. Waugh,
and Martin H. Greenberg

Rutledge Hill Press
Nashville, Tennessee

Published in Nashville, Tennessee, by Rutledge Hill Press, Inc., 211
Seventh Avenue North, Nashville, Tennessee 37219

Typography by Bailey Typography, Nashville, Tennessee
Cover design by Harriette Bateman

Library of Congress Cataloging-in-Publication Data

Dixie ghosts.

  1. Ghost stories, American — Southern States.
2. Southern States — Fiction. I. McSherry, Frank D.
II. Waugh, Charles, III. Greenberg, Martin Harry.
PS648.G48D5 1988   813'.0872   88-1991
ISBN 0-934395-73-X

Manufactured in the United States of America
      6 7 8 — 94

Table of Contents

From the Misty Dark

"Here we are, alone, in this shadowy house. . . . *Fred! Who's that behind you?*"

Ghosts.

Here they come. Stalking through the ages. Thin, filmy things in white rustling down dark halls on windy nights or sitting across from you in broad daylight—real as roast beef—until they disappear into thin air. The dead who return. . . .

Are they hallucinations? Shakespeare called them "daggers of the mind proceeding from the heat-oppressed brain." Or are they evidence that the universe we live in may be stranger than we know?

Ghosts have appeared in literature as long as writing has existed. From the lore of primitive tribesmen, to the ancient Greeks and Homer whose hero Ulysses crossed the underground river to the land of ghosts, to Pliny the Younger who told of haunted houses in Rome, to the Renaissance and the poet Dante who sang of ghosts, they have evoked a fascination in writer and reader alike.

Who can forget Shakespeare's scene in which the Prince of Denmark mounts the castle walls to confront the dreadful thing (the image of his dead father) that walks the starlit battlements, only to learn of a secret murder? Or Macbeth, and he alone, seeing the ghost of the man he had killed (his former friend and general Banquo) appear at the royal feast and sit down in Macbeth's royal chair?

And for good reason. Ghosts act with a purpose. Some writers suggest, or imply, that those who see the ghosts do, too, that some inner need calls the ghost to them.

Perhaps. We do not know.

If ghosts represent unfinished business—love and hate—so important that death itself cannot bar the way to its completion, then we can see why the ghost stories gathered here gain from being placed in one of the most romantic settings imaginable, the American South.

The South is haunted by more than ghosts. For all its renowned natural beauty, the South is haunted by a history of horrors the rest of the nation has never known. No other Americans have been so bloodily defeated in war, endured an army of occupation or struggled with the costs of slavery and its aftermath. No other Americans have been controlled by a code of honor that made compromise in anything almost impossible or have seen their economic strength shattered for generations. There is a darkness in the heart of the land.

In commenting on the South, horror writer Robert Mc-Cammon said that in spite of its beauty and greatness, there was a loneliness in the South that goes back to the "cultured" civilization—with all its contradictions—destroyed in the Civil War: "great lavish balls and plantations and lynchings and unspeakable brutalities, genteel culture and horrid secrets of blood and birth all mingled together." Perhaps, as he suggests, this past holds a great power over literature of the supernatural.

Though it is changing, the old South—with its unfinished business—is a land made for ghosts and literature. The collection of stories presented in DIXIE GHOSTS has the power to produce shudders like a cold breeze on a hot night that precedes the coming of the storm.

See for yourself.

—Frank D. McSherry, Jr.
McAlester, Oklahoma

Acknowledgments

"Wish You Were Here"—Copyright © 1965 by Richard Hardwick. Reprinted by permission of the Scott Meredith Literary Agency, Inc., 845 Third Avenue, New York, NY 10022

"Drawer 14"—Copyright © 1965 by H. S. D. Publications. Reprinted by permission of the author.

"Poor Little Saturday"—Copyright © 1956 by King-Size Publications, Inc. Reprinted by permission of Lescher & Lescher, Ltd.

"Dead Man's Story"—Copyright © 1938 by Howard Rigsby. First appeared in *Argosy* Magazine as "I'll Be Glad When You're Dead." Reprinted by permission of John Hawkins Associates, Inc.

"One Foot in the Grave"—Copyright © 1948 by *Weird Tales*. Reprinted by permission of Kirby McCauley, Ltd.

"The Guns of William Longley"—Copyright © 1967 by Fawcett Publications, Inc. Reprinted by permission of Brandt & Brandt Literary Agents, Inc.

"The Stormsong Runner"—Copyright © 1979, 1986 by Jack L. Chalker. Reprinted by permission of the author.

"What of the Night"—Copyright © 1980 by Mercury Press, Inc. From *The Magazine of Fantasy and Science Fiction*. Reprinted by permission of Karl Edward Wagner, Literary Executor for Manly Wade Wellman.

DIXIE GHOSTS

While the postman brought Buzzy final notices from Ace TV, he brought Charlie letters from his dead wife. . . .

ONE

Wish You Were Here
Richard Hardwick

The idiosyncrasies of most people end with death and are only rarely recalled afterward, with decreasing frequency and accuracy, in reminiscences of their friends and acquaintances. Martha Adamson, however, true to her form in life, was not like most people in death. Or so it seemed. She was still a bit on the peculiar side.

Charlie Adamson came to me scarcely a month after his wife's funeral. He was pale, and though the afternoon was cool after the rains we had been having almost daily, a fine beading of perspiration stood out on his forehead.

"Buzzy," he said, plopping down in one of the rockers on my porch. My real name is Henry Busby, but as far back as I can remember folks have just called me "Buzzy." "Buzzy," said Charlie, "you knew Martha as well as anybody, including myself. Would you say she might have had any . . . any odd powers?"

"Depends on what you mean by odd, Charlie," I said as diplomatically as possible. I hauled out the old briar and dug it down into the tobacco pouch.

"Well," Charlie went on, "let me ask you something else. Do you believe there's a life after death?"

"I suppose I do. What are you getting at?"

He reached quickly into the inside pocket of his well-tailored suit and pulled out an envelope. "Just this! If I didn't know Martha's handwriting, I'd say somebody was pulling a pretty lousy joke on me, and one in darned poor taste!"

He shoved the envelope, a squarish pink one, at me. I took it and plucked out the letter. It was short, and having

1

known Martha all of her forty-seven years on this earth, I immediately recognized her neat, prim hand. It read, without salutation or signature, as follows:

The grave is fine, Charles, dear. Wish you were here.

I clamped the pipe between my teeth and laid the letter on my lap while I struck a match. I puffed a little blue cloud and picked up the letter again.

"It sure looks like her handwriting," I said. "How'd you get it?"

"Look at the envelope! Postmarked right here in Binsville yesterday! Came in the regular delivery today."

"In that case, Charlie," I said, giving the letter back to him, "I'd say you hit the nail on the head. Somebody is pulling a pretty lousy joke on you."

He shook his head vehemently. "That's her handwriting, Buzzy! I'd know it anywhere!"

"There are such things as forgeries. And there are people around this town who would go to pretty good lengths to put a fright into you."

"What do you mean by that?"

I leaned back and puffed on the pipe, then I turned and looked him squarely in the eye. "We've known each other ever since you came here about twenty years ago, haven't we, Charlie?"

"It's twenty-five years, Buzzy, and yes, we have. Fact is, Martha and I didn't have a closer friend in Binsville than you."

"All right. So let's stop pussyfooting around. Some folks think you killed Martha."

"She was killed when the car ran off the road and hit that tree south of town!"

"Sure she was. That's exactly what the official death certificate said. Death by accident."

He stuffed the letter back into his pocket. "You were the first one to come along after the wreck. People trust you, Buzzy. You testified at the inquest that Martha was dead and I was unconscious. Why would anybody think I killed her?"

I reached over casually and took the corner of his jacket lapel and rubbed the rich material slowly between my thumb and forefinger. "How many men in this whole country can afford a suit like that? Two hundred and fifty if it cost a penny."

"Three hundred and a quarter," he said dully, slumping back in the rocker. "For her money, is that it?"

"In a nutshell."

He stood up suddenly, straight as a ramrod, jaws knotting. "That still don't satisfy me about the letter! I'm going to have a handwriting expert examine it!"

I saw Charlie again three days later. He had been up to Atlanta, he said, and from the looks of him he had doubled his intake of gin while maybe halving the vermouth. Charlie was one of those martini men. Very dry.

"Well?" I said.

He sighed. "I took all kinds of samples of her handwriting—checks, letters, grocery lists. Went to three different experts, and every one of them is ready to stake his reputation that Martha wrote that letter, no doubt about it."

Just about then old Mr. Grubb, the postman, came through my gate, stumbled around the empty cans and trash, and gave me the usual assortment of bills and occupant throwaways.

"Might as well save myself a trip up that driveway of yours, Mr. Adamson," he said to Charlie. "Here's a few things for you."

I had barely opened the bill from the Ace TV shop and glimpsed the blood-red stamp that read "LAST WARNING" and something about legal action, when Charlie let out a little squeak and dropped his mail to the porch floor.

"What's the matter?"

"It's—it's—"

Perspiration was popping out of his forehead like sap out of a skinned pine, and his eyes were sort of starting from the sockets. There was one letter still clutched in his hand, and I reached over and took it.

It was the same handwriting, on the same pink stationery.

Charles Dear [Martha had called him that from the beginning],

Please—please have some drain tile installed at the foot of the hill below the sycamore tree! With all this rain I have been positively afloat for the past week! The beautiful silk lining of the casket is all moldy and my blue organdy is absolutely ruined! Please, Charles dear, have this done without delay. Mr. Fenwick should give you a good price.

Your,
Martha

I got up and went into the house and brought out a half-empty bottle of vodka that had been in the cabinet for months. Charlie didn't even wait for me to go back for a glass.

I put Charlie Adamson in my bed that night and I slept on the couch. He had sent me on an urgent mission up the hill to his place for gin and vermouth after the vodka was gone, and by the time he had his fill of his favorite beverage, there was nothing left to do but drag him off to bed. I never could have gotten him up the hill by myself.

As I was tucking him in, I looked at his slack face and I could not help recalling the night of the wreck. He had looked the same then, except for a small streak of blood where his head had hit the steering wheel. It really hadn't been a bad wreck. Charlie couldn't have been going more than twenty or so when they hit that oil slick and whammed into the tree.

That was what got the talk started. Charlie had been little more than stunned, but Martha had received a massive skull fracture that killed her outright, apparently when she went forward into the dashboard. Folks with suspicious turns of mind whispered around that Charlie had set the whole thing up and killed her after purposely running the car into a tree.

Of course, there was no proof, but if it hadn't been for me, it might have looked pretty bad for him in a circumstantial way. Most of these same old folks could remember back when I was courting Martha. She was Martha Malone then, the only child of old man A. D. Malone, rest his soul, who owned something like half the land in the whole county. The good half.

Naturally, I was more than a little shaken up when Charlie Adamson came down from Atlanta on some kind of business with old man A. D., met Martha, and, within a month, married her. I had already made pretty detailed plans for my life as a country gentleman, bringing back the glory that once was the Busbys'.

Folks knew I had to be telling the truth when I said I saw the wreck happen, and when I got to the car Charlie was unconscious and Martha was dead.

After getting that second letter and drinking so much vodka and gin, Charlie declined the offer to join me for breakfast next morning. I sat there at my little table near the woodstove and had a big plate of grits and sidemeat and three eggs, sunny-side up and soft as baby oysters.

"Charlie," I said, stirring the eggs into the grits, "don't you think you ought to go to the police about this?"

He stumbled across from the bed to the sideboard where the gin bottle stood from the night before. He poured a hefty slug into a dirty glass, and without so much as uncorking the vermouth, turned it up. It seemed to steady him a bit after a few moments, and he came and sat down at the table.

"What would I tell them, Buzzy? That—that my dear departed wife is writing me letters from the cemetery?" He shook his head and poured another three fingers. "No thanks!"

Charlie went, like they say, from bad to worse after that. He drank night and day, and entirely stopped shaving or combing his hair. His three-hundred-and-twenty-five-dollar suit grew splotched and wrinkled, and anybody who didn't know him would have taken Charlie for a bum.

He came staggering down the hill almost every day to my place, bringing his bottle along with him. Whenever old Mr. Grubb happened by while he was there, Charlie would duck into the house and he wouldn't come out till the postman had delivered my mail and gone on.

It must have been about ten days after he got the letter about the drain tile. Charlie, as usual, was sitting in the rocker with a big dent in a bottle of gin. He didn't see old Grubb till he was standing right there in front of us.

"Well, hello there, Mr. Adamson," the postman said. He handed me Ace TV's positively and absolutely final notice and then with a little lick of his thumb he drew a pink envelope out of his bag and pushed it into Charlie's shaking hands. "Save me a trip up that driveway of yours."

Charlie just sat there for the next five minutes, staring open-mouthed at the letter. When I saw that's all he could do, I reached over and took it. It was another one from Martha, alright, and I read it to him. She thanked him for the drain tile (Charlie had called Mr. Fenwick about it the very next day after getting the letter) and went on to register a complaint about the worms. She asked him to check with Cal Lumpkin at the nursery about what might get rid of them. She went on to say how they tickled and she couldn't scratch.

That was the end of the line for Charlie Adamson. He left the gin bottle, empty, there on the porch and hightailed a crooked line up the hill. It wasn't more than two or three minutes before I heard the gun go off up there in the big house. It sounded to me like both barrels at once.

I sat there rocking slowly back and forth, and after a while I smiled. I never had been much for smiling, especially after Charlie and Martha went off on what I figured would be my honeymoon.

Just about everybody's got a weakness, I figure. Martha's was being a little on the peculiar side. Charlie's, if he had one, was dry martinis. I think mine was revenge. I started planning it fifteen years ago when I tossed that handful of rice after the newlyweds.

When they came back I acted like the same old Buzzy, and as the years went by both of them would come to me with their little problems. I was always a real good listener. I found that in between nods a good listener can get in a few licks of his own. So gradually, just a little at a time, I worked Martha around to believing that Charlie might try to kill her some day. After that, I kind of slipped her the idea of writing a series of letters from the grave, as it were, and letting me keep them. I promised her that if anything suspicious ever happened to her, and Charlie wasn't punished, I'd start mailing the letters. Martha wrote nearly sixty of them in all, fitted for dry weather, cold, hot, just about everything. Some were real corkers. I burned what was left after Charlie shot himself.

That finished the last half of my revenge. The night I found Charlie and Martha in the wreck, I had the first half of it. I killed Martha that night. I felt I ought to drag it out for my dear old pal Charlie.

Charlie has been dead a month now and is buried out there on the hillside next to Martha. That big shady old sycamore is over them. That should have been the end of it. But it wasn't. Old Mr. Grubb came by about fifteen minutes ago, and there, mixed in with the advertisements and bills, was a little pink envelope with a faint perfumey smell. There was a short, friendly note inside. It went like this:

> You naughty, naughty Buzzy-Wuzzy [Martha was the only one who ever called me that.] Who would have ever thought it of you! But Charles dear and I have agreed to be charitable and let bygones be bygones. We know you must be lonesome without us. The Busby plot is right next to the Malones', so you just hurry on out, and it'll be like old times. Just the three of us . . .
>
> Martha

I know I had a bottle of vodka around here someplace. I must invite old Mr. Grubbs to share it with me.

Born in Georgia in 1923, Richard Hardwick was educated at Emory University and the University of Georgia. During World War II, he served as a Japanese-English interpreter for the army. Since 1960 he has been a freelance writer, largely of short mysteries to the leading magazines in the field, including Ellery Queen's Mystery Magazine, Manhunt, *and* Alfred Hitchcock's Mystery Magazine, *in addition to books for young adults, non-fiction, and true crime. His best known mysteries are* The Plotters *(1965) and* Tis the Season to Be Deadly *(1966).*

TWO

Drawer 14
Talmage Powell

No cracks about my job, please. I've already taken more than enough ribbing from campus cutups. I don't relish being night attendant at the Asheville city morgue, but there are compensations.

For one thing, the job gave me a chance to complete my college work in daytime and do considerable studying at night between catnaps and the light, routine duties.

In their tagged and numbered drawers, the occupants weren't going to disturb me while I was cracking a brain cell on a problem in calculus. Or so I thought.

This particular night I relieved Olaf Daly, like always. Olaf was a man stuck with a job because of his age and a game leg. He lived each day only for the moment when he could flee his profession, as it were. Like always, he grunted a hello and a goodbye in the same breath, the game leg assisting him out of the morgue with surprising alacrity.

Alone in the deep silence of the anteroom, I dropped my thermos, transistor radio, and a couple of textbooks on the desk. I pulled the heavy record book toward me to give it a rundown.

Olaf had made his daily entries in his neat, spidery handwriting. Male victim of drowning. Man and woman dead in auto crash. Wino who didn't wake up when his bed caught fire. Male loser of a knife fight. Woman found dead in river.

Olaf's day had been routine. Nothing had come in like the dilly of last week.

She had been a pitiful, dirty, lonely old woman who had lived in a hovel. Crazy as a scorched moth, she had slipped into a dream world where she wasn't dirty, or old, or for-saken at all. Instead, she had believed she was the Fourth Witch of Endor, with power over the forces of darkness.

The slum section being a breeding ground for ignorance and superstition, some of her neighbors had taken the Fourth Witch of Endor seriously. She had looked the part, with a skull-like face, a beaked nose with a wart on the end, a toothless mouth accenting a long and pointed chin, and strings of dirty hair hanging lank about her sunken cheeks. She had eked out a half-starved living by telling fortunes, performing incantations, predicting winning numbers, and selling love potions and spells. To her credit, she never had gone in for the evil eye, her neighbors reported. If she couldn't put a good hex on a person, she had refused to hex him at all.

On a very hot and humid night, the Fourth Witch of En-dor had mounted the roof of her tenement. Nobody knew for sure whether she had slipped or maybe taken a crack at flying to the full moon. Anyhow, she had been scraped off the asphalt six stories below, brought here, and deposited in drawer 14. She had lain in the refrigerated cubicle for four days before an immaculate son had flown in from a distant state to claim the body.

She hadn't departed a moment too soon for Olaf Daly. "I swear," the old man had said, "there's a hint of a smell at drawer 14, like you'd figure sulphur and brimstone to smell."

I hadn't noticed. The only smells assailing my nostrils were those in a chem lab where I was trying hard to keep up with the class.

I turned from the record book for a routine tour of the building.

Lighted brightly, the adjoining room was large, chill, and barren. The floor was spotless gray tile with a faint, antisep-tic aroma. Across the room was the double doorway to the outside ramp where the customers were brought in. Near the door was the long, narrow, marble-topped table mounted on casters. Happily, it was empty at the moment, scrubbed clean, waiting for inevitable use. The refrigeration equipment made a low, whispering sound, more felt than heard.

To my right, like an outsized honeycomb, was the bank of drawers where the dead were kept for the claiming, or eventual burial at city expense.

Each occupied drawer was tagged, like with a shipping ticket or baggage check, the tag being attached with thin wire to the proper drawer handle when the body was checked in.

I whistled softly between my teeth, just for the sake of having some sound, as I started checking the tags against my mental tally from the record book.

As I neared drawer 14, I caught myself on the point of sniffing. Instead of sniffing, I snorted. "That Olaf Daly." I muttered. "He and his smell of sulphur and brimstone!"

A couple steps past drawer 14 I rocked up on my toes, turned my head, then my whole body around.

Olaf had not listed an occupant for drawer 14, but the handle was tagged. I bent forward slightly, reached. The whistle sort of dripped to nothing off my lips.

I turned the tag over casually the first time; then a second and third time, considerably faster.

I straightened and gave my scalp a scratch. Both sides of the tag were blank. Olaf was old, but far from senile. This wasn't like him at all, forgetting to fill in a drawer tag.

Then I half grinned to myself. The old coot was playing a joke on me. I didn't know he had it in him.

The whistle returned to my lips with a wise note, but not exactly appreciative. I took hold of the handle and gave it a yank. The drawer slid open on its rollers. The whistle keened to a thin wail and broke.

The girl in the drawer was young. She was blonde. She was beautiful, even in death.

I stood looking at her with my toes curling away from the soles of my shoes. The features of her face were lovely, the skin like pale tan satin. Her eyes were closed as if she were merely sleeping, her long lashes like dark shadows. She was clothed in a white nylon uniform with a nurse's pin on the collar. The only personal adornment was an I.D. bracelet of delicate golden chain and plaque. The plaque was engraved with initials: Z. L.

I broke my gaze away from the blonde girl and hurried back to the anteroom. At the desk, I jerked the record book toward me. I didn't want to misjudge old man Daly.

11

I moved my finger down the day's entries. Hesitated. Repeated the process. Went to the previous day by turning a page. Then to the day before that. Nobody, definitely, had been registered in drawer 14.

I puckered, but couldn't find a whistle as I turned again to the door of the morgue room. There was a glass section in the upper portion of the door. I looked through the glass. I didn't have to open the door. I'd left drawer 14 extended, and blonde Z. L. was still there, bigger than life, as big as death.

Carefully, I sat down at the desk, took out my handkerchief, wiped my forehead.

I took a long, deliberate breath, picked up the phone and dialed Olaf Daly's number. While his phone rang, I sneaked a glance in the direction of the morgue room.

Olaf's wife answered sleepily, along about the sixth or seventh ring. No, I couldn't speak to Olaf because he hadn't come home yet.

Then she added suddenly, in a kindlier tone, "Just a minute. I think I hear him coming now."

Olaf got on the line with a clearing of his throat. "Yah, what is it?"

"This is Tully Branson, Mr. Daly."

"I ain't available for stand-in duty if some of your college pals have cracked a keg someplace."

"No, sir," I said. "I understand, Mr. Daly. It's just that I need the information on the girl in drawer 14."

"Ain't nobody in drawer 14, Tully."

"Yes, sir. There's a girl in drawer 14. A blonde girl, Mr. Daly, far too young and nice looking to have to die. I'm sure you remember. Only you forgot the record book when she was brought in."

I heard Mrs. Daly asking Olaf what was it. The timber of his voice changed as he spoke in the direction of his wife. "I think young Branson brought straight whisky in his thermos tonight."

"No, sir," I barked at Olaf. "I need it, but I haven't got any whisky. All I've got is a dead blonde girl in drawer 14 that you forgot to make a record of."

"How could I do a thing like that?" Olaf demanded.

"I don't know," I said, "but you did. She's right here. If you don't believe me, come down and have a look."

"I think I'll do just that, son! You're accusing me of a mighty serious thing!"

He slammed the phone down so hard it stabbed me in the eardrum. I hung up with a studied gentleness, lighted a cigarette, poured some coffee from the thermos, lighted a cigarette, took a sip of coffee, and lighted a cigarette.

I had another swallow of coffee, reached for the package, and discovered I already had three cigarettes spiraling smoke from the ashtray. I gave myself a sickly grin and butted out two of the cigarettes to save for later.

With his game leg, Olaf arrived with the motion of a schooner mast on a stormy sea. I returned his glare with a smile that held what smug assurance I was able to muster. Then I bowed him into the morgue room.

He went through the swinging door, with me following closely. Drawer 14 was still extended. He didn't bother to cross all the way to it. Instead, after one look, he whirled on me.

"Branson," he snarled in rage, "if I was twenty years younger I'd bust your nose! You got a nerve, dragging a tired old man back to this stinking place. And just when I'd decided you was one of the nicer members of the younger generation too!"

"But Mr. Daly . . ."

"Don't 'but' me, you young pup! I'll put you on report for this!"

I took another frantic look at drawer 14. She was there, plain as anything. Blonde, and beautiful, and dead.

Olaf started past me, shoving me aside. I caught hold of his arm. I was chicken—and just about ready to molt. "Old man," I yelled, "you see her. I know you do!"

"Get your mitts offa me," he yelled back. "I see exactly what's there. I see an empty drawer. About as empty as your head."

I clutched his arm, not wanting to let go. "I don't know what kind of joke this is . . ."

"And neither do I," he said, shouting me down. "But it's a mighty poor one!"

"Then look at that drawer, old man, and quit horsing around."

"I've looked all I need to. Nothing but an overgrown juvenile delinquent would think up such a shoddy trick to oust a poor old man out of his house!"

He jerked his arm free of my grip, stormed through the door, past the anteroom. At the front door of the building, which was down a short corridor, he stopped, turned, and shook his finger at me.

"You cruel young crumb," he said, "you better start looking for another job tomorrow, if I have anything to do with it!" With that, he was gone.

I'd followed him as far as the anteroom. I turned slowly, looked through the glass pane into the morgue room. A dismal groan came from me. Z. L. still occupied drawer 14.

"Be a good girl," I heard myself mumbling, "and go away. I'll close my eyes, and you just go away."

I closed my eyes, opened them. But she hadn't gone away.

I groped to the desk chair and collapsed. I didn't sit long, on account of a sudden flurry of business which was announced by the buzzer at the service door.

The skirling sound, coming suddenly, lifted me a couple feet off the desk chair. When I came down, I was legging it across the morgue room.

Smith and Macklin, from the meat wagon, were sliding an old guy in tattered clothing from a stretcher to the marble-topped table.

"He walked in front of a truck," Smith said.

"No I.D.," Macklin said. "Ice him as a John Doe."

"Kinda messy, ain't he, Branson?" Smith grinned at me as he pulled the sheet over the John Doe. Smith was always egging me because he knew my stomach wasn't the strongest.

"Yeah," I said. "Kinda." I blew some sweat off my upper lip. "Not like the girl. No marks on her."

"Girl?"

"Sure," a note of eagerness slipped into my voice. "The beautiful blonde. The one in drawer 14."

Smith and Macklin both looked at the open, extended drawer. Then they looked at each other.

14

"Tully, old boy," Macklin said, "how you feeling these days?"

"Fine," I said, a strip of ice forming where my forehead was wrinkling.

"No trouble sleeping? No recurrent nightmares?"

"Nope," I said. "But the blonde in 14 . . . if you didn't bring her in, then maybe Collins and Snavely can give me the rundown on her."

Smith and Macklin sort of edged from me. Then Smith's guffaw broke the morgue stillness. "Beautiful blonde, drawer 14, where the poor old demented woman was . . . Sure, Branson, I get it."

Macklin looked at his partner uncertainly. "You do?"

"Simple," Smith said, sounding relieved. "Old Tully here gets bored. Just thought up a little gag to rib us, huh, Tully?"

It was obvious they didn't see the girl and weren't going to see her. If I insisted, I knew suddenly, I was just asking for trouble. So I let out a laugh about as strong as skimmed milk. "Sure," I said. "Got to while away the tedium, you know."

Smith punched me in the ribs with his elbow. "Don't let your corpses get warm, Tully old pal." He departed with another belly laugh. But Macklin was still throwing worried looks over his shoulder at me as he followed Smith out.

I hated to see the outside door close behind them. I sure needed some company. For the first time, being the only living thing in the morgue caused my stomach to shrink to the size of a cold, wrinkled prune.

I skirted drawer 14 like I was crossing a deep gorge on a bridge made of brittle glass.

"Go away," I muttered to Z. L. "You're not real. Not even a dead body. Just a—an *image* that nobody can see but me. So go away!"

My words had no effect whatever on the image. They merely frightened me a little when I caught the tone in which I was conversing with a nonexistent dead body.

Back at the anteroom desk, I sat and shivered for several seconds. Then an idea glimmered encouragingly in my mind. Maybe Olaf Daly, Smith, and Macklin were all in on the gag. Maybe Z. L. had been brought in by Collins and Snavely, who tooled the meat wagon on the dayshift, and

15

everybody had thought it would be a good joke to scare the pants off the bright young college man.

Feeling slightly better, I reached for the phone and called Judd Lawrence. A golfing pal of my father's, Judd was a plainclothes detective attached to homicide. He'd always seemed to think well of me; had, in fact, recommended me for the job here.

Judd wasn't home. He was pulling a three-to-eleven P.M. tour of duty. I placed a second call to police headquarters. Judd had signed out, but they caught him in the locker room.

"Tully Branson, Mr. Lawrence."

"How goes it, Tully?"

"I got a problem."

"Shoot." There was no hesitation in his big, hearty voice.

"Well, uh . . . seems like the record is messed up on one of our transients. A girl. Blonde girl. A nurse. Her initials are Z. L."

"You ought to call Olaf Daly, Tully."

"Yes, sir. But you know how Olaf is when he gets away from here. Anyhow, he's in dreamland by this time and I sure hate to get him riled up. He gets real nasty."

Judd boomed a laugh. "Can't say that I blame him. That all you've got on the girl?"

"Just what I've given you. She's certainly no derelict, furthest thing in the world from that. Girl like her, dead from natural causes, would be in a private funeral home, not here."

"So the fact that she's in the morgue means she died violently," Judd said.

"I guess it has to mean that."

"Murder?"

"Can't think of anything else," I said. "It has to be a death under suspicious circumstances."

"Okay, Tully. I'll see what I can turn up for you."

"Sure hate to put you to the trouble."

"Trouble?" he said. "No trouble. Couple phone calls is all it should take."

"I sure appreciate it, Mr. Lawrence."

I hung up. While I was waiting for Judd Lawrence to call me back, I sneaked to the door of the morgue room and let my gaze creep to the glass pane to make sure the image was still in drawer 14.

It was. I shuffled back to the desk, feeling like I was a tired old man.

When the phone rang finally, I snatched it up. "City morgue. Tully Branson speaking."

"Judd here, Tully."

"Did you . . ."

"Negative from homicide, Tully. No blondes with initials Z. L., female, have been murdered in the last twenty-four hour period."

"Oh," I said, gagging, giving vent to a moan of real anguish.

"Checked with nurse's registry," Judd was saying. "There is a nurse answering your description. Young, blonde, just finished training. Her name is Zella Langtry. Lives at 711 Eastland Avenue. She recently went to work at City Hospital. But if any violence occurred to her, it's been in the past half-hour. She just checked off duty when the graveyard shift reported on."

His words, coupled with the image in drawer 14, left one crazy, wild possibility. The inspiration was so weird it turned the hair on my scalp to needles.

"Mr. Lawrence, I have the most terrible feeling Zella Langtry will never reach home alive."

"What is that? What are you saying, Tully?"

"The Fourth Witch of Endor . . ." I gabbled. "She was a kindly soul at heart. Never put a bad hex on anybody. Just good ones."

"What in the blathering world are you carrying on about?" Judd asked sharply. "Tully, you been drinking?"

"No, sir."

"Feel all right?"

"I—uh . . . Yes, sir, and thanks a lot, Mr. Lawrence."

Twenty minutes later, my jalopy rolled to a stop on Eastland Avenue. I got out, started walking along looking for numbers. I knew I was in the right block, and I located number 711 easily enough. It was a small, white cottage with a skimpy yard that attempted to look more wholesome than its lower-class surroundings.

The place was dark, quiet, peaceful.

I was standing there feeling like seventy kinds of fool when the whir of a diesel engine at the street intersection caught my attention. I looked toward the sound, saw a municipal bus lumbering away.

From the shadows of a straggly maple tree, I watched the shadowy figure of a girl coming along Eastland in my direction. But she wasn't the only passenger who had got off the bus. Behind her was a taller, heavier shadow, that of a man. My breathing thinned as I took in the scene.

She realized he was behind her. She started walking faster. So did the man. She looked over her shoulder. She stepped up the pace even more, almost running now.

The man's shoes slapped quick and hard against the sidewalk. The girl's scream was choked off as the man slammed against her.

They were struggling on the sidewalk, the man locking her throat in the crook of his elbow, the girl writhing and kicking.

I went from under the maple tree like invisible trumpets were urging me on with a blood-rousing fanfare. The man heard me coming, released the girl. I piled into him with a shoulder in his midsection.

He brought a knee up hard. It caught me on the point of the chin. I sat down on the sidewalk, and the man turned and ran away.

Firm but gentle hands helped me to my feet. I looked into the eyes of Zella Langtry for the first time. They were very nice, smoky and grateful in the shadowy night.

"You all right?" I asked, getting my breath back.

"I am now, thanks to you. And you?"

"Fine," I said. "Just fine now."

She was regaining her composure. "Lucky thing for me you were around at the right moment!"

"I—uh—just happened to be passing," I said. "Maybe I'd better walk you to your destination. Won't do any good to report that guy now. Didn't get a look at him. Never would catch him."

"I was going home," she said. "I live just down the street."

We walked along, and she told me her name was Zella, and I told her mine was Tully. When we got to her front door, we looked at each other, and I asked if I could call her some time, and she said any time a phone was handy.

I watched her go inside. I was whistling as I returned to the jalopy.

Inside the morgue, I headed straight for drawer 14. If my theory was correct, the image of Zella Langtry wouldn't be in the drawer, now that she had been rescued from the jaws of death, as it were.

I stood at drawer 14, taking a good, long look. My theory was right as far as it went.

The image of Zella Langtry was no longer in the drawer. The new one was quite a lovely redhead.

The author of more than six hundred short stories, mostly mystery and suspense, Talmage Powell was born in North Carolina in 1920. Except for a short stint as police reporter, he has been a professional writer all his life. His first novel, The Smasher, *appeared in 1959; his Florida private eye, Ed Rivers, stars in five novels, including* The Girl's Number Doesn't Answer *(1959). His fast-moving stories are ingenious and frequently peopled with a large cast of characters.*

There was more than one way to look at the lonely witch woman in the sleepy south Georgia town who befriended the little boy who haunted the lonely plantation. . . .

THREE

Poor Little Saturday
Madeleine L'Engle

The witch woman lived in a deserted, boarded-up plantation house, and nobody knew about her but me. Nobody in the nosey little town in south Georgia where I lived when I was a boy knew that if you walked down the dusty main street to where the post office ended it, and then turned left and followed that road a piece until you got to the rusty iron gates of the drive to the plantation house, you could find goings on would make your eyes pop out. It was just luck that I found out. Or maybe it wasn't luck at all. Maybe the witch woman wanted me to find out because of Alexandra. But now I wish I hadn't because the witch woman and Alexandra are gone forever and it's much worse than if I'd never known them.

Nobody'd lived in the plantation house since the Civil War when Colonel Londermaine was killed and Alexandra Londermaine, his beautiful young wife, hung herself on the chandelier in the ball room. A while before I was born some northerners bought it but after a few years they stopped coming and people said it was because the house was haunted. Every few years a gang of boys or men would set out to explore the house but nobody ever found anything, and it was so well boarded up it was hard to force an entrance, so by and by the town lost interest in it. No one climbed the wall and wandered around the grounds except me.

I used to go there often during the summer because I had bad spells of malaria when sometimes I couldn't bear to lie on the iron bedstead in my room with the flies buzzing

21

around my face, or out on the hammock on the porch with the screams and laughter of the other kids as they played torturing my ears. My aching head made it impossible for me to read, and I would drag myself down the road, scuffling my bare sunburned toes in the dust, wearing the tattered straw hat that was supposed to protect me from the heat of the sun, shivering and sweating by turns. Sometimes it would seem hours before I got to the iron gates near which the brick wall was lowest. Often I would have to lie panting on the tall prickly grass for minutes until I gathered strength to scale the wall and drop down on the other side.

But once inside the grounds it seemed cooler. One funny thing about my chills was that I didn't seem to shiver nearly as much when I could keep cool as I did at home where even the walls and the floors, if you touched them, were hot. The grounds were filled with live oaks that had grown up unchecked everywhere and afforded an almost continuous green shade. The ground was covered with ferns which were soft and cool to lie on, and when I flung myself down on my back and looked up, the roof of leaves was so thick that sometimes I couldn't see the sky at all. The sun that managed to filter through lost its bright pitiless glare and came in soft yellow shafts that didn't burn you when they touched you.

One afternoon, a scorcher early in September, which is usually our hottest month (and by then you're fagged out by the heat anyhow), I set out for the plantation. The heat lay coiled and shimmering on the road. When you looked at anything through it, it was like looking through a defective pane of glass. The dirt road was so hot that it burned even through my calloused feet and as I walked clouds of dust rose in front of me and mixed with the shimmying of the heat. I thought I'd never make the plantation. Sweat was running into my eyes but it was cold sweat, and I was shivering so that my teeth chattered as I walked. When I managed finally to fling myself down on my soft green bed of ferns inside the grounds I was seized with one of the worst chills I'd ever had in spite of the fact that my mother had given me an extra dose of quinine that morning and some 666 Malaria Medicine to boot. I shut my eyes tight and clutched the ferns with my hands and teeth to wait until the chill had passed, when I heard a soft voice call:

"Boy."

I thought at first I was delirious, because sometimes I got lightheaded when my bad attacks came on; only then I remembered that when I was delirious I didn't know it; all the strange things I saw and heard seemed perfectly natural. So when the voice said, "Boy," again, as soft and clear as the mocking bird at sunrise, I opened my eyes.

Kneeling near me on the ferns was a girl. She must have been about a year younger than I. I was almost sixteen so I guess she was fourteen or fifteen. She was dressed in a blue and white gingham dress; her face was very pale, but the kind of paleness that's supposed to be, not the sickly pale kind that was like mine showing even under the tan. Her eyes were big and very blue. Her hair was dark brown and she wore it parted in the middle in two heavy braids that were swinging in front of her shoulders as she peered into my face.

"You don't feel well, do you?" she asked. There was no trace of concern or worry in her voice. Just scientific interest.

I shook my head. "No," I whispered, almost afraid that if I talked she would vanish, because I had never seen anyone here before, and I thought that maybe I was dying because I felt so awful, and I thought maybe that gave me the power to see the ghost. But the girl in blue and white checked gingham seemed as I watched her to be good flesh and blood.

"You'd better come with me," she said. "She'll make you all right."

"Who's she?"

"Oh—just Her," she said.

My chill had begun to recede by now, so when she got up off her knees, I scrambled up, too. When she stood up her dress showed a white ruffled petticoat underneath it, and bits of green moss had left patterns on her knees and I didn't think that would happen to the knees of a ghost, so I followed her as she led the way towards the house. She did not go up the sagging, half-rotted steps which led to the veranda about whose white pillars wisteria vines climbed in

23

wild profusion, but went around to the side of the house where there were slanting doors to a cellar. The sun and rain had long since blistered and washed off the paint, but the doors looked clean and were free of the bits of bark from the eucalyptus tree which leaned nearby and which had dropped its bits of dusty peel on either side; so I knew that these cellar stairs must frequently be used.

The girl opened the cellar doors. "You go down first," she said. I went down the cellar steps which were stone, and cool against my bare feet. As she followed me she closed the cellar doors after her and as I reached the bottom of the stairs we were in pitch darkness. I began to be very frightened until her soft voice came out of the black.

"Boy, where are you?"

"Right here."

"You'd better take my hand. You might stumble."

We reached out and found each other's hands in the darkness. Her fingers were long and cool and they closed firmly around mine. She moved with authority as though she knew her way with the familiarity born of custom.

"Poor Sat's all in the dark," she said, "but he likes it that way. He likes to sleep for weeks at a time. Sometimes he snores awfully. Sat, darling!" she called gently. A soft, bubbly, blowing sound came in answer, and she laughed happily. "Oh, Sat, you are sweet!" she said, and the bubbly sound came again. Then the girl pulled at my hand and we came out into a huge and dusty kitchen. Iron skillets, pots, and pans were still hanging on either side of the huge stove, and there was a rolling pin and a bowl of flour on the marble topped table in the middle of the room. The girl took a lighted candle off the shelf.

"I'm going to make cookies," she said as she saw me looking at the flour and the rolling pin. She slipped her hand out of mine. "Come along." She began to walk more rapidly. We left the kitchen, crossed the hall, went through the dining room, its old mahogany table thick with dust although sheets covered the pictures on the walls. Then we went into the ball room. The mirrors lining the walls were spotted and discolored; against one wall was a single delicate gold chair, its seat cushioned with pale rose and silver woven silk; it seemed extraordinarily well preserved. From the ceiling hung the huge chandelier from which Alexandra Londermaine had hung herself, its prisms catching and breaking up into a hundred colors the flickering of the candle and the few shafts of light that managed to slide in through the boarded-up windows. As we crossed the ball room the girl began to dance by herself, gracefully, lightly, so that her full blue and white checked gingham skirts flew out around her. She looked at herself with pleasure in the old mirrors as she danced, the candle flaring and guttering in her right hand.

"You've stopped shaking. Now what will I tell Her?" she said as we started to climb the broad mahogany staircase. It was very dark so she took my hand again, and before we had reached the top of the stairs I obliged her by being seized by another chill. She felt my trembling fingers with satisfaction. "Oh, you've started again. That's good." She slid open one of the huge double doors at the head of the stairs.

As I looked in to what once must have been Colonel Londermaine's study I thought that surely what I saw was a scene in a dream or a vision in delirium. Seated at the huge table in the center of the room was the most extraordinary woman I had ever seen. I felt that she must be very beautiful, although she would never have fulfilled any of the standards of beauty set by our town. Even though she was seated I felt that she must be immensely tall. Piled up on the table in front of her were several huge volumes, and her finger was marking the place in the open one in front of her, but she was not reading. She was leaning back in the carved chair, her head resting against a piece of blue and gold embroidered silk that was flung across the chair back, one hand gently stroking a fawn that lay sleeping in her lap. Her eyes were closed and somehow I couldn't imagine what color they would be. It wouldn't have surprised me if they had been shining amber or the deep purple of her velvet robe. She had a great quantity of hair, the color of mahogany in firelight, which was cut quite short and seemed to be blown wildly about her head like flame. Under her closed eyes were deep shadows, and lines of pain about her mouth. Otherwise there were no marks of age on her face but I would not have been surprised to learn that she was any age in the world—a hundred, or twenty-five. Her mouth was large and mobile and she was singing something in a deep, rich voice. Two cats, one black, one white, were coiled up, each on a book, and as we opened the doors a leopard stood up quietly beside her, but did not snarl or move. It simply stood there and waited, watching us.

The girl nudged me and held her finger to her lips to warn me to be quiet, but I would not have spoken—could not, anyhow, my teeth were chattering so from my chill which I had completely forgotten, so fascinated was I by this woman sitting back with her head against the embroidered silk, soft deep sounds coming out of her throat. At last these sounds resolved themselves into words, and we listened to her as she sang. The cats slept indifferently, but the leopard listened, too:

> I sit high in my ivory tower,
> The heavy curtains drawn.
> I've many a strange and lustrous flower,
> A leopard and a fawn
>
> Together sleeping by my chair
> And strange birds softly winging,
> And ever pleasant to my ear
> Twelve maidens' voices singing.
>
> Here is my magic maps' array,
> My mystic circle's flame.
> With symbol's art He lets me play,
> The unknown my domain,
>
> And as I sit here in my dream
> I see myself awake,
> Hearing a torn and bloody scream,
> Feeling my castle shake . . .

Her song wasn't finished but she opened her eyes and looked at us. Now that his mistress knew we were here the leopard seemed ready to spring and devour me at one gulp, but she put her hand on his sapphire-studded collar to restrain him.

26

"Well, Alexandra," she said, "Who have we here?"

The girl, who still held my hand in her long, cool fingers, answered, "It's a boy."

"So I see. Where did you find him?"

The voice sent shivers up and down my spine.

"In the fern bed. He was shaking. See? He's shaking now. Is he having a fit?" Alexandra's voice was filled with pleased interest.

"Come here, boy," the woman said.

As I didn't move, Alexandra gave me a push, and I advanced slowly. As I came near, the woman pulled one of the leopard's ears gently, saying, "Lie down, Thammuz." The beast obeyed, flinging itself at her feet. She held her hand out to me as I approached the table. If Alexandra's fingers felt firm and cool, hers had the strength of the ocean and the coolness of jade. She looked at me for a long time and I saw that her eyes were deep blue, much bluer than Alexandra's, so dark as to be almost black. When she spoke again her voice was warm and tender: "You're burning up with fever. One of the malaria bugs?" I nodded. "Well, we'll fix that for you."

When she stood and put the sleeping fawn down by the leopard, she was not as tall as I had expected her to be; nevertheless she gave an impression of great height. Several of the bookshelves in one corner were emptied of books and filled with various shaped bottles and retorts. Nearby was a large skeleton. There was an acid stained wash basin, too; that whole section of the room looked like part of a chemist's or physicist's laboratory. She selected from among the bottles a small amber colored one, and poured a drop of the liquid it contained into a glass of water. As the drop hit the water there was a loud hiss and clouds of dense smoke arose. When it had drifted away she handed the glass to me and said, "Drink. Drink, my boy!"

My hand was trembling so that I could scarcely hold the glass. Seeing this, she took it from me and held it to my lips.

"What is it?" I asked.

"Drink it," she said, pressing the rim of the glass against my teeth. On the first swallow I started to choke and would have pushed the stuff away, but she forced the rest of the burning liquid down my throat. My whole body felt on fire. I

27

felt flame flickering in every vein and the room and everything in it swirled around. When I had regained my equilibrium to a certain extent I managed to gasp out again, "What is it?"

She smiled and answered:

Nine peacocks' hearts, four bats' tongues,
A pinch of moondust and a hummingbird's lungs.

Then I asked a question I would never have dared ask if it hadn't been that I was still half drunk from the potion I had swallowed, "Are you a witch?"

She smiled again, and answered, "I make it my profession."

Since she hadn't struck me down with a flash of lightning, I went on. "Do you ride a broomstick?"

This time she laughed. "I can when I like."

"Is it—is it very hard?"

"Rather like a bucking bronco at first, but I've always been a good horsewoman, and now I can manage very nicely. I've finally progressed to sidesaddle, though I still feel safer astride. I always rode my horse astride. Still, the best witches ride sidesaddle, so . . . Now run along home. Alexandra has lessons to study and I must work. Can you hold your tongue or must I make you forget?"

"I can hold my tongue."

She looked at me and her eyes burnt into me like the potion she had given me to drink. "Yes, I think you can," she said. "Come back tomorrow if you like. Thammuz will show you out."

The leopard rose and led the way to the door. As I hesitated, unwilling to tear myself away, it came back and pulled gently but firmly on my trouser leg.

"Good-bye, boy," the witch woman said. "And you won't have any more chills and fever."

"Good-bye," I answered. I didn't say thank you. I didn't say good-bye to Alexandra. I followed the leopard out.

She let me come every day. I think she must have been lonely. After all I was the only thing there with a life apart from hers. And in the long run the only reason I have had a life of my own is because of her. I am as much a creation of

28

the witch woman's as Thammuz the leopard was, or the two cats, Ashtaroth and Orus (it wasn't until many years after the last day I saw the witch woman that I learned that those were the names of the fallen angels).

She did cure my malaria, too. My parents and the townspeople thought that I had outgrown it. I grew angry when they talked about it so lightly and wanted to tell them that it was the witch woman, but I knew that if ever I breathed a word about her I would be eternally damned. Mamma thought we should write a testimonial letter to the 666 Malaria Medicine people, and maybe they'd send us a couple of dollars.

Alexandra and I became very good friends. She was a strange, aloof creature. She liked me to watch her while she danced alone in the ball room or played on an imaginary harp—thought sometimes I fancied I could hear the music. One day she took me into the drawing room and uncovered a portrait that was hung between two of the long boarded up windows. Then she stepped back and held her candle high so as to throw the best light on the picture. It might have been a picture of Alexandra herself, or Alexandra as she might be in five years.

"That's my mother," she said. "Alexandra Londermaine."

As far as I knew from the tales that went about town, Alexandra Londermaine had given birth to only one child, and that still-born, before she had hung herself on the chandelier in the ball room—and anyhow, any child of hers would have been Alexandra's mother or grandmother. But I didn't say anything because when Alexandra got angry she became ferocious like one of the cats, and was given to leaping on me, scratching and biting. I looked at the portrait long and silently.

"You see, she has on a ring like mine," Alexandra said, holding out her left hand, on the fourth finger of which was the most beautiful sapphire and diamond ring I had ever seen, or rather, that I could ever have imagined, for it was a ring apart from any owned by even the most wealthy of the townsfolk. Then I realized that Alexandra had brought me in here and unveiled the portrait simply that she might show

29

me the ring to better advantage, for she had never worn a ring before.

"Where did you get it?"

"Oh, she got it for me last night."

"Alexandra," I asked suddenly, "how long have you been here?"

"Oh, a while."

"But how long?"

"Oh, I don't remember."

"But you must remember."

"I don't. I just came—like Poor Sat."

"Who's Poor Sat?" I asked, thinking for the first time of whoever it was that had made the gentle bubbly noises at Alexandra the day she found me in the fern bed.

"Why, we've never shown you Sat, have we!" she exclaimed. "I'm sure it's all right, but we'd better ask Her first."

So we went to the witch woman's room and knocked. Thammuz pulled the door open with his strong teeth and the witch woman looked up from some sort of experiment she was making with test tubes and retorts. The fawn, as usual, lay sleeping near her feet. "Well?" she said.

"Is it all right if I take him to see Poor Little Saturday?" Alexandra asked her.

"Yes, I suppose so," she answered. "But no teasing," and turned her back to us and bent again over her test tubes as Thammuz nosed us out of the room.

We went down to the cellar. Alexandra lit a lamp and took me back to the corner furthest from the doors, where there was a stall. In the stall was a two-humped camel. I couldn't help laughing as I looked at him because he grinned at Alexandra so foolishly, displaying all his huge buck teeth and blowing bubbles through them.

"She said we weren't to tease him," Alexandra said severely, rubbing her cheek against the preposterous splotchy hair that seemed to be coming out, leaving bald pink spots of skin on his long nose.

"But what—" I started.

"She rides him sometimes." Alexandra held out her hand while he nuzzled against it, scratching his rubbery lips against the diamond and sapphire of her ring. "Mostly She talks to him. She says he is very wise. He goes up to Her room sometimes and they talk and talk. I can't understand a word they say. She says it's Hindustani and Arabic. Sometimes I can remember little bits of it, like: *iderow, sorcabatcha,* and *anna bihed bech.* She says I can learn to speak with them when I finish learning French and Greek."

Poor Little Saturday was rolling his eyes in delight as Alexandra scratched behind his ears. "Why is he called Poor Little Saturday?" I asked.

Alexandra spoke with a ring of pride in her voice. "I named him. She let me."

"But why did you name him that?"

"Because he came last winter on the Saturday that was the shortest day of the year, and it rained all day so it got light later and dark earlier than it would have if it had been nice, so it really didn't have as much of itself as it should, and I felt so sorry for it I thought maybe it would feel better if we named him after it . . . she thought it was a nice name!" she turned on me suddenly.

"Oh, it is! It's a fine name!" I said quickly, smiling to myself as I realized how much greater was this compassion of Alexandra's for a day than any she might have for a human being. "How did She get him?" I asked.

"Oh, he just came."

"What do you mean?"

"She wanted him so he came. From the desert."

"He *walked!*"

"Yes. And swam part of the way. She met him at the beach and flew him here on the broom stick. You should have seen him. She was still all wet and looked so funny. She gave him hot coffee with things in it."

"What things?"

"Oh, just things."

Then the witch woman's voice came from behind us. "Well, children?"

It was the first time I had seen her out of her room. Thammuz was at her right heel, the fawn at her left. The cats, Ashtaroth and Orus, had evidently stayed upstairs. "Would you like to ride Saturday?" she asked me.

Speechless, I nodded. She put her hand against the wall and a portion of it slid down into the earth so that Poor Little Saturday was free to go out. "She's sweet, isn't she?" the witch woman asked me, looking affectionately at the strange, bumpy-kneed, splay-footed creature. "Her grandmother was very good to me in Egypt once. Besides, I love camel's milk."

"But Alexandra said she was a he!" I exclaimed.

"Alexandra's the kind of woman to whom all animals are he except cats, and all cats are she. As a matter of fact, Ashtaroth and Orus are she, but it wouldn't make any difference to Alexandra if they weren't. Go on out, Saturday. Come on!"

Saturday backed out, bumping her bulging knees and ankles against her stall, and stood under a live oak tree. "Down," the witch woman said. Saturday leered at me and didn't move. "Down, sorcabatcha!" the witch woman commanded, and Saturday obediently got down on her knees. I clambered up onto her, and before I had managed to get at all settled she rose with such a jerky motion that I knocked my chin against her front hump and nearly bit my tongue off. Round and round Saturday danced while I clung wildly to her front hump and the witch woman and Alexandra rolled on the ground with laughter. I felt as though I were on a very unseaworthy vessel on the high seas, and it wasn't long before I felt violently seasick as Saturday pranced among the live oak trees, sneezing delicately.

At last the witch woman called out, "Enough!" and Saturday stopped in her tracks, nearly throwing me, and kneeling laboriously. "It was mean to tease you," the witch woman said, pulling my nose gently. "You may come sit in my room with me for a while if you like."

There was nothing I liked better than to sit in the witch woman's room and to watch her while she studied from her books, worked out strange looking mathematical problems, argued with the zodiac, or conducted complicated experiments with her test tubes and retorts, sometimes filling the room with sulphurous odors or flooding it with red or blue light. Only once was I afraid of her, and that was when she danced with the skeleton in the corner. She had the room flooded with a strange red glow and I almost thought I could see the flesh covering the bones of the skeleton as they danced together like lovers. I think she had forgotten that I was sitting there, half hidden in the wing chair, because when they had finished dancing and the skeleton stood in the corner again, his bones shining and polished, devoid of any living trappings, she stood with her forehead against one of the deep red velvet curtains that covered the boarded-up windows and tears streamed down her cheeks. Then she went back to her test tubes and worked feverishly. She never alluded to the incident and neither did I.

As winter drew on she let me spend more and more time in the room. Once I gathered up courage enough to ask her about herself, but I got precious little satisfaction.

"Well, then, are you maybe one of the northerners who bought the place?"

"Let's leave it at that, boy. We'll say that's who I am. Did you know that my skeleton was old Colonel Londermaine? Not so old, as a matter of fact; he was only thirty-seven when he was killed at the battle of Bunker Hill—or am I getting him confused with his great-grandfather, Rudolph Londermaine? Anyhow he was only thirty-seven, and a fine figure of a man, and Alexandra only thirty when she hung herself for love of him on the chandelier in the ballroom. Did you know that the fat man with the red mustaches has been trying to cheat your father? His cow will give sour milk for seven days. Run along now and talk to Alexandra. She's lonely."

When the winter had turned to spring and the camellias and azaleas and Cape Jessamine had given way to the more lush blooms of early May, I kissed Alexandra for the first time, very clumsily. The next evening when I managed to get away from the chores at home and hurried out to the plantation, she gave me her sapphire and diamond ring which she had swung for me on a narrow bit of turquoise satin. "It will keep us both safe," she said, "if you wear it always. And then when we're older we can get married and you can give it back to me. Only you mustn't let anyone see it, ever, ever, or She'd be very angry."

I was afraid to take the ring but when I demurred Alexandra grew furious and started kicking and biting and I had to give in.

Summer was almost over before my father discovered the ring hanging about my neck. I fought like a witch boy to keep him from pulling out the narrow ribbon and seeing the

33

ring, and indeed the ring seemed to give me added strength and I had grown, in any case, much stronger during the winter than I had ever been in my life. But my father was still stronger than I, and he pulled it out. He looked at it in dead silence for a moment and then the storm broke. That was the famous Londermaine ring that had disappeared the night Alexandra Londermaine hung herself. That ring was worth a fortune. Where had I got it?

No one believed me when I said I had found it in the grounds near the house—I chose the grounds because I didn't want anybody to think I had been in the house or indeed that I was able to get in. I don't know why they didn't believe me; it still seems quite logical to me that I might have found it buried among the ferns.

It had been a long, dull year, and the men of the town were all bored. They took me and forced me to swallow quantities of corn liquor until I didn't know what I was saying or doing. When they had finished with me I didn't even manage to reach home before I was violently sick and then I was in my mother's arms and she was weeping over me. It was morning before I was able to slip away to the plantation house. I ran pounding up the mahogany stairs to the witch woman's room and opened the heavy sliding doors without knocking. She stood in the center of the room in her purple robe, her arms around Alexandra who was weeping bitterly. Overnight the room had completely changed. The skeleton of Colonel Londermaine was gone, and books filled the shelves in the corner of the room that had been her laboratory. Cobwebs were everywhere, and broken glass lay on the floor; dust was inches thick on her work table. There was no sign of Thammuz, Ashtaroth or Orus, or the fawn, but four birds were flying about her, beating their wings against her hair.

She did not look at me or in any way acknowledge my presence. Her arm about Alexandra, she led her out of the room and to the drawing room where the portrait hung. The birds followed, flying around and around them. Alexandra had stopped weeping now. Her face was very proud and pale and if she saw me miserably trailing behind them she gave no notice. When the witch woman stood in front of the portrait the sheet fell from it. She raised her arm; there was a great cloud of smoke; the smell of sulphur filled my nostrils, and when the smoke was gone, Alexandra was gone, too. Only the portrait was there, the fourth finger of the left hand now bearing no ring. The witch woman raised her hand again and the sheet lifted itself up and covered the portrait. Then she went, with the birds, slowly back to what had once been her room, and still I tailed after, frightened as I had never been before in my life, or have been since.

She stood without moving in the center of the room for a long time. At last she turned and spoke to me.

"Well, boy, where is the ring?"

"They have it."

"They made you drunk, didn't they?"

"Yes."

"I was afraid something like this would happen when I gave Alexandra the ring. But it doesn't matter . . . I'm tired . . ." She drew her hand wearily across her forehead.

"Did I—did I tell them everything?"

"You did."

"I—I didn't know."

"I know you didn't know, boy."

"Do you hate me now?"

"No, boy, I don't hate you."

"Do you have to go away?"

"Yes."

I bowed my head. "I'm so sorry . . ."

She smiled slightly. "The sands of time . . . Cities crumble and rise and will crumble again and breath dies down and blows once more . . ."

The birds flew madly about her head, pulling at her hair, calling into her ears. Downstairs we could hear a loud pounding, and then the crack of boards being pulled away from a window.

"Go, boy," she said to me. I stood rooted, motionless, unable to move. "GO!" she commanded, giving me a mighty push so that I stumbled out of the room. They were waiting for me by the cellar doors and caught me as I climbed out. I had to stand there and watch when they came out with her. But it wasn't the witch woman, my witch woman. It was *their* idea of a witch woman, someone thousands of years old, a disheveled old creature in rusty black, with long wisps of gray hair, a hooked nose, and four wiry black hairs springing out of the mole on her chin. Behind her flew the four birds and suddenly they went up, up, into the sky, directly in the path of the sun until they were lost in its burning glare.

Two of the men stood holding her tightly, although she wasn't struggling, but standing there, very quiet, while the others searched the house, searched it in vain. Then as a group of them went down into the cellar I remembered, and by a flicker of the old light in the witch woman's eyes I could see that she remembered, too. Poor Little Saturday had been forgotten. Out she came, prancing absurdly up the cellar steps, her rubbery lips stretched back over her gigantic teeth, her eyes bulging with terror. When she saw the witch woman, her lord and master, held captive by two dirty, insensitive men, she let out a shriek and began to kick and lunge wildly, biting, screaming with the blood-curdling, heart-rending screams that only a camel can make. One of the men fell to the ground, holding a leg in which the bone had snapped from one of Saturday's kicks. The others scattered in terror, leaving the witch woman standing on the veranda supporting herself by clinging to one of the huge wisteria vines that curled around the columns. Saturday clambered up onto the veranda, and knelt while she flung herself between the two humps. Then off they ran, Saturday still screaming, her knees knocking together, the ground shaking as she pounded along. Down from the sun plummeted the four birds and flew after them.

Up and down I danced, waving my arms, shouting wildly until Saturday and the witch woman and the birds were lost in a cloud of dust, while the man with the broken leg lay moaning on the ground beside me.

Born in New York City in 1917, Madeleine L'Engle was educated at Smith College and Columbia University. During World War II she taught for the Committee for Refugee Education, helping victims of Nazi terror settle in the United States; later she taught at St. Hugh's School in New York. A specialist in children's books, she is best known for her science fiction novel A Wrinkle in Time, *which won the Newbery Medal in*

1963, the Hans Christian Andersen Runner-Up Award in 1964, the Sequoyah Award in 1965, and the Lewis Carroll Shelf Award in 1965. She has also written a number of shorter works, such as the charming—and somewhat sinister—"Poor Little Saturday."

Tough old Joe Root had met bigger and meaner adversaries than this Yankee, and he wasn't going to give in so easily. . . .

FOUR

Dead Man's Story
Howard Rigsby

Live and walkin' I war runty, but ask anybody and they'll tell you there war no tougher man to be found in all Florida. From the time I war coltish I war stringy, but them what tried to whup me allus vowed they'd sight rather tangle with a 'gator 'cause they war easier hurted than Joe Root—that's me, or what is left of me, what with shootin', drownin', buryin', and sech.

For sixty year I lived over on the west coast and war a game warden for twenty of 'em and I know every swampy piece and piney stretch and bayou from Port Saint Joe to Pensacola. I can tell you to the minute when the young quail'll hatch out and lookin' at a deer track I can tell you where he's goin' and what he's thinkin'. I fought and et and hunted bear and panther and wild boar and they has fought me and some tried eatin' me. I can call out so's you'd think it war a loony bird and I know all the leaves and herbs and grasses that is good for what ails you. Rattlers and moccasins bit me so much that after while they paid me no mind 'cause they knowed that all their pisen couldn't hurt me. No sir, it war no critter got me here where I be, lyin' in the ground, it war a man, and of all the ornery varmints and belly crawlers in God's world he war that most low-down of the lot.

It war in March and I come at night, workin' up the spits and islands, up from Panama City. There war a moon and the gulf war quiet and shinin' like clean steel and, when I cut the motor of my launch, shorewards I heered the cats pacin' in the bresh and the deer movin' through the palmettoes up

39

towards the springs which is on the long key that stretches out into the Choctawhatchee Bay. It war all so purty and quiet that I almost fergit what I come for. Then back in the bresh I heered a gun. There war two shots and I knowed right off it war a 12-gauge pump. That war real suspectful 'cause there ain't a passel of pumpers 'mong the county folks and it war ten year since I knowed of a person livin' up that way where the shots come from. It war no jackin' gang I figgered 'cause I knowed they'd been workin' the springs on the key. They had a fast boat which they run up in and they'd settle in the scrub there and shine their light when the deer was drinkin'.

Well, I set there with the gulf slappin' gentle 'gainst the boat and figgered a spell, listenin', and then I headed up to where a bayou cut in that'd take me to where them shots come from.

I rowed easy up the bayou with my 30–30 'crost my knees and it war dark with the cypress meetin' overhead and trailin' mossy streamers down into the boat. I heered 'gators rollin' off the bank and sighin' and their eyes shined at me. About two miles up the bayou I seen the light. It war in the cabin where nobody lived since ole man Jackson died in it ten year before. I set there a thinkin' on it and driftin' over toward the landin' that war all rotted and then I seen the boat layin' there covered with a tarp. I edged up 'long her and she war a nice cruiser, all mahogany and fitted out with brass and I bet as fast as anythin' on the whole gulf. It war too nice for any jacker boat and I seen no reason for it bein' there. But it war my duty to see who fired them shots. There war a little patch of cleared land near the cabin which war a fine-lookin' place for a man with a 12-gauge pumper to pick off a deer when it come up in the moonlight to kick 'mong the ole turnip and potato beds and graze on the wild hay that war sproutin' there.

I tied my boat to a gleamin' deck cleat on the cruiser's bow and got out on the landin' and a rotted board cracked like a rifle shot under my foot. The door of the cabin swung open sudden and a man stood there sightin' out. There war a huntin' knife in his one hand and the other war jammed into his pocket.

"Who's there?" he hollered and I knowed right off it war a Yankee.

"Steady," I tole him. "Ain't no cause for alarmin'."

His eyes foun' me and he seemed to relax. "What you want?"

I begun walkin' up to the door of the cabin. When I war near up to him I said, "I want that buck deer yore makin' sech a mess of skinnin' in there."

He war a big man, built like a bear, with long thick arms and black as a bear. "Now is that a nice way to ask for a thing?" he said. "And you been peekin'. How you know I shot a buck deer? And how you knowin' I never before skinned one?"

How I knowed war real simple. First off I could smell freshkilt deer and buck smells stronger than doe. And I knowed he war makin' a mess 'cause iffen he bled the critter proper there war no need for him to get a speck of blood on his hands, but his hands war all blood.

"Never mind how I come to know," I said. "I'm a game warden, and you and that buck deer is comin' with me."

He laughed. "Why I thought you was only beggin' for a piece of it. Come in, Mister Warden, and tell me what's the rap." Then he got a bottle and two glasses and tole me to set and have a drink.

I war needin' a drink, I war right hongry for one, but I war not drinkin' no liquor with him. "You better pack yore fixin's," I tole him sharp. "I aim to tote you and that deer over there on the table back to Panama City tonight."

He taken a drink. "You mean to say you can't kill no deer in Florida?" he said jest like he war being real polite, but he war really mean and fumin' underneath.

"We got a season," I tole him steady, "jest like whatever state you may be t'home in, mister, and them that kills out of season pays a hundred dollars fine and goes to jail for a piece to boot."

"But between us there won't be no trouble," he said. "I didn't know your rules, Mister Game Warden, but I always pay when I done wrong." He pulled a roll of bills on me then and it war bigger money and more of it than I ever seen. He tooken two bills off from the roll. "Here," he said, "is your fine and another century for yourself."

"Put yore money in yore pants."

Still starin' at me with them little varmint eyes he war peelin' off more bills. "You can tell me when to stop," he said.

I said, "You can stop now. Yore money won't buy that buck deer you kilt, er me, er the Florida law. Now bundle yore traps, mister, and come along with me."

He put his money away and laughed downright insultin'. "I have bought bigger men than you, and I have bought more law than all you got." He moved sudden then, like a rattler strikin', and grabbed the barrel of my 30-30. "And bigger men than you has come to take me," he said. "But I ain't gone with 'em."

I war careless I admit. I shouldn't a took no more chanct with him than I would of with a he bear in matin' time. But most men caught for killin' a buck deer won't go to fightin' desperate. They'll gen'ly try to buy off but they won't go tanglin' with guns.

"Yore makin' a mistake," I tole him.

"There ain't no pint-sized cracker game warden can take me in."

I said, "I'm a deppity, too. And I taken bigger men than you. Some I had to bloody up, but I taken 'em."

The hand that war sunk in his pocket come out slow with a nasty little gun in it. "Won't be no blood this time unless it's your own," he said. "Now sit down and we'll talk this over like sensible men."

He had me and I war boilin'. I had made a mistake and I had a feelin' even then that maybe it war the kind of a mistake a man don't git a chanct to make more'n once in a lifetime. And when I dived for him and heered that nasty little gun roarin' in my ears I knowed it.

I got it in the belly and I got it bad, but it taken more'n a little pop-gun like what he had to stop Joe Root. I rasseled with him for my own gun which he war still holdin' with one hand on the barrel.

"Ain't you a tough little banty," he muttered and he war grinnin' with a deadly pisen grin.

The little gun went off ag'in and my left side turned all numbed from where I gotten it in the shoulder. I let go rasselin' for my own gun sudden and I slammed him and knocked him back so his next shot war wild and then I war a-comin' at him and I seen fear in his eyes then.

He gotten me good as I closed with him and I could feel the bullet gnawin' at the gristle in my chest, but I had got my hands on him now and he let out a scream and clubbed me on the head with the gun and each time he hit me he war cryin', "Go down! Go down! Ain't you human? Go down! You're dead!"

Then he slammed two more shots into me and pushed me away and he war like a crazy man now when I come back and started to choke him. But after a bit I begin to feel I war dead and the hand I war chokin' him with wouldn't hold no more and I slid down to his feet. But my eyes war open and I war a starin' up at him accusin' and my arm war wrapped tight around his feet.

His breath war comin' hard and he war sort of moanin' and he stared down at me and there war fear of me in his eyes. He tried to walk and get away from me but my arm war like iron 'round his legs and fin'ly he had to bend down and club at it with his gun to get loose. He taken a drink then and collected his self together a little bit.

"You was the toughest guy I ever kilt," he said. "Even big Tony wasn't half as hard, and all the others . . ." He stopped and taken another drink and looked down at where I war starin' at him with my bloody lips drawn back grinnin'. And he tried to laugh but it war shaky and not mirthful. "A skinny little old string-bean like you," he went on. "Me—Mike Mitchell—almost gettin' dragged to jail by a little old cracker game warden, and for just killin' a deer, a lousy little deer. Why I can see them headlines they would of had up north." He taken another drink. "Well there won't be no headlines now, 'cause I got you—you tough little old rooster you. Hey!—quit starin' at me! You got no right to stare and grin at people. You're dead! Don't you know it?"

I gurgle in my throat and he jumps straight up and drops the glass he war holdin'. His eyes war wide and starin' and he said feverish, "I'm goin' to get rid of you right now. I'm

43

goin' to get you out of here. I'm goin' to sink you in the water so's you'll know you're dead, and I'll know it, too. And there ain't no one will ever find you."

He taken me by the heels and I war dragged out of the cabin and down to the old landin'. He gotten rope from his cruiser and trussed me up real awkward then he gotten him some stone and a rusty ole iron plowshare ole man Jackson use to have. He tied these to me and dumped me in my boat.

I war towed behind that shiny cruiser out into Choctawhatchee and there I war dumped and my launch set adriftin' and as he spilled me into the water that big black Yankee said, "Goodbye, old rooster." But as I went my lips war pulled back in a tight grin and my eyes war starin' at him so he let me go quick. Then I went down into that water I knowed all my life with the fishes scuttlin' out of my way and the ole moon shinin' down on my face and the shadder of the cruiser's bottom moved over me with a noise like soft thunder in another world and I war restin' in the silt, rockin' easy in the warm ole arms of the gulf. But I war not a happy body for my job war not yet done.

Rockin' there while the moon shined down through the water and the fishes played in the weavin' bottom grass, the ropes what tied my legs war rubbin', rubbin' as I rocked, rubbin' on ole man Jackson's plowshare. By mornin' I war a free body, movin' and driftin' about under the water with on'y a rock or two still trailin' on my ropes. Now the water war all light inside with the sun and the tide war flowin' up the little bayou and I went twistin' and driftin' 'long with it. It was a real nice day, and different, for the teal and mallard war a-lookin' down through the water at me quizzical and I seen the roots of the cypress instead of their tops, as usual.

Goin' up the bayou an ole gran'pa 'gator bumped 'longside of me and looked me over, but I guess he seen I war ole, too, and no tender morsel and he only flapped his jaws disdainful. He come down on the rope, silly critter, and swum off with it, not even knowin' he had it, and as the rope unwinded from me I war twisted and turned and then, s'prisin' quick, I war floatin' spang on top of the bayou right next to ole man Jackson's landin'.

I laid floatin' in the sun and the grin war froze for good now on my face and my eyes war starin' toward the cabin. Smoke war comin' from the chimney and after a bit the Yankee come out and looked around. Sudden he stiffened and, shadin' his eye, he come edgin' down toward the landin'. And when he seen it war really me he begun to shake and sort of moan. Then he whupped out his little gun what done for me and started firin' wild and silly at me.

He quit that in a minute and calmed down. He gotten in his cruiser and let her drift over to where I war floatin', beginnin' to swell a bit, and taken holt my coat with a gaff.

"How come you got loose?" he asked me. "Why didn't you stay put? Can't you leave me be? Quit starin'!"

I kept right on starin' when he drug me into the boat, and as he paddled over to the landin' he war mutterin', "I'll get rid of you. I'm goin' to bury you, and then there won't be no doubt in any body's mind but what you're dead."

And, shore nuff, that war what he done to me next. He drug me back into the palmettoes where there war a swampy piece and he digged a bit and then he put me in the muddy hole.

"There," said he, shovelin' muck on me, "this is the last I'll see of you. You won't stare and grin at me no more, you old monkey. This here is a grave and you're in it, so you are dead."

It was mighty dark, and wet too, and after a bit I could feel the blind little critters in the ground with me, a movin' and a pushin' at me, wonderin' who I war and how I come to be there. Most any other body, done up and shot through and drowned as I war, would of been right satisfied to rest there. But I war not. I war no peaceful body 'cause my job war not yet done.

There war no sech thing as time in that dark and a body had no way of knowin' how long it had been there. It might been years and it might been a hour when I heered a noise like horses on a road a long ways off. And soon the sound come closer and the swamp begun a movin' and a shakin' over me. Then somethin' tugged on me and there war a snortin' and a gruntin'.

It war wild hogs and purty soon they got me most out of the swamp, snortin' and fightin' over me. But it were mostly a game with 'em. I war too tough and stringy for any critter, even pigs, to think of eatin' and after a bit them hogs galloped off, leavin' me head and shoulders out of the swamp, starin' and grinnin' toward ole man Jackson's cabin which war just beginnin' to show as the ground mist war liftin' and the sun comin' up.

It war another purty mornin'. Over in the bresh a buck deer sniffed and wrinkled up his nose and then went gallivantin' off aflauntin' his tail. And for a spell a possum set up in a pine tree a-watchin' and thinkin' me over.

The first buzzard come along to investigate about ten o'clock. He moseyed around in big circles, cagy and ready to go, but when he seen I war never goin' nowhere nor do nobody hurt he come down gradual on a hummock near me. Soon as he sets there war a dozen of his brethern come from nowhere and begun circlin' me, takin' council. And it war about that time that the door of the cabin opened and the Yankee come out with a axe, walkin' toward the scrub to cut his self some wood.

When he seen the buzzards he stopped sudden and purty soon he come walkin' toward me slow and as he come closer I seen his eyes war blood-shot and wild like a man with hants who war drinkin' and not sleepin' nights. The buzzards leaved and went flappin' up and then the Yankee seen me pokin' up out of the swamp, starin' and grinnin', and his face went as pale as if he war the hant and not me.

He stood there shakin' and starin' back at me and little bubbles come to his lips, just like a deer which the houn's has runned most to death. Then sudden he turnt away and went over to a old pitch pine log and begun to hack him pieces offen it with his axe. When he gotten a lot he taken the load down back of the cabin to a dry spot. Then he come back to where I war.

"You won't stay buried and you won't stay drowned," he tole me feverish. "Maybe you'll stay burnt up!"

Then he taken me and he drug me down to that stack of pitch pine and he war laughin' like mad as he done it.

I war awful wet from the water and the muck and the fire couldn't make no real headway on me, but I steam a lot and I sizzle and pop and as the wood burnt out the stack shifts and suddenly I rolt off right to his feet and laid there lookin' up at him. And he screamed out so that every critter in the bresh for miles war shocked and quiet.

"Go away from me!" he tole me, blubberin' like a woman. "You ain't dead. Get up and walk and go away. I didn't go to kill you—honest."

It war quite a spell that time before he left off shakin' and blubberin' and then he went to the cabin and come out in a minute drinkin' from a bottle. He war a bit more brashy now. "You ain't goin' to scare me," he said, "dead or alive. And there ain't none of your cracker friends goin' to come here and find you. I'm goin' to get rid of you again and this time you are goin' to stay dead like a kilt man should." Then he drug me back down to his boat and put me aboard. "The sharks'll eat you," he tole me, "'cause they'll eat anything, and we're goin' to find us some."

We come out into the Choctawhatchee roarin' but when the Yankee seen the boat on the other side of the key he throttled down. Leavin' the cruiser idle along he come and hove me into one of the lockers that run along the sides and which had cushions on the lids for settin'. I war swelled up some and it war all he could do to stuff me into the locker and when he got me there the lid wouldn't quite close. He left me there and went back to the wheel and I heered him cuss and say, "Now what do they want?"

I knowed what they war wantin' 'cause I had seen that other boat belonged to ole Dan Meade, Sheriff of Choctawhatchee County, and my ole partner in the warden business, Goose Winters, war with him. They had found my launch floatin' empty and they war out a lookin' for me.

But there I was, stuffed helpless in a locker and like as not they'd on'y hail the Yankee and ask had he seen me. And, shore nuff, after a bit Dan Meade called out and tole us to heave to. And then there war the scrape of his boat 'longside.

"I'm in a hurry," the Yankee tole him.

Sheriff Meade cleared his throat out and I heered him spit. "You all got a fine boat here," he said. "A mighty nice boat for a man what's in a hurry. Where might you be hurryin'?"

"That's my business."

"Well, it's mine, too," Meade said and there war a pause while I could tell he war showin' off his star. "I'll jest take a look at yore licenses for this little ole hurry boat, iffen you don't mind."

Then the cruiser swayed and Dan Meade come board and there war nothin' I could do, layin' there helpless and him so clost and no way to tell him 'bout what had happened. He walked right past me into the little cabin and I heered Goose who stayed in the launch say, "Some critter been doin' a sight of bleedin' 'round you, feller."

The Yankee said, "It's just from a—from a rabbit I kilt."

"He must of put up a purty good fight," Goose said. "A real tough little rabbit, war he?"

Then Sheriff Meade come out of the cabin and the Yankee asked him, "You satisfied, Mister Sheriff?"

Meade said nothin'. He war standin' right over where I be in the locker and after a bit he says slow, "You smell somethin', Goose?"

I heered Goose sniff. "Well I say I do," he said. "Our friend here in this hurry boat war tellin' me about a tough rabbit what he kilt. Maybe he got hit 'round here somewhere."

"That so," Meade remarked real cordial. "Well I would of sworn it war tough but no rabbit. Tell me about it, friend, whilst I set and smoke a minute."

There war a real frightenin' cry from the Yankee then and first thing I know the sheriff has set down on top of the locker, squashin' me down and in my swole condition it war not endurable.

"What you go shoutin' like that for?" the sheriff asked the Yankee.

I could almost hear him thinkin' fast and then he come out with a long story of how his own brother war too sick and dying down in Key West and he war in a terrible hurry to get down there and his voice war so nervous and shaky that I guess he made it seem like the truth to the sheriff.

"Well I don't want to holt no man goin' to his dyin' brother," the sheriff said and he moves his legs like he war goin' to git up and I war right sick with my own helplessness to tell him I war there right under where he war settin' and that the Yankee war lyin'. I seen I would never have no peace now and would end up in a shark's belly with my job not done and the Yankee goin' off unhurted by law or man for killin' that buck deer.

"Well I sure thank you," the Yankee said, real smooth now, "and when I get to my brother I'm goin' to tell him how nice you were to me and I know it will make him get well."

"Well now," the sheriff said, sort of embarrassed. "Shucks, friend, I on'y done my duty. But that is a beautiful thought. It's a real purty sentiment and I hope yore brother does git well and good."

"Hit's purty but it don't change the way this boat smells," Goose said.

His nose went sniff.

"Well, I can't holt a man for a bad smell," the sheriff said. "We'll be goin'."

He got up offen me and when he did all my hope of salvation went with him. I wanted bad to tell him the smell war me, but there war nothin' I could do and it war bad to know he war shakin' that Yankee's hand. Then, just as the sheriff war climbin' over the side somethin' happened that war as big a surprise to me as it war to any body else.

When the sheriff got his self up off that locker it had relieved me a lot and now I heered a long windy sigh and it war me and I never heered a gladder sound.

For jest a spell there war a silence on the Choctawhatchee and you could hear the birds callin' way back up in the bresh and then they war so much sudden movin' about and hollerin' that I thought the cruiser would go plumb to the bottom.

Fin'ly it calmed a bit and the Yankee war blubberin' ag'in. "Don't open it," he war beggin'. "Please don't open it. He'll be layin' there laughin' at me and lookin' with them eyes. I'll talk. I'll tell you about everything. I'm Mike Mitchell and I kilt Tony Ginelli and I did that job at the Unity Bank. You can send me north or put me in jail, but please don't open it now."

Sheriff Meade paid him no mind. He opened the locker and, like Mister Mitchell said, I war layin' there grinnin' and starin', but I war a peaceful body now for my job war done.

Mister Mitchell covered up his face with his hands whilst Dan Meade and old Goose looked down at me.

"How do, Joe," Goose said before he seen for sure I couldn't answer.

"Why there war no need to confess all them things, Mister Mitchell," Sheriff Meade said after a bit. "You done the biggest killin' you'll ever do right here. And there won't be no need to send you north. We'll handle you, friend. And jest to make shore you don't git away whilst we tows you back to town, I'm goin' to chain you to this here locker where old Joe Root can keep his eyes on you."

Co-author with Dorothy Heyward of the Broadway musical South Pacific, *Howard Rigsby sets much of his best fiction in the Deep South. Born in Colorado in 1909, he was educated at San Mateo Junior College, San Jose State College, and the University of Nevada. The author's short stories have appeared in the* Saturday Evening Post *and* Ladies' Home Journal, *among others. Rigsby was editor of* Argosy, *where his* Voyage to Leandro *first appeared as a serial in 1938. He has written Broadway plays, television scripts—*Rawhide *is his best known—and numerous novels, including* Lucinda, *which made the* New York Times' *list of the Year's Ten Best Mysteries in 1954.*

Though Henry's foot had been severed in an accident, it still seemed a "part" of him. . . .

FIVE

One Foot in the Grave
Davis Grubb

It was all over. And now Henry was lying, comfortable and easy, between the cool sheets in the room off Doc Sandy's office. It was really amazing. There was scarcely any pain to it at all. As a matter of fact, Henry, staring at the pale, yellow ceiling of the bedroom in the doctor's house, felt actually more rested and quiet than he had felt in years. He smiled. All those months of talking safety to his men in the sawmill—it was ironic. And then it came to him: how it had happened—his walking through the big, pine-fragrant lumber room with Ed Smiley, his foreman—his foot catching suddenly in a crack—the sudden, wild fear as he pitched forward headlong toward the great, whirring blade of the rip-saw—Ed's big hands grabbing his shoulder, throwing him, saving his life. Then the numbness in his foot and the sickness and that was all there was to it until now: Henry lying comfortably and quietly between the sheets.

Doc Sandy's face between him and the ceiling now.

"How's it feel, Henry?"

"I'm all right," he could hear his voice saying, far away. "I'm really all right. But you know something, John? It's a funny thing—. I really can't understand how it could be."

"What's that, Henry?"

"My foot," he said. "The one that's gone. I can't understand how it could be. It—itches."

And it sounded so ridiculous that he laughed in spite of himself.

"It not only itches," he said, "but it feels cold. Especially the big toe."

"That's not strange," said Doc Sandy. "That often happens, Henry. You see—the foot's still there in a way. And in a way it isn't. The part that's still there is in your brain. Or in your soul—it's a hard thing to explain—."

Henry shut his eyes then and began to shake weakly with laughter.

"What's funny, Henry?"

"I win that bet, John," Henry said. "It's a technicality, I'll admit, but I win it. You can't deny that."

And he could hear Doc Sandy laughing and cursing and saying yes Henry was right, he had won the bet, and Henry shut his eyes, remembering the night the bet was made—the cold winter night—Henry and Doc Sandy playing three-cushion billiards in the Recreation Pool Room and drinking beer and talking about death. Doc Sandy had bet Henry that he would be under the ground before Henry would and Henry had bet him that it would be the other way around and they put down their cues and shook hands on it and agreed that whoever survived was to pay for the other one's funeral.

"Yes," Henry kept saying. "I win. I win by a foot, John. And I intend to see you give that foot the best funeral that money can buy."

Then the doctor's nurse was giving him a drink; the glass straw was between his lips and the good, cold water was soothing to his parched throat. He could hear Doc Sandy lighting his old pipe and then he could smell the sweet, dry fragrance of the burning tobacco.

"John," he said.

"Yes, Henry."

"John, I keep wondering a funny thing. I keep wondering which—which place my foot went to. It was part of me—so it must be part of my soul. It's a funny thing to wonder but I just can't help it. I mean—when the rest of me goes over—will my foot be waiting there to join me again? John, it gives you the funniest feeling in the world to think of a foot—a single, solitary foot wandering around eternity—waiting—. I can't help wondering where it's gone and where it's waiting—in the Good Place or—."

Henry shut his eyes and began to laugh again.

"What's funny, Henry?"

"My foot!" Henry laughed. "I swear it, John. When I said that a second ago—when I said I wondered where it had gone—so help me, John!—it felt hot!"

Nobody could have been nicer to Henry than his secretary Margaret and his foreman Ed Smiley were those next couple of weeks. Henry stayed in the cot at Doc Sandy's office until he was able to get around on crutches and there wasn't a single night that Ed and Margaret missed coming to see him and almost always they brought something—ice cream from Beam's Confectionary or maybe a big spray of sweet shrubs from Judge Bruce's backyard.

Margaret was a queer little person in her early thirties—blonde and pretty in a way that nobody ever noticed particularly—living alone in the Bruces' boarding house on Lafayette Avenue—going to the movies every Saturday with Ed Smiley and then afterwards having an ice-cream soda with him at Beam's. Henry, like many bachelors, often fancied himself quite a match-maker and he was fond of reflecting that, had it not been for him, Ed and Margaret would never have met. He was continually asking the girl when she was going to get married and Margaret, at this, would blush warmly and busy herself in the papers on the desk. Henry never teased Ed about it—knowing, as a man, that Ed had his own good reasons for waiting. But it was something he thought about a lot during those two weeks in bed. And it was a pleasant relief—to think about this—nights when his foot would not let him sleep—nights when the plagued, absent thing felt so cold that he could have sworn that it wandered alone among the mountains of the moon—nights when the rain hurled itself against the windows of the doctor's house and Henry, shivering in the warm cot off the doctor's office, could feel the cold, dreadful wet of the March night between his toes. One night he could stand it no longer. It was late—past midnight—and Doc Sandy had gone to bed long hours before. Just the same Henry had to know. He had to talk. He called for a long time before he heard the doctor's slippers whispering down the kitchen stairs.

"John," he said. "I know it's silly. You'll swear I've gone loco or something—."

"Want a sleeping pill, Henry?"

"No," he said. "It's not that, John. I swear you'll think I've gone loco—."

"What, Henry?"

"It's just this," Henry said. "I've got to know for sure. Did you bury it, John? I know it was just a joke at first and we kidded about the bet and all that and you said you'd had a little coffin made and buried the fool thing in back of the saw-mill under the puzzle-tree. You think I'm loco but—."

"I did bury it, Henry," said the doctor. "I swear I did."

"You swear it?"

"I swear it," said the doctor. "Look here, Henry. Get a grip on yourself! You're going to be up and around in a day or so—on crutches for a while—then we'll get you a foot that'll be as good as new! You'll never miss it!"

Henry shut his eyes and pressed the back of his head hard into the pillow. His hands were wet with perspiration.

"It's funny your saying that, John. It's very funny."

"What's funny, Henry?"

"That I'll never miss it. It's very funny—your putting it like that. It's what's been going through my head all night. The feeling that—that somehow—*it* misses *me*."

There wasn't much trick to the crutches after a few days. It was a little hard getting the knack of them at first but, within a week, Henry was getting around almost as easily as before. And within two weeks he was able to get up and downstairs to his room over the mill office without any help at all. In a month the place was healed enough so that Doc Sandy was able to fix him up with an artificial foot. Henry felt a little better about it and began to get his sleep at night now that he knew the doctor had really buried the thing. Then one day he began to worry again and asked the doctor to take him down back of the sawmill and show him the little grave.

"You're the damnedest fool I ever did see, Henry!" Doc Sandy said, laughing. "Getting all upset over a fool joke."

"Did you put a shoe on it?" Henry said, staring solemnly at the little mound under the puzzle-tree.

"Certainly," said the doctor. "And a brand new shoe at that—the pair you bought at Jim Purdy's sale the week before the accident. Never been worn."

"Is there a sock on it, too?" whispered Henry.

"Damn it all, man—!"

"Is there?" he said.

"Yes!" cried the doctor. "Yes, damn it, there's a sock on it!"

"You didn't put it on straight," Henry said, shaking his head a little sorrowfully. "You put it on crooked, John. It pinches my toe!"

That night it began. Night was the time when it always happened. Henry would go to bed, knowing that he was perfectly sane, knowing that the thing could not be true. Yet it was true. It was happening. It was as real as life itself. Sometimes it would be just a pressure on the sole—as if he were standing somewhere, waiting for a train perhaps. And then it would begin—the gentle, pulsing padding—the lift and fall of walking—the easy thud of brick pavement beneath the foot—the soft crush of leaves or grass. And Henry would lie quaking and sweating beneath the quilt and stare with wild sorrow and horror into the shuddering dark. The foot—his foot—apart from him—was walking somewhere—going someplace—living its own life without any help from him. Then he made another discovery that seemed more incredible and awful than any of the rest of it. It was that the foot always seemed to be going the same distance—walking along the same ways—the same street. Henry got so that he could count the number of steps on the brick pavement and then, after a pause, steps soft and yielding beneath the heel, then another pause and something different again—wooden floor perhaps—then the slower, measured climbing of a stairway.

One night after it had stopped Henry sprang from his bed in a frenzy of fear. Snatching his clothes from the back of the chair by his bed he dressed quickly, lighted the oil lamp and went out back to the puzzle-tree. Fetching a shovel from the tool-shed behind the saw-mill he began to dig. When the spade scraped on the wooden box Henry's heart flew to his mouth. Digging, clawing with his hands, panting and perspiring like a man in a fever, he dragged the little box into the lantern light, pried off the lid with the tip of the spade and stared within. For a moment he was sure he had lost his mind. He lifted it out and looked closely to be sure. The sole. The sole of the brand-new shoe from Jim Purdy's store. He remembered the day he had bought those shoes. He had never worn them. But the sole. It was scuffed and scratched. Worn.

They were shooting pool that afternoon in the Recreation—Henry and Doc Sandy.

"Henry," said the doctor, chalking his cue-stick and squinting low along the cushions for a massé shot. "Ed Smiley was in to see me this morning."

"Ed?" said Henry. "Doesn't look like there's anything wrong with him. He's the perfect picture of health!"

Doc Sandy shot and missed.

"It wasn't about himself that he came to see me, Henry," he said. "It was about Margaret. Your Margaret. She's not well, Henry. I'll tell you frankly—I prescribed a couple of weeks' vacation. She's run down—nervous. Ed said he didn't want to ask you and you know Margaret. She'd never ask you."

"I hadn't noticed her," Henry said. "I really never pay any attention to her, John. You know how it is. You just take somebody like Margaret for granted—year after year. Sure! Sure, I'll give her two weeks off—a month if she needs it! Thanks for telling me, John."

Supper time. Walking home down Lafayette Avenue. Poor little Margaret. Henry felt like a slave-driver. Never realizing what a drab little world it must have been for her all those years—day after day in that glum, dingy office, laboring over the books in that proper, lace-like little hand of hers, keeping his office neat and dusted. When Henry opened the office door he heard her. She was crying. Then he saw her: slumped among the papers on the desk, her hands over her face, her shoulders shaking with sobs.

Henry stood there wondering what to do, feeling terrible about it. He cleared his throat.

"Margaret," he said. "Margaret."

She stood up slowly and turned, facing him. Her face was streaked and wet with tears—plainer and more homely than he had ever seen her—the face under the washed blonde hair tired and old.

"Don't touch me," she whispered. She was shuddering violently and clutching her handkerchief into a tight wet ball. "Don't come near me! Let me alone! Oh when will you let me alone!"

Henry felt behind him for a chair and sat down with a thump.

"I—I don't understand, he began. What do you mean, Margaret?—Let you alone—."

"What do I mean!" she whispered. "What do I mean! You ask me that! You dare to ask me that!"

"I—I don't—. I don't understand," he said. He reached in the pocket of his alpaca coat for a handkerchief to mop the perspiration from his upper lip.

She seemed almost crouching, ready to spring on him. ·

"Last night," she whispered fiercely, the knuckles of her thin, red hands shining white with rage. "Last night!—the night before last! How many nights! Lying there listening for your footsteps on the pavement—the creaking of the gate—your footsteps on the tanbark walk—then lying there waiting for your footsteps on the stairs. Those nights! My God! The things you told me—the things you promised me! You said we'd be married! You said—you said you'd kill me if you ever lost me! You ask me what I mean! Those nights! In my room! In my arms!"

She sprang forward and struck him across the face with the flat of her hand. Henry didn't feel the blow. He sat staring through the girl—beyond her.

"My—footsteps?" he whispered.

She was on the floor now, at his feet, covering his hands with kisses.

"I'm sorry," she wailed. "Oh I'm sorry. I didn't mean to do that! Oh I didn't. Forgive me, dearest! It's just that—I couldn't stand it! I couldn't! At first—the first night—I thought it was a dream when I heard your footsteps and then the door opened and I saw it was you—. It was like seeing a ghost. I couldn't believe it. Those nights—they've seemed like a dream—unreal, wonderful!"

"My footsteps?" he whispered again, rising, pushing her away from him, stepping over her sobbing, shaking shoulders and walking like a sleeper out the door and up the steps to his room. He lay down with his clothes on and stared unseeing at the ceiling, moving over the yellow, guttering light of the gas flame by the bedroom door.

A soul within him—a hidden, secret other him—a tenant of his heart that the foot had claimed for its own and taken with it to the grave! Margaret. He had never so much as looked at her. He had never seen her. She was a piece of furniture. A desk. A chair. A ledger with the lacy, sorrowful love letter of commerce on its pages.

"My footstep," he said aloud to the walls.

Footsteps. Down the pavement of the shady street in the secret moment of the night—footsteps up the tanbark walk of the Bruces' boarding house—footsteps up the stairs—the hesitation and then the open door.

Then he was hearing her flat, tired voice—still and composed now. He turned his head on the pillow. She was standing in the bedroom door—looking at him. She had on her cheap little flowered hat and the coat with the touching curl of dusty fur about the collar.

"I'm sorry to bother you again," she said. "I won't bother you any more. You won't ever have to bother with me again. The books are in order. I'm leaving town with Ed Smiley tonight. He's going to marry me."

Then she was gone. Henry listened to her quick footsteps going down the stairs. The street door slammed and the clock in the town hall struck six times. He lay back—sad, regretful, but at the same time relieved. It was all over now. Perhaps tonight he could sleep. Sleep! That El Dorado of peace that he had long ceased hoping for. Henry shut his eyes. He had stopped trembling. It was dark outside the window—the heavy wine dark of early April. Then in a moment it began again.

Footsteps. The foot. Fast now. Faster than it had ever been. Along the damp pavements of the small town night. Running. The thud was almost painful on his sole. Then a pause. Then the running again—up the springy, yielding softness of tanbark—under the trees bursting with dark greenness in the moonless April night. Up the wooden steps—two—four—six—eight. Henry shut his eyes and clenched his teeth against the scream that struggled in his throat. Ten—twelve—. The landing now. Up the hall—. His fingers tore through the linen sheet beneath him. The door—the open door. He felt he was fainting—his eyes started from his head. Then it began—not on the sole now but on the toe—a smashing violent rhythm on the toe of his foot—a remorseless, brutal thudding that made his leg ache to the very hip. Then it stopped. The padding, running thud again—down the steps—through the tanbark—through the dark—the mossy pavements of the April night—then, at last, like a benediction it was still.

He lay on the bed for a long while before getting up. Then he went slowly down the stairs, down the path to the shed, down to the puzzle-tree with the spade in his shaking fingers. Like a madman he dug. His fingers ached and the nails broke as he clawed the box from the earth, ripped the wooden lid loose and stared at the thing within. He was standing there at dawn when Doc Sandy and the sheriff came down the path. Not moving. Just standing looking at the foot in his hand and the shoe—its toe all dark with something sticky and some wisps of washed blonde hair.

Born in Moundsville, West Virginia, in 1919, Davis Grubb studied painting at the Carnegie Institute of Technology at Pittsburgh before eye problems forced him to leave that field forever. That his writing retains his artistic vision is evidenced by several novels being made into successful films, including The Night of the Hunter *(1953) and* A Dream of Kings *(1955). Grub is known for his skillful utilization of the macabre in his short stories; many of his best have been collected in two volumes,* Twelve Tales of Suspense and the Supernatural *(1964) and* The Siege of 813 *(1987). He died in 1984.*

*When Waco gave Jim Anderson the guns Bill Longley had worn, neither man
really believed the legends about them. . . .*

SIX

The Guns of William Longley

Donald Hamilton

We'd been up north delivering a herd for old man
Butcher the summer I'm telling about. I was nineteen at the
time. I was young and big, and I was plenty tough, or
thought I was, which amounts to the same thing up to a
point. Maybe I was making up for all the years of being that
nice Anderson boy, back in Willow Fork, Texas. When your
dad wears a badge, you're kind of obliged to behave yourself around home so as not to shame him. But Pop was
dead now, and this wasn't Texas.

Anyway, I was tough enough that we had to leave Dodge
City in something of a hurry after I got into an argument
with a fellow who, it turned out, wasn't nearly as handy with
a gun as he claimed to be. I'd never killed a man before. It
made me feel kind of funny for a couple of days, but like I
say, I was young and tough then, and I'd seen men I really
cared for trampled in stampedes and drowned in rivers on
the way north. I wasn't going to grieve long over one bellig-
erent stranger.

It was on the long trail home that I first saw the guns one
evening by the fire. We had a blanket spread on the ground,
and we were playing cards for what was left of our pay—
what we hadn't already spent on girls and liquor and general hell-raising. My luck was in, and one by one the others
dropped out, all but Waco Smith, who got stubborn and
went over to his bedroll and hauled out the guns.

"I got them in Dodge," he said. "Pretty, ain't they? Fellow
I bought them from claimed they belonged to Bill Longley."

61

"Is that a fact?" I said, like I wasn't much impressed. "Who's Longley?"

I knew who Bill Longley was, all right, but a man's got a right to dicker a bit, and besides I couldn't help deviling Waco now and then. I liked him all right, but he was one of those cocky little fellows who asks for it. You know the kind. They always know everything.

I sat there while he told me about Bill Longley, the giant from Texas with thirty-two killings to his credit, the man who was hanged twice. A bunch of vigilantes strung him up once for horse-stealing he hadn't done, but the rope broke after they'd ridden off and he dropped to the ground, kind of short of breath but alive and kicking.

Then he was tried and hanged for a murder he had done, some years later in Giddings, Texas. He was so big that the rope gave way again and he landed on his feet under the trap, making six-inch-deep footprints in the hard ground—they're still there in Giddings to be seen, Waco said, Bill Longley's footprints—but it broke his neck this time and they buried him nearby. At least a funeral service was held, but some say there's just an empty coffin in the grave.

I said, "This Longley gent can't have been so much, to let folks keep stringing him up that way."

That set Waco off again, while I toyed with the guns. They were pretty, all right, in a big carved belt with two carved holsters, but I wasn't much interested in leatherwork. It was the weapons themselves that took my fancy. They'd been used, but someone had looked after them well. They were handsome pieces, smooth-working, and they had a good feel to them. You know how it is when a firearm feels just right. A fellow with hands the size of mine doesn't often find guns to fit him like that.

"How much do you figure they're worth?" I asked, when Waco stopped for breath.

"Well, now," he said, getting a sharp look on his face, and I came home to Willow Fork with the Longley guns strapped around me. If that's what they were.

I got a room and cleaned up at the hotel. I didn't much feel like riding clear out to the ranch and seeing what it looked like with Ma and Pa gone two years and nobody looking after things. Well, I'd put the place on its feet again one of these days, as soon as I'd had a little fun and saved a little money. I'd buckle right down to it, I told myself, as soon as Junellen set the date, which I'd been after her to do since before my folks died. She couldn't keep saying forever we were too young.

I got into my good clothes and went to see her. I won't say she'd been on my mind all the way up the trail and back again, because it wouldn't be true. A lot of the time I'd been too busy or tired for dreaming, and in Dodge City I'd done my best *not* to think of her, if you know what I mean. It did seem like a young fellow engaged to a beautiful girl like Junellen Barr could have behaved himself better up there, but it had been a long dusty drive and you know how it is.

But now I was home, and it seemed like I'd been missing Junellen every minute since I left, and I couldn't wait to see her. I walked along the street in the hot sunshine feeling light and happy. Maybe my leaving my guns at the hotel had something to do with the light feeling, but the happiness was all for Junellen, and I ran up the steps to the house and knocked on the door. She'd have heard we were back, and she'd be waiting to greet me, I was sure.

I knocked again and the door opened and I stepped forward eagerly. "Junellen—" I said, and stopped foolishly.

"Come in, Jim," said her father, a little turkey of a man who owned the drygoods store in town. He went on smoothly: "I understand you had quite an eventful journey. We are waiting to hear all about it."

He was being sarcastic, but that was his way, and I couldn't be bothered with trying to figure what he was driving at. I'd already stepped into the room, and there was Junellen with her mother standing close, as if to protect her, which seemed kind of funny. There was a man in the room, too, Mr. Carmichael from the bank, who'd fought with Pa in the war. He was tall and handsome as always, a little heavy nowadays but still dressed like a fashion plate. I couldn't figure what he was doing there.

It wasn't going at all the way I'd hoped, my reunion with Junellen, and I stopped, looking at her.

"So you're back, Jim," she said. "I heard you had a real exciting time. Dodge City must be quite a place."

There was a funny hard note in her voice. She held herself very straight, standing there by her mother, in a blue-flowered dress that matched her eyes. She was a real little lady, Junellen. She made kind of a point of it, in fact, and Martha Butcher, old man Butcher's kid, used to say about Junellen Barr that butter wouldn't melt in her mouth, but that always seemed like a silly saying to me, and who was Martha Butcher anyway, just because her daddy owned a lot of cows?

Martha'd also remarked about girls who had to drive two front names in harness, as if one wasn't good enough, and I'd told her it surely wasn't if it was a name like Martha, and she'd kicked me on the shin. But that was a long time ago when we were all kids.

Junellen's mother broke the silence in her nervous way: "Dear, hadn't you better tell Jim the news?" She turned to Mr. Carmichael. "Howard, perhaps you should—"

Mr. Carmichael came forward and took Junellen's hand, "Miss Barr has done me the honor to promise to be my wife," he said.

I said, "But she can't. She's engaged to me."

Junellen's mother said quickly, "It was just a childish thing, not to be taken seriously."

I said, "Well, I took it seriously!"

Junellen looked up at me. "Did you, Jim? In Dodge City, did you?" I didn't say anything. She said breathlessly, "It doesn't matter. I suppose I could forgive. . . . But you have killed a man. I could never love a man who has taken a human life."

Anyway, she said something like that. I had a funny feeling in my stomach and a roaring sound in my ears. They talk about your heart breaking, but that's where it hit me, the stomach and the ears. So I can't tell you exactly what she said, but it was something like that.

I heard myself say, "Mr. Carmichael spent the war peppering Yanks with a peashooter, I take it."

"That's different—"

Mr. Carmichael spoke quickly. "What Miss Barr means is that there's a difference between a battle and a drunken brawl, Jim. I am glad your father did not live to see his son wearing two big guns and shooting men down in the street.

He was a fine man and a good sheriff for this county. It was only for his memory's sake that I agreed to let Miss Barr break the news to you in person. From what we hear of your exploits up north, you have certainly forfeited all right to consideration from her."

There was something in what he said, but I couldn't see that it was his place to say it. "You agreed?" I said. "That was mighty kind of you sir, I'm sure." I looked away from him. "Junellen—"

Mr. Carmichael interrupted. "I do not wish my fiancée to be distressed by a continuation of this painful scene. I must ask you to leave, Jim."

I ignored him. "Junellen," I said, "is this what you really—"

Mr. Carmichael took me by the arm. I turned my head to look at him again. I looked at the hand with which he was holding me. I waited. He didn't let go. I hit him and he went back across the room and kind of fell into a chair. The chair broke under him. Junellen's father ran over to help him up. Mr. Carmichael's mouth was bloody. He wiped it with a handkerchief.

I said, "You shouldn't have put your hand on me, sir."

"Note the pride," Mr. Carmichael said, dabbing at his cut lip. "Note the vicious, twisted pride. They all have it, all these young toughs. You are too big for me to box, Jim, and it is an undignified thing, anyway. I have worn a sidearm in my time. I will go to the back and get it, while you arm yourself."

"I will meet you in front of the hotel, sir," I said, "if that is agreeable to you."

"It is agreeable," he said, and went out.

I followed him without looking back. I think Junellen was crying, and I know her parents were saying one thing and another in high, indignant voices, but the funny roaring was in my ears and I didn't pay too much attention. The sun was very bright outside. As I started for the hotel, somebody ran up to me.

"Here you are, Jim." It was Waco, holding out the Longley guns in their carved holsters. "I heard what happened. Don't take any chances with the old fool."

I looked down at him and asked, "How did Junellen and her folks learn about what happened in Dodge?"

He said, "It's a small town, Jim, and all the boys have been drinking and talking, glad to get home."

"Sure," I said, buckling on the guns. "Sure."

It didn't matter. It would have got around sooner or later, and I wouldn't have lied about it if asked. We walked slowly toward the hotel.

"Dutch LeBaron is hiding out back in the hills with a dozen men," Waco said. "I heard it from a man in a bar."

"Who's Dutch LeBaron?" I asked. I didn't care, but it was something to talk about as we walked.

"Dutch?" Waco said. "Why Dutch is wanted in five states and a couple of territories. Hell, the price on his head is so high now even Fenn is after him."

"Fenn?" I said. He sure knew a lot of names. "Who's Fenn?"

"You've heard of Old Joe Fenn, the bounty hunter. Well, if he comes after Dutch, he's asking for it. Dutch can take care of himself."

"Is that a fact?" I said, and then I saw Mr. Carmichael coming, but he was a ways off yet and I said, "You sound like this Dutch fellow was a friend of yours—"

But Waco wasn't there any more. I had the street to myself, except for Mr. Carmichael, who had a gun strapped on outside his fine coat. It was an army gun in a black army holster with a flap, worn cavalry style on the right side, butt forward. They wear them like that to make room for the saber on the left, but it makes a clumsy rig.

I walked forward to meet Mr. Carmichael, and I knew I would have to let him shoot once. He was a popular man and a rich man and he would have to draw first and shoot first or I would be in serious trouble. I figured it all out very coldly, as if I had been killing men all my life. We stopped, and Mr. Carmichael undid the flap of the army holster and pulled out the big cavalry pistol awkwardly and fired and missed, as I had known, somehow, that he would.

Then I drew the right-hand gun, and as I did so I realized that I didn't particularly want to kill Mr. Carmichael. I mean, he was a brave man coming here with his old cap-and-ball pistol, knowing all the time that I could outdraw and outshoot him with my eyes closed. But I didn't want to be killed, either, and he had the piece cocked and was about to fire again. I tried to aim for a place that wouldn't kill him, or cripple him too badly, and the gun wouldn't do it.

I mean, it was a frightening thing. It was like I was fighting the Longley gun for Mr. Carmichael's life. The old army revolver fired once more and something rapped my left arm lightly. The Longley gun went off at last, and Mr. Carmichael spun around and fell on his face in the street. There was a cry, and Junellen came running and went to her knees beside him.

"You murderer!" she screamed at me. "You hateful murderer!"

It showed how she felt about him, that she would kneel in the dust like that in her blue-flowered dress. Junellen was always very careful of her pretty clothes. I punched out the empty and replaced it. Dr. Sims came up and examined Mr. Carmichael and said he was shot in the leg, which I already knew, being the one who had shot him there. Dr. Sims said he was going to be all right, God willing.

Having heard this, I went over to another part of town and tried to get drunk. I didn't have much luck at it, so I went into the place next to the hotel for a cup of coffee. There wasn't anybody in the place but a skinny girl with an apron on.

I said, "I'd like a cup of coffee, ma'am," and sat down.

She said, coming over, "Jim Anderson, you're drunk. At least you smell like it."

I looked up and saw that it was Martha Butcher. She set a cup down in front of me. I asked, "What are you doing here waiting tables?"

She said, "I had a fight with Dad about . . . well, never mind what it was about. Anyway, I told him I was old enough to run my own life and if he didn't stop trying to boss me around like I was one of the hands, I'd pack up and leave. And he laughed and asked what I'd do for money, away from home, and I said I'd earn it, so here I am."

It was just like Martha Butcher, and I saw no reason to make a fuss over it like she probably wanted me to.

"Seems like you are," I agreed. "Do I get sugar, too, or does that cost extra?"

She laughed and set a bowl in front of me. "Did you have a good time in Dodge?" she asked.

"Fine," I said, "Good liquor. Fast games. Pretty girls. Real pretty girls."

"Fiddlesticks," she said. "I know what you think is pretty. Blond and simpering. You big fool. If you'd killed him over her, they'd have put you in jail, at the very least. And just what are you planning to use for an arm when that one gets rotten and falls off? Sit still."

She got some water and cloth and fixed up my arm where Mr. Carmichael's bullet had nicked it.

"Have you been out to your place yet?" she asked.

I shook my head. "Figure there can't be much out there by now. I'll get after it one of these days."

"One of these days!" she said. "You mean when you get tired of strutting around with those big guns and acting dangerous—." She stopped abruptly.

I looked around, and got to my feet. Waco was there in the doorway, and with him was a big man, not as tall as I was, but wider. He was a real whiskery gent, with a mat of black beard you could have used for stuffing a mattress. He wore two gunbelts, crossed, kind of sagging low at the hips.

Waco said, "You're a fool to sit with your back to the door, Jim. That's the mistake Hickok made, remember? If instead of us it had been somebody like Jack McCall—"

"Who's Jack McCall?" I asked innocently.

"Why, he's the fellow shot Wild Bill in the back. . . ." Waco's face reddened. "All right, all right. Always kidding me. Dutch, this big joker is my partner, Jim Anderson. Jim, Dutch LeBaron. He's got a proposition for us."

I tried to think back to where Waco and I had decided to become partners, and couldn't remember the occasion. Well, maybe it happens like that, but it seemed like I should have had some say in it.

"Your partner tells me you're pretty handy with those guns," LeBaron said, after Martha'd moved off across the room. "I can use a man like that."

"For what?" I asked.

"For making some quick money over in New Mexico territory," he said.

I didn't ask any fool questions, like whether the money was to be made legally or illegally. "I'll think about it," I said.

Waco caught my arm. "What's to think about? We'll be rich, Jim!"

I said, "I'll think about it, Waco."

LeBaron said, "What's the matter, sonny, are you scared?"

I turned to look at him. He was grinning at me, but his eyes weren't grinning, and his hands weren't too far from those low-slung guns.

I said, "Try me and see."

I waited a little. Nothing happened. I walked out of there and got my pony and rode out to the ranch, reaching the place about dawn. I opened the door and stood there, surprised. It looked just about the way it had when the folks were alive, and I half expected to hear Ma yelling at me to beat the dust off outside and not bring it into the house. Somebody had cleaned the place up for me, and I thought I knew who. Well, it certainly was neighborly of her, I told myself. It was nice to have somebody show a sign that they were glad to have me home, even if it was only Martha Butcher.

I spent a couple of days out there, resting up and riding around. I didn't find much stock. It was going to take money to make a going ranch of it again, and I didn't figure any credit at Mr. Carmichael's bank was anything to count on. I couldn't help giving some thought to Waco and LeBaron and the proposition they'd put before me. It was funny. I'd think about it most when I had the guns on. I was out back practicing with them one day when the stranger rode up.

He was a little, dry elderly man on a sad-looking white horse he must have hired at the livery stable for not very much, and he wore his gun in front of his left hip with butt to the right for a cross draw. He didn't make any noise coming up. I'd fired a couple of times before I realized he was there.

"Not bad," he said when he saw me looking at him. "Do you know a man named LeBaron, son?"

"I've met him," I said.

"Is he here?"

"Why should he be here?"

"A bartender in town told me he'd heard you and your sidekick, Smith, had joined up with LeBaron, so I thought you might have given him the use of your place. It would be more comfortable for him than hiding out in the hills."

"He isn't here," I said. The stranger glanced toward the house. I started to get mad, but shrugged instead. "Look around if you want to."

"In that case," he said, "I don't figure I want to." He glanced toward the target I'd been shooting at, and back to me. "Killed a man in Dodge, didn't you, son? And then stood real calm and let a fellow here in town fire three shots at you, after which you laughed and pinked him neatly in the leg."

"I don't recall laughing," I said. "And it was two shots, not three."

"It makes a good story, however," he said. "And it is spreading. You have a reputation already, did you know that, Anderson? I didn't come here just to look for LeBaron. I figured I'd like to have a look at you, too. I always like to look up fellows I might have business with later."

"Business?" I said, and then I saw that he'd taken a tarnished old badge out of his pocket and was pinning it on his shirt. "Have you a warrant, sir?" I asked.

"Not for you," he said. "Not yet."

He swung the old white horse around and rode off. When he was out of sight, I got my pony out of the corral. It was time I had a talk with Waco. Maybe I was going to join LeBaron and maybe I wasn't, but I didn't much like his spreading it around before it was true.

I didn't have to look for him in town. He came riding to meet me with three companions, all hard ones if I ever saw any.

"Did you see Fenn?" he shouted as he came up. "Did he come this way?"

"A little old fellow with some kind of badge?" I said. "Was that Fenn? He headed back to town, about ten minutes ahead of me. He didn't look like much."

"Neither does the devil when he's on business," Waco said. "Come on, we'd better warn Dutch before he rides into town."

I rode along with them, and we tried to catch LeBaron on the trail, but he'd already passed with a couple of men. We saw their dust ahead and chased it, but they made it before us, and Fenn was waiting in front of the cantina that was LeBaron's hangout when he was in town.

We saw it all as we came pounding after LeBaron, who dismounted and started into the place, but Fenn came forward, looking small and inoffensive. He was saying something and holding out his hand. LeBaron stopped and shook hands with him, and the little man held onto LeBaron's hand, took a step to the side, and pulled his gun out of that cross-draw holster left-handed, with a kind of twisting motion.

Before LeBaron could do anything with his free hand, the little old man had brought the pistol barrel down across his head. It was as neat and coldblooded a thing as you'd care to see. In an instant, LeBaron was unconscious on the ground, and Old Joe Fenn was covering the two men who'd been riding with him.

Waco Smith, riding beside me, made a sort of moaning sound as if he'd been clubbed himself. "Get him!" he shouted, drawing his gun. "Get the dirty, sneaking bounty hunter!"

I saw the little man throw a look over his shoulder, but there wasn't much he could do about us with those other two to handle. I guess he hadn't figured us for reinforcements riding in. Waco fired and missed. He never could shoot much, particularly from horseback. I reached out with one of the guns and hit him over the head before he could shoot again. He spilled from the saddle.

I didn't have it all figured out. Certainly it wasn't a very nice thing Mr. Fenn had done, first taking a man's hand in friendship and then knocking him unconscious. Still, I didn't figure LeBaron had ever been one for giving anybody a break; and there was something about the old fellow standing there with his tarnished old badge that reminded me of Pa, who'd died wearing a similar piece of tin on his chest. Anyway, there comes a time in a man's life when he's got to make a choice, and that's the way I made mine.

71

Waco and I had been riding ahead of the others. I turned my pony fast and covered them with the guns as they came charging up—as well as you can cover anybody from a plunging horse. One of them had his pistol aimed to shoot. The left-handed Longley gun went off and he fell to the ground. I was kind of surprised. I'd never been much at shooting left-handed. The other two riders veered off and headed out of town.

By the time I got my pony quieted down from having that gun go off in his ear, everything was pretty much under control. Waco had disappeared, so I figured he couldn't be hurt much; and the new sheriff was there, old drunken Billy Bates who'd been elected after Pa's death by the gambling element in town, who hadn't liked the strict way Pa ran things.

"I suppose it's legal," Old Billy was saying grudgingly. "But I don't take it kindly, Marshal, your coming here to serve a warrant without letting me know."

"My apologies, Sheriff," Fenn said smoothly. "An oversight, I assure you. Now, I'd like a wagon. He's worth seven-hundred and fifty dollars over in New Mexico Territory."

"No decent person would want that kind of money," Old Billy said sourly, swaying on his feet.

"There's only one kind of money," Fenn said. "Just as there's only one kind of law, even though there's different kinds of men enforcing it." He looked at me as I came up. "Much obliged, son."

"*Por nada,*" I said. "You get in certain habits when you've had a badge in the family. My daddy was sheriff here once."

"So? I didn't know that." Fenn looked at me sharply. "Don't look like you're making any plans to follow in his footsteps. That's hardly a lawman's rig you wearing."

I said, "Maybe, but I never yet beat a man over the head while I was shaking his hand, Marshal."

"Son," he said, "my job is to enforce the law and maybe make a small profit on the side, not to play games with fair and unfair." He looked at me for a moment longer. "Well, maybe we'll meet again. It depends."

"On what?" I asked.

"On the price," he said. "That price on your head."

"But I haven't got—"

"Not now," he said. "But you will, wearing those guns. I know the signs. I've seen them before, too many times. Don't count on having me under obligation to you, when your time comes. I never let personal feelings interfere with business. . . . Easy, now," he said, to a couple of fellows who were lifting LeBaron, bound hand and foot, into the wagon that somebody had driven up. "Easy. Don't damage the merchandise. I take pride in delivering them in good shape for standing trial, whenever possible."

I decided I needed a drink, and then I changed my mind in favor of a cup of coffee. As I walked down the street, leaving my pony at the rail back there, the wagon rolled past and went out of town ahead of me. I was still watching it, for no special reason, when Waco stepped from the alley behind me.

"Jim!" he said. "Turn around, Jim!"

I turned slowly. He was a little unsteady on his feet, standing there, maybe from my hitting him, maybe from drinking. I thought it was drinking. I hadn't hit him very hard. He'd had time for a couple of quick ones, and liquor always got to him fast.

"You sold us out, you damn traitor!" he cried. "You took sides with the law!"

"I never was against it," I said. "Not really."

"After everything I've done for you!" he said thickly. "I was going to make you a great man, Jim, greater than Longley or Hickok or any of them. With my brains and your size and speed, nothing could have stopped us! But you turned on me! Do you think you can do it alone? Is that what you're figuring, to leave me behind now that I've built you up to be somebody?"

"Waco," I said, "I never had any ambitions to be—"

"You and your medicine guns!" he sneered. "Let me tell you something. Those old guns are just something I picked up in a pawnshop. I spun a good yarn about them to give you confidence. You were on the edge, you needed a push in the right direction, and I knew once you started wearing a flash rig like that, with one killing under your belt already, somebody'd be bound to try you again, and we'd be on our

73

way to fame. But as for their being Bill Longley's guns, don't make me laugh!"

I said, "Waco—"

"They's just metal and wood like any other guns!" he said. "And I'm going to prove it to you right now! I don't need you, Jim! I'm as good a man as you, even if you laugh at me and make jokes at my expense. . . . *Are you ready, Jim?*"

He was crouching, and I looked at him, Waco Smith, with whom I'd ridden up the trail and back. I saw that he was no good and I saw that he was dead. It didn't matter whose guns I was wearing, and all he'd really said was that he didn't know whose guns they were. But it didn't matter, they were my guns now, and he was just a little runt who never could shoot for shucks, anyway. He was dead, and so were the others, the ones who'd come after him, because they'd come, I knew that.

I saw them come to try me, one after the other, and I saw them go down before the big black guns, all except the last, the one I couldn't quite make out. Maybe it was Fenn and maybe it wasn't. . . .

I said, "To hell with you, Waco. I've got nothing against you, and I'm not going to fight you. Tonight or any other time."

I turned and walked away. I heard the sound of his gun behind me an instant before the bullet hit me. Then I wasn't hearing anything for a while. When I came to, I was in bed, and Martha Butcher was there.

"Jim!" she breathed. "Oh, Jim . . . !"

She looked real worried, and kind of pretty, I thought, but of course I was half out of my head. She looked even prettier the day I asked her to marry me, some months later, but maybe I was a little out of my head that day, too. Old Man Butcher didn't like it a bit. It seems his fight with Martha had been about her cleaning up my place, and his ordering her to quit and stay away from that young troublemaker, as he'd called me after getting word of all the hell we'd raised up north after delivering his cattle.

He didn't like it, but he offered me a job, I suppose for Martha's sake. I thanked him and told him I was much obliged, but I'd just accepted an appointment as Deputy

U.S. Marshal. Seems like somebody had recommended me for the job, maybe Old Joe Fenn, maybe not. I got my old gun out of my bedroll and wore it tucked inside my belt when I thought I might need it. It was a funny thing how seldom I had any use for it, even wearing a badge. With that job, I was the first in the neighborhood to hear about Waco Smith. The news came from New Mexico Territory. Waco and a bunch had pulled a job over there, and a posse has trapped them in a box canyon and shot them to pieces.

I never wore the other guns again. After we moved into the old place, I hung them on the wall. It was right after I'd run against Billy Bates for sheriff and won that I came home to find them gone. Martha looked surprised when I asked about them.

"Why," she said, "I gave them to your friend, Mr. Williams. He said you'd sold them to him. Here's the money."

I counted the money, and it was a fair enough price for a pair of second-hand guns and holsters, but I hadn't met any Mr. Williams.

I started to say so, but Martha was still talking. She said, "He certainly had an odd first name, didn't he? Who'd christen anybody Long Williams? Not that he wasn't big enough. I guess he'd be as tall as you, wouldn't he, if he didn't have that trouble with his neck?"

"His neck?" I said.

"Why, yes," she said. "Didn't you notice when you talked to him, the way he kept his head cocked to the side. Like this."

She showed me how Long Williams had kept his head cocked to the side. She looked real pretty doing it, and I couldn't figure how I'd ever thought her plain, but maybe she'd changed. Or maybe I had. I kissed her and gave her back the gun money to buy something for herself, and went outside to think. Long Williams, William Longley. A man with a wry neck and a man who was hanged twice. It was kind of strange, to be sure, but after a time I decided it was just a coincidence. Some drifter riding by just saw the guns through the window and took a fancy to them.

I mean, if it had really been Bill Longley, if he was alive and had his guns back, we'd surely have heard of him by now down at the sheriff's office, and we never have.

75

The creator of secret agent Matthew Helm, Donald Hamilton was born in Sweden in 1916 and immigrated to the United States in 1924. Educated at the University of Chicago, he has been a full-time writer since 1946. Many of Hamilton's novels have been made into films, including The Big Country (1957), starring Gregory Peck and Charlton Heston. The two worlds of the ruthless killer and the Western combine in the haunting "The Guns of William Longley."

More than most, Père Lebas should know all about sin and guilt. . . .

SEVEN

The Soul of Rose Dédé
M. E. M. Davis

The child pushed his way though the tall weeds, which were dripping with the midsummer-eve midnight dew-melt. He was so little that the rough leaves met above his head. He wore a trailing white gown whose loose folds tripped him, so that he stumbled and fell over a sunken mound. But he laughed as he scrambled to his feet—a cooing baby laugh, taken up by the inward-blowing Gulf wind, and carried away to the soughing pines that made a black line against the dim sky.

His progress was slow, for he stopped—his forehead gravely puckered, his finger in his mouth—to listen to the clear whistle of a mockingbird in the live-oak above his head; he watched the heavy flight of a white night-moth from one jimson-weed trumpet to another; he strayed aside to pick a bit of shining punk from the sloughing bark of a rotten log; he held this in his closed palm as he came at last into the open space where the others were.

"Holà, 'Tit-Pierre!" said André, who was half reclining on a mildewed marble slab, with his long black cloak floating loosely from his shoulders, and his hands clasped about his knees. "Holà! Must thou needs be ever a-searching! Have I not told thee, little Hard-Head, that she hath long forgotten thee?"

His voice was mocking, but his dark eyes were quizzically kind.

The child's under-lip quivered, and he turned slowly about. But Père Lebas, sitting just across the narrow footway, laid a caressing hand on his curly head. "Nay, go thy way, 'Tit Pierre," he said, gently; "André does but tease. A mother hath never yet forgot her child."

77

"Do you indeed think he will find her?" asked André, arching his black brows incredulously.

"He will not find her," returned the priest. "Margot Caillion was in a far country when I saw her last, and even then her grandchildren were playing about her knees. But it harms not the child to seek her."

They spoke a soft provincial French, and the familiar *thou* betokened an unwonted intimacy between the hollow-cheeked old priest and his companion, whose forehead wore the frankness of early youth.

"I would the child could talk!" cried the young man, gayly. "Then might he tell us somewhat of the women that ever come and go in yonder great house."

The priest shuddered, crossing himself, and drew his cowl over his face.

'Tit-Pierre, his gown gathered in his arm, had gone on his way. Nathan Pilger, hunched up on a low, irregular hummock against the picket-fence, made a speaking-trumpet of his two horny hands, and pretended to hail him as he passed. 'Tit-Pierre nodded brightly at the old man, and waved his own chubby fist.

The gate sagged a little on its hinges, so that he had some difficulty in moving it. But he squeezed through a narrow opening, and passed between the prim flower-beds to the house.

It was a lofty mansion, with vast wings on either side, and wide galleries, which were upheld by fluted columns. It faced the bay, and a covered arcade ran from the entrance across the lawn to a gay little wooden kiosk, which hung on the bluff over the water's edge. A flight of stone steps led up to the house. 'Tit-Pierre climbed these laboriously. The great carved doors were closed, but a blind of one of the long French windows in the west wing stood slightly ajar. 'Tit-Pierre pushed this open. The bedchamber into which he peered was large and luxuriously furnished. A lamp with a crimson shade burned on its claw-footed gilt pedestal in a corner; the low light diffused a rosy radiance about the room. The filmy curtains at the windows waved to and fro softly in the June night wind. The huge old-fashioned, four-posted bed, overhung by a baldachin of carved wood with satin linings, occupied a deep alcove. A woman was sleeping there beneath the lace netting. The snow-white bed-linen followed the contours of her rounded limbs, giving her the look of a recumbent marble statue. Her black hair, loosed from its heavy coil, spread over the pillow. One ex-quisite bare arm lay across her forehead, partly concealing her face. Her measured breathing rose and fell rhythmically on the air. A robe of pale silk that hung across a chair, dainty lace-edged garments tossed carelessly on an antique lounge—these seemed instinct still with the nameless, sub-tle grace of her who had but now put them off.

On a table by the window, upon whose threshold the child stood atiptoe, was set a large crystal bowl filled with water-lilies. Their white petals were folded; the round, red-lined green leaves glistened in the lamp light. One long bud, rolled tightly in its green and brown sheath, hung over the fluted edge of the bowl, swaying gently on its flexible stem. 'Tit-Pierre gazed at it intently, frowning a little, then put out a small forefinger and touched it. A quick thrill ran along the stem; the bud moved lightly from side to side and burst suddenly into bloom; the slim white petals quivered; a trem-ulous, sighing, whispering sound issued from the heart of gold. The child listened, holding the fragrant disk to his pink ear, and laughed softly.

He moved about the room, examining with infantile curi-osity the costly objects scattered upon small tables and ranged upon the low, many-shelved mantel.

Presently he pushed a chair against the foot of the bed, climbed upon it, lifted the netting, and crept cautiously to the sleeper's side. He sat for a moment regarding her. Her lips were parted in a half-smile; the long lashes which swept her cheeks were wet, as if a happy tear had just trembled there. 'Tit-Pierre laid his hand on her smooth wrist, and touched timidly the snowy globes that gleamed beneath the open-work of her night-dress. She threw up her arm, turn-ing her face full upon him, unclosed her large, luminous eyes, smiled, and slept again.

With a sigh, which seemed rather of resignation than of disappointment, the child crept away and clambered again to the floor.

Outside the fog was thickening. The dark waters of the bay lapped the foot of the low bluff; their soft, monotonous moan was rising by imperceptible degrees to a higher key. The scrubby cedars, leaning at all angles over the water, were shaken at intervals by heavy puffs of wind, which drove the mist in white, ragged masses across the shelled road, over the weedy neutral ground, and out into the tops of the sombre pines. The red lights in a row of sloops at anchor over against Cat Island had dwindled to faintly glimmering sparks. The watery flash of the revolving light in the light-house off the point of the island showed a black wedge-shaped cloud stretching up the seaward sky.

Nathan Pilger screwed up his eye and watched the cloud critically. André followed the direction of his gaze with idle interest, then turned to look again at the woman who sat on a grassy barrow a few paces beyond Père Lebas.

"She has never been here before," he said to himself, his heart stirring curiously. "I would I could see her face!"

Her back was towards the little group; her elbow was on her knee, her chin in her hand. Her figure was slight and girlish; her white gown gleamed ghostlike in the wan light.

"Naw, I bain't complainin', nor nothin'," said the old sailor, dropping the cloud, as it were, and taking up a broken thread of talk; "hows'ever, it's tarnation wearyin' a-settin' here so studdy year in an' year out. Leas'ways," he added, shifting his seat to another part of the low mound, "fer an old sailor sech as I be."

"If one could but quit his place and move about, like 'Tit-Pierre yonder," said André, musingly, "it would not be so bad. For myself, I would not want—"

"The child is free to come and go because his soul is white. There is no stain upon 'Tit-Pierre. The child hath not sinned." It was the priest who spoke. His voice was harsh and forbidding. His deep-set eyes were fixed upon the tall spire of Our Lady of the Gulf, dimly outlined against the sky beyond an intervening reach of clustering roofs and shaded gardens.

André stared at him wonderingly, and glanced half furtively at the stranger, as if in her presence, perchance, might be found an explanation of the speaker's unwonted bitterness of tone. She had not moved. "I would I could see her face!" he muttered, under his breath. "For myself," he went on, lifting his voice, "I am sure I would not want to wander far. I fain would walk once more on the road along the curve of the bay; or under the pines, where little white patches of moonlight fall between the straight, tall tree-trunks. And I would go sometimes, if I might, and kneel before the altar of Our Lady of the Gulf."

Nathan Pilger grunted contemptuously. "What a lan'lub-ber ye be, Andry!" he said, his strong nasal English con-trasting oddly with the smooth foreign speech of the others. "What a lan'lubber ye be! Ye bain't no sailor, like your fa-ther afore ye. Tony Dewdonny hed as good a pair o' sea-legs as ever I see. Lord! if there wa'n't no diffickulties in the way, Nathan Pilger 'd ship fer some port a leetle more furrin than the shadder of Our Lady yunder! Many's the deck I've walked," he continued, his husky voice growing more and more animated, "an' many's the vi'ge I've made to outland-ish places. Why, you'd oughter see Arkangel, Andry. Here's the north coast o' Rooshy"—he leaned over and traced with his forefinger the rude outlines of a map on the ground; the wind lifted his long, gray locks and tossed them over his wrinkled forehead; "here's the White Sea; and here, off the mouth of the Dewiny River, is Arkangel. The Rooshan men in that there town, Andry, wears petticoats like women; whilse down here, in the South Pacific, at Taheety, the folks don't wear no clo'es at all to speak of! You'd oughter see Taheety, Andry. An' here, off Guinea—"

"All those places are fine, no doubt," interrupted his lis-tener, "Arkangel and Taheetee and Guinee"—his tongue tripped a little over the unfamiliar names—"but, for myself, I do not care to see them. I find it well on the bay shore here, where I can see the sloops come sailing in through the pass, with the sun on their white sails. And the little boats that rock on the water! Do you remember, Silvain," he cried, turning to the priest, "how we used to steal away before sunrise in my father's little fishingboat, when we were boys, and come back at night with our backs blistered by the sun and our arms aching, hein? That was before you went away to France to study for the priesthood. Ah, but those were good times!" He threw back his head and laughed joyously. His dark hair, wet with the mist, lay in loose rings on his forehead; his fine young face, beardless but manly, seemed almost lustrous in the pale darkness. "Do you remember,

Silvain? Right where the big house stands, there was Jacques Caillion's steep-roofed cottage, with the garden in front full of pinks and mignonette and sweet herbs; and the vine-hung porch where 'Tit-Pierre used to play, and where Margot Caillion used to stand shading her eyes with her arm, and looking out for her man to come home from sea."

"Jack Caillion," said Nathan Pilger, "was washed overboard from the *Suzanne* in a storm off Hatteras in '11—him and Dunc Cook and Ba'tist' Roux."

"The old church of Our Lady of the Gulf," the young man continued, "was just a stone's-throw this side of where the new one was built; back a little is our cottage, and your father's, Silvain; and in the hollow beyond Justin Roux has his blacksmith's forge."

He paused, his voice dying away almost to a whisper. The waves were beating more noisily against the bluff, filling the silence with a sort of hoarse plaint; the fog—gray, soft, impenetrable—rested on them like a cloud. The moisture fell in an audible drip-drop from the leaves and the long, pendent moss of the live-oaks. A mare, with her colt beside her, came trotting around the bend of the road. She approached within a few feet of the girl, reared violently, snorting, and dashed away, followed by the whinnying colt. The clatter of their feet echoed on the muffled air. The girl, in her white dress, sat rigidly motionless, with her face turned seaward.

André lifted his head and went on, dreamily: "I mind me, most of all, of one day when all the girls and boys of the village walked over to Bayou Galère to gather water-lilies. Margot Caillion, with 'Tit-Pierre in her hand, came along to mind the girls. You had but just come back from France in your priest's frock, Silvain. You were in the church door when we passed, with your book in your hand." A smothered groan escaped the priest, and he threw up his arm as if to ward off a blow. "And you were there when we came back at sunset. The smell of the pines that day was like balm. The lilies were white on the dark breast of the winding bayou. Rose Dédé's arms were heaped so full of lilies that you could only see her laughing black eyes above them. But Lorance would only take a few buds. She said it was a kind of sin to take them away from the water where they grew. Lorance was ever—"

The girl had dropped her hands in her lap, and was listening. At the sound of her own name she turned her face towards the speaker.

"Lorance!" gasped André. "Is it truly you, Lorance?"

"Yes, it is I, André Dieudonné," she replied, quietly. Her pale girlish face, with its delicate outlines, was crowned with an aureole of bright hair, which hung in two thick braids to her waist; her soft brown eyes were a little sunken, as if she had wept overmuch. But her voice was strangely cold and passionless.

"But . . . when did you . . . come, Lorance?" André demanded, breathlessly.

"I came," she said, in the same calm, measured tone, "but a little after you, André Dieudonné. First 'Tit-Pierre, then you, and then myself."

"Why, then—" he began. He rose abruptly, gathering his mantle about him, and leaned over the marble slab where he had been sitting. *"'Sacred to the memory of André Antoine Marie Dieudonné,'"* he read, slowly, slipping his finger along the mouldy French lettering, *"'who died at this place August 20th, 1809. In the 22d year of his age.'* Eighty years and more ago I came!" he cried. "And you have been here all these years, Lorance, and I have not known! Why, then, did you never come up?"

She did not answer at once. "I was tired," she said, presently, "and I rested well down there in the cool, dark silence. And I was not lonely . . . at first, for I heard Margot Caillion passing about, putting flowers above 'Tit-Pierre and you and me. My mother and yours often came and wept with her for us all—and my father, and your little brothers. The sound of their weeping comforted me. Then . . . after a while . . . no one seemed to remember us any more."

"Margot Caillion," said Nathan Pilger, "went back, when her man was drownded, to the place in France where she was born. The others be all layin' in the old church-yard yunder on the hill . . . all but Silvann Leebaw an' me."

She looked at the old man and smiled gravely. "A long time passed," she went on, slowly. "I could sometimes hear you speak to 'Tit-Pierre, André Dieudonné; . . . and at last some men came and dug quite near me; and as they pushed their spades through the moist turf they talked about the good Père Lebas; and then I knew that Silvain was coming." The priest's head fell upon his breast; he covered his face with his hands and rocked to and fro on his low seat. "Not long after, Nathan Pilger came. Down there in my narrow chamber I have heard above me, year after year, the murmur of your voices on St. John's eve, and ever the feet of 'Tit-Pierre, as he goes back and forth seeking his mother. But I cared not to leave my place. For why should I wish to look upon your face, André Dieudonné, and mark there the memory of your love for Rose Dédé?"

Her voice shook with a sudden passion as she uttered the last words. The hands lying in her lap were twisted together convulsively; a flush leaped into her pale cheeks.

"Rose Dédé!" echoed André, amazedly. "Nay, Lorance, but I never loved Rose Dédé! If she perchance cared for me—"

"Silence, fool!" cried the priest, sternly. He had thrown back his cowl; his eyes glowed like coals in his white face; he lifted his hand menacingly. "Thou wert ever a vain puppet, André Dieudonné. It was not for such as thou that Rose Dédé sinned away her soul! Was it *thou* she came at midnight to meet in the lone shadows of these very live-oaks? Hast *thou* ever worn the garments of a priest? . . . They shunned Rose Dédé in the village . . . but the priest said mass at the altar of Our Lady of the Gulf, . . . and the wail of the babe was sharp in the hut under the pines, . . . and it ceased to breathe, . . . and the mother turned her face to the wall and died, . . . and my heart was cold in my breast as I looked on the dead faces of the mother and the child. . . . They lie under the pine-trees by Bayou Galère. But the priest lived to old age; . . . and when he died, he durst not sleep in consecrated ground, but fain would lie in the shadows of the live oaks, where the dark eyes of Rose Dédé looked love into his."

His wild talk fell upon unheeding ears. 'Tit-Pierre had come out of the house. He was nestling against Nathan Pilger's knee. He held a lily-bud in one hand, and with the other he caressed the sailor's weather-beaten cheek.

"'Tit-Pierre," whispered the old man, "that is Lorance Baudrot. Do you remember her, 'Tit-Pierre?" The child smiled intelligently. "Lorance was but a slip of a girl when I come down here from Cape Cod—cabin-boy aboard the *Mary Ann*. She was the pretties' lass on all the bay shore. An' I—I loved her, 'Tit-Pierre. But I wa'n't no match agin Andry Dewdonny; an' I know'd it from the fust. Andry was the likelies' lad hereabout, an' the harnsomes'. I see that Lorance loved him. An' when the yaller-fever took him, I see her a-droop-in' an' a-droopin' tell she died, an' she never even know'd I loved her. Her an' Andry was laid here young, 'Tit-Pierre, 'longside o' you. I lived ter be pretty tol'able old; but when I hed made my last v'ige, an' was about fetchin' my las' breath, I give orders ter be laid in this here old buryin'-groun' some'er's clost ter the grave o' Lorance Baudrot."

His voice was overborne by André's exultant tones. "Lorance!" he cried, "did you indeed love me?—*me!*"

Her dark eyes met his frankly, and she smiled.

"Ah, if I had only known!" he sighed—"if I had only known, Lorance, I would surely have lived! We would have walked one morning to Our Lady of the Gulf, with all the village-folk about us, and Silvain—the good Père Lebas— would have joined our hands. . . . My father would have given us a little plot of ground; . . . you would have planted flowers about the door of our cottage; . . . our children would have played in the sand under the bluff. . . ."

A sudden gust of wind blew the fog aside, and a zigzag of flame tore the wedge-shaped cloud in two. A greenish light played for an instant over the weed-grown spot. The mocking-bird, long silent in the heart of the live-oak, began to sing.

"All these years you have been near me," he murmured, reproachfully, "and I did not know." Then, as if struck by a breathless thought, he stretched out his arms imploringly. "I love you, Lorance," he said. "I have always loved you. Will you not be my wife now? Silvain will say the words, and 'Tit-Pierre, who can go back and forth, will put this ring, which was my mother's, upon your finger, and he will bring me a curl of your soft hair to twist about mine. I cannot come to you, Lorance; I cannot even touch your hand. But when I go down into my dark place I can be content dreaming of you. And on the blessed St. John's eves I will know you are mine, as you sit there in your white gown."

As he ceased speaking, Père Lebas, with his head upon his breast, began murmuring, as if mechanically, the words which preface the holy sacrament of marriage. His voice faltered, he raised his head, and a cry of wonder burst from his lips. For André had moved away from the mouldy gravestone and stood just in front of him. Lorance, as if upborne on invisible wings, was floating lightly across the intervening space. Her shroud enveloped her like a cloud, her arms were extended, her lips were parted in a rapt smile. Nathan Pilger, with 'Tit-Pierre in his arms, had limped forward. He halted beside André, and as the young man folded the girl to his breast, the child reached over and laid an open lily on her down-drooped head.

The priest stared wildly at them, and struggled to rise, but could not. As he sank panting back upon the crumbling tomb, his anguish overcame him. "My God!" he groaned hoarsely, "I, only I, cannot move from my place. *The soul of Rose Dédé hangs like a millstone about my neck!*"

Even as he spoke, the cloud broke with a roar. The storm—black, heavy, thunderous—came rushing across the bay. It blotted out, in a lightning's flash, the mansion which stands on the site of Jacques Caillion's hut, and the weedgrown, ancient, forgotten graveyard in its shadow.

. . . And a bell in the steeple of Our Lady of the Gulf rang out the hour.

Born in Alabama in 1852, Mary Evelyn Moore Davis was the precocious daughter of a Massachusetts doctor-turned cotton planter. Educated by tutors on the family's Texas plantation, she first published strongly pro-Confederate poems during the Civil War and following the war married former Confederate calvary Major T. E. Davis, editor of the Houston Telegraph. *One of the first writers to use black dialect for literary purposes, she, wrote such novels and memoirs as* War Times at La Rose Blanche *(1888) and* The Little Chevalier *(1903).*

When he came to educate them, he learned something from their "ignorant" superstitions. . . .

EIGHT

The Stormsong Runner
Jack L. Chalker

I wonder who's in charge of cold weather for this region. I'd like to talk to them. You see, I—no, I'm not crazy. Or maybe I am. It would simplify things enormously if I were.

Look, let me explain it to you. About three years ago, I graduated from college in Pittsburgh. There I was, twenty-two, fresh, eager, armed with a degree in elementary education. All scholarship, no problems. I sailed through.

And back then, as now, that degree and half a buck bought a large coffee to go.

So I drifted, bummed around, took any job I could get, while firing off applications to dozens of school districts. The baby boom's over, though—there were few openings, none that wouldn't make you cut your throat in a couple of years.

I was on the road to failing the most important course of all—life. I started drinking, blowing pot and sniffing coke, and was in and out involved with a bunch of flaky girls more into that than I was.

What rescued me was, oddly enough, an accident. I was driving a girlfriend's old clunker when this fellow ran a light and hit me broadside. A couple of weeks in the hospital, a lurking lawyer I'd known from high school, and I suddenly had a good deal of the other guy's insurance company's money.

I bought a place down in southern West Virginia, up in the hills in the middle of nowhere, and tried to get my head on straight. It was peaceful in those mountains, and quiet; the little town about three miles away had the few necessities of life available, and the people were friendly, if a little curious about why such a rich city feller would move down there. Grass is greener syndrome, I suppose.

As I wandered the trails of my first summer, I made some acquaintance with the people who lived further back, primitive, clannish, and isolated from even the tiny corner of the twentieth century that permeated the little town. I even got shot at when I discovered that they still do indeed have stills back there—and got blind stinking drunk when we straightened it out.

The grinding poverty of these people was matched only by their lack of knowledge about how destitute they really were. State social workers and welfare people sometimes trekked up there, but they encountered hostility mixed with pride. And, in a way, I admired the mountain folk all the more for it, for in some things they were richer than anyone in this uncertain world—their sense of family, the closeness between people, the love of nature and the placement of a person's worth above all else—these were things my own culture had long ago lost, called corny and hick.

Most of these people were illiterate, and so were their kids. Most of the time the kids were kept hidden when the state people came up—these folk were too poor to afford shoes, pens and pencils, and all the other costly paraphernalia of our "free" school system. They preferred to ignore the state laws on education as much as they did the federal ones on making moonshine.

Well, I talked to some of the state people, who knew of the problem but could do little about it, and convinced someone in the welfare department that I could make a contribution. They accepted my teaching certificate, and I became a *per diem* teacher to the hill people on the West Virginia State Department of Education. Not much, but it was a job, and I was needed here. The only way these people were ever going to break the bonds of poverty and isolation was through education, at least in the basics. I was determined that my students—perhaps a dozen at the start—would be able to read and write and do simple, practical sums before I was through—and that's more than most modern high school graduates in urban areas can do these days.

It was tough to get some of those parents to agree, but when the first snow fell in early October I had a group. We met in my house—a two-story actual log cabin, but with only two large rooms (one more than I needed). The kids were fun, and eager learners. I wound up with an ominous thirteen, but it was perfect—each one got individual attention from me, and I got to know them well. When they ran into trouble, I'd go up to their shacks, stomach lined as much as possible with yogurt or cream against the inevitable parental hospitality, and we'd have extra lessons. In this way I sneakily started teaching some of the parents as well.

Their ages ranged from nine to fourteen, but they all started off evenly—they were ignorant as hell. And I got help—the state was so pleased to make any kind of a dent in the region that they sent us everything from hot-lunch supplies to pens, pencils, crayons, and even some simple books, obviously years old and discovered in some Charleston elementary school's basement but perfect for us.

Schooling was erratic and unconventional. The snow was extremely deep at times, the weather as fierce as the Canadian northwoods, and there were whole weeks when contact was impossible. Yet, as spring approached progress had been made; their world was a little wider. They were mostly on Dick and Jane, but they were *reading,* and they were already adding and subtracting on a basic level.

And they taught me, too. We spent time in those woodlands watching deer and coon, and, as spring arrived, they showed me the best spots for viewing the wonderful flowers and catching the biggest fish.

They were close to nature and were, in fact, a part of it. It sometimes made me hesitate in what I was doing. "Poor" is such a relative term.

Only one of the students was a real puzzle—a girl of ten or eleven (who knew for sure?) named Cindy Lou Whittler, the only child of a poor woman who made out as best she could while tending the grave of her husband just out back. She was fat and acne-ridden, and awkward as hell; the other kids would have made her the butt of their cruel jokes in normal circumstances, but they steered clear of her. She sat off by herself, talked only haltingly and only when prompted—and you could cut the tension with a knife.

They were scared to death of her.

Finally I could stand it no longer, and had a talk with Billy Bushman. He was the oldest of the group, the most worldly-wise, and was the natural class leader.

"Billy," I asked him one day, "you've got to tell me. Why are you and everybody else scared of Cindy Lou?"

He shuffled uneasily and glanced around. "'Cause she a witcher woman," he replied softly. "You do somthang she don' liak, she sing th' stormsong an' thas all fo you."

A little more prompting brought the rest of the story. They thought—knew—she was a witch, and they believed she could cause lightning and thunder.

I felt sorry for the girl. Superstition is rampant among the ignorant (and some not so ignorant, come to think of it) and an idea based on it, once formed, is almost impossible to dislodge. Seems a couple of years back she and a boy had had a fight, and she threatened him. A couple of days later, he was struck by lightning and killed.

Such are legends born.

Shortly after, contemplating her sullen loneliness in the corner, I called her aside after class and talked to her about it. Getting any response from her was like pulling teeth.

"Cindy Lou, I know the others think you're a witch," I told her, feeling genuinely sorry for her, "and I know how lonely you must be."

She smiled a little, and the hurt that was always in her eyes seemed to lessen.

"I heard the story about the boy," I told her, trying to tread cautiously but to open her up.

"Didn't kill nobody," she replied at last. "Couldn't."

"I know," I told her. "I understand."

Finally she couldn't hold it in any longer, and started crying. I tried to soothe and comfort her, glad the hurt was coming out. To cure a boil—even one in the soul—it must first be lanced so tears can flow.

"I jest make 'em liak ah'm told ta," she sobbed. "Ah caint tell 'em what ta do."

This threw me for a loop. In my smug urban superiority it had never occurred to me that she might believe it, too.

90

"Who tells you?" I asked softly. "Who tells you to bring the thunderstorms?"

"Papa come sometimes," she replied, still sniffling. "He say ah got to make 'em. That everybody's got a reason for bein' heah an' mine's doin' this."

I understood now. I knew. An ugly, fat little girl *would* see her father, now two years dead, and she would rationalize her loneliness and ugliness somehow. This was in the character of these people so much a part of nature and the hills—she wasn't the ugly duckling, no, she was the most important person, most powerful person in the whole area.

She made the thunderstorms for southern West Virginia—and she was here for that purpose.

It made life livable.

The beginning of spring meant the onrush of thunderstorms as the warmer air now moving in struck the mountains; and as they increased in frequency, so did her loneliness, isolation—and pride. As the kids became more scared of her, she knew she had power—over them, over all.

She made the storms. She.

I tried to teach them a little basic meteorology, to sneakily dispel this fantasy for the rest of them, but they nodded, told me the answers I wanted to hear, and kept on believing that Cindy Lou made the storms. Outsiders couldn't understand. And this gave them some pride, too—for they were smugly confident that, for all my education, they knew for sure something that was beyond me.

It was the middle of May now, and my job had been among the most enjoyable and rewarding that I could imagine. I started to pick up other students as word got around, and began to travel as well, to teach some of the adults who managed to swallow just enough of that fierce pride to get me to help them.

One day I was coming back from one such student—he was seventy if he was a day, and I had him up to Dr. Seuss—when I passed near the Whittler house. I decided to stop by and see how Cindy Lou and her terribly suffering mother, the oldest thirty-six I had ever seen, were getting along. Classes were infrequent now; in spring these people planted and worked hard to eke out their subsistence.

As I approached the house, I thought I heard Cindy Lou's voice coming from inside, and I hesitated, as if a great hand were lain upon me. Frozen, her words drifted through the crude wooden shack to me.

"No, Papa!" she cried out fiercely. "Ah caint do this'n! You caint ask me! You know the wata's too high now. A big'n liak this'll flood the whole valley—maybe the town, too!"

And then there came the sound I'll never forget—the one that made the hairs on my neck stand up.

"You do liak yo' papa say!" came a deep, gravelly and oddly hollow man's voice. "Ah ain't got no choice in this mattah and neither do you. Leave them choices to them what knows bettah. You do it, now, heah? You know what happen if'n you don't!"

Suddenly the spell that seemed to hold me broke, and I stood for a moment, uneasily shivering. I considered not dropping in, just going on, but I finally decided it was my duty. I knew one thing for sure—somebody definitely *did* tell Cindy Lou to make the storms; she could never have made that voice outside a recording studio.

I had to know who was feeding her this. I knocked.

For a while there was no answer. Then, just as I was about to give up, the door creaked open and Cindy Lou peered out.

She'd been crying, I could see, but she was glad to see me and asked me in.

"Mama's gone ta town," she explained. "Cleanin' Mr. Summil's windas."

I walked into the one-room shack that I'd been in many times before. There was no back door, and only the most basic furnishings.

There was no one else in the shack but the two of us.

My stomach started turning a little, but I got a grip on myself.

"Cindy Lou?" I asked anxiously. "Where's the man who was just here? I heard voices."

She shrugged. "Papa dead, you know. Cain't hang around fo' long," she explained so matter-of-factly that it was more upsetting than the voice itself. I shifted subjects, the last refuge of the nervous.

92

"You've been crying," I noted.

She nodded seriously. "Papa want me t'do a big'n tonight. You been by the dam today?"

I shook my head slowly. There was a small earthen dam used to trap water. Part of it was tapped for town use, and the small lake it backed up made the best fishing in the area. I had walked by there only a half hour or so earlier; the water was already to the top, ready to spill over, this mostly from the runoff of melting snow from the hard winter.

"If'n it rain big, that dam'll bust," she said flatly.

Again I nodded. It was true—I'd complained to the county about that dam, pleaded with them to shore it up, but it was low on the priority list—not many voters in these parts.

"Ah din't kill that boy," she continued, getting more anxious, "but if'n I do what Papa want, ah'll kill a lot of folk sure."

And that, too, was true—if the dam burst and nobody heeded any warnings. I tried to think of an answer that would comfort her. I was terribly afraid of what would happen to her if that dam *did* break in a storm. She paid a heavy price for assumed guilt by others; this one she'd blame on herself, and I was sure she couldn't handle that.

"What happens if you don't bring the storm?" I asked gently.

She was grim, face set, and her voice sounded almost as dead and hollow as that man's eerie tones had been.

"Terrible thangs" was all she could tell me.

I didn't want to leave her, but when I heard that the storm was set for before midnight, and that her mother probably wouldn't come home until the next day, I decided I had to act. Cindy Lou refused to come with me, and I had little choice, I was afraid that she might kill herself to keep from doing her terrible task, and I needed reinforcement. I made for town and Mrs. Whittler.

It took me over an hour to get there, and another half hour to find her. She seemed extremely alarmed, and it was the first time I'd heard her curse, but she and I rushed back to where no cars could go as quickly as possible.

Clouds obscured the sky, and no stars showed through that low ceiling as sundown caught us still on the rutted path to the shack. Ordinarily, no problem—it was usually cloudy on this side of the mountains—but that deepening blackness seemed somehow alive, threatening now as we neared the shack.

We burst in suddenly, and I quickly lit a kerosene lantern. The shack was empty.

"My God! My God!" Mrs. Whittler moaned. "What has that rascal done to mah poor baby?"

"Think!" I urged her. "Where would she go?"

She shook her head sadly from side to side. "I dunno. Nowheres. Everywheres. Too dark to see her anyways if she din't wanta be seen."

It was true, but I didn't want to face it. Nothing is more terrible than knowing you are impotent in a crisis.

There was a noticeable lowering of the temperature. The barometer was falling so fast that you could feel it sink. There was a mild rumble off in the distance.

"There must be *something* we can do!" I almost screamed in frustration.

She chewed on her lower lip a moment. Then, suddenly, her head came up, and there was fire in her eyes. "There's one thang!" she said firmly, and walked out of the shack. I followed numbly.

We walked around to the back in the almost complete darkness. Small flashes of lightning gave a sudden, intermittent illumination, like a few frames of a black and white movie.

She stood there at the grave of her husband, the little wooden cross the only sign that someone was buried there.

"Jared Whittler!" she screamed. "You cain't do this to our daughta! She's ours! Ours! *Please,* oh, God! You was always a good man, Jared! *In the name of God, she's all I've got!*"

It seemed then that the lightning picked up, and thunder roared and echoed among the darkened hills.

Now, suddenly, there was a cosmic fireworks display; sharp, piercing streaks of lightning seemed to flash all around us, thunder boomed, and the wind picked up to tremendous force.

It started to rain, a few hard drops at first, then faster and faster, until we were engulfed in a terrible torrent.

And yet we stood there transfixed, in front of that little cross, and we prayed, and we pleaded, oblivious to the weather.

Suddenly, through it all, we heard a roaring sound unlike any of the storm. I turned slowly, the terror of reality in my soul.

"Oh, my God!" I managed. "There goes the dam!"

There was a sound like a tidal wave moving closer to us, then passing us somewhere to our backs, and continuing on down into the valley below.

As suddenly as it came on, the rain stopped. Both of us still stood there, soaked to the skin, now ankle-deep in mud. Now the storm was just a set of dull flashes in the distance to the east, and a few muted rumbles of what it had been.

She turned to me then. Though I couldn't really see her, I knew that she was stoic as all hill folk were in disaster.

"You're soaked," she said quietly. "Come in and git dried off. There'll be work to do in the town tonight."

I was shocked, numb, and silently, without thought, I followed her into the shack where, by the light of the kerosene lantern, she fished out some ragged towels for me to use.

We said nothing to each other. There was nothing left to say.

Suddenly there was a noise outside, and slowly, hesitantly, the old door opened on creaking hinges.

"Cindy Lou!" her mother almost whispered, and then ran and hugged her, holding the child to her bosom. Cindy Lou cried and hugged her mother all the more.

After a time, Mrs. Whittler turned her loose and looked at her. "Lord! You a mess!" she exclaimed, and went over and threw the girl a towel.

I stood there dumbly, trying to think of something to say. She sensed it, and looked up at me.

"Ah went to the dam," she said softly. "If'n it was gonna go, ah wanted to be goin' with it. Papa come to me then, say, 'These things hav'ta happen sometimes.' He say you goes when th' time comes, but it wasn't mah time, that you an' Mama was heah, callin' fo' me."

"It had to happen—your papa's right about that. If it hadn't been this time, then a few days from now," I consoled.

She shrugged.

"Ah couldn't do it. Papa got the man in charge of eastern Kentucky to do it," she said. "Papa say he don't want me doin' this no mo'. He gon' try ta git me changed to handlin' warm days."

And that was it.

We spent days cleaning up the mess; my cabin was the highest ground near the town, so it became rescue headquarters and temporary shelter. It'll take months to dig that silt out of the town itself, but, miraculously, no lives had been lost.

The state says they'll do something real soon now. By that time I'll be dead of old age, of course—but, no, I'll die of helping everybody with the red tape first.

Cindy Lou? Well, she seems happier now, convinced that she's switched jobs to something potentially less lethal. I go up there often. The kids still aren't all that friendly, but I take Cindy Lou with me on my rounds; realistically, I know I'm the father figure she craves, and she is almost like a daughter to me, but, what the hell. You get to analyzing why you do something and you go nuts.

And my students? More each day seem to show up, ages five to eighty-five. No teacher can find more satisfaction in his work than I do.

Every time there's a thunderstorm, though, I get to thinking—and I'm not sure that's good, either.

The weather bureau had predicted that storm; the Charleston paper showed a front right where a front should have been, and I looked at back issues and that front had been moving across the country for three days. Anybody used to this mountain country could tell a storm was brewing that day.

And that man's voice? I don't know. I'm not sure whether Cindy Lou's voice can go that low or not, but . . . it must have, mustn't it? She hasn't seen Papa much these days, she tells me. He's mad at her, and she doesn't care at all.

And yet, creeping into my mind some lonely, storm-tossed nights, I can't help thinking; what if it's true? Is it truly a disturbing thought or is it, in some way, equally comforting, for if such things actually are it gives some meaning to practically everyone's usually dull life.

Does each of us have a specific purpose here on Earth? Are some of us teachers to those who need us, and others stormsong runners?

Born in Virginia in 1944 and educated at Towson State College and Johns Hopkins University, Jack L. Chalker is a science fiction fan turned publisher turned writer. In 1960 he founded Mirage fiction. Chalker's first novel, A Jungle of Stars *(1976) earned him the John Campbell Award as Best New Writer in 1977. Recent titles include* Children of Flux and Anchor *and* When the Changewinds Blow.

When Dale Parr was stranded in front of the isolated old house, it was empty—
at least until he fell asleep. . . .

NINE

What of the Night
Manly Wade Wellman

First he felt savage desperation that his car had stalled on what had nearly ceased to be a mountain road, with the first spiteful raindrops falling in the sunset. A moment later, gratitude that the car had made its dull stop almost in the yard of a house he hadn't seen, there among shadowy trees and bushes. Surely the owners would take him in, help him.

He'd sought these southern highlands to indulge a young man's whim. His grandfather had been born hereabouts, had prospered in a big town to eastward and had never gone back. So he himself had driven here to explore. Heading away from Asheville, away from paved roads, he had trundled through a land of heights and hollows and forests. Just once he had stopped under shady walnuts, to eat most of his picnic lunch. But then, going on, his road had grown snakily narrow and he had turned off on this gravelly sidetrack in hopes of finding a way back again. All he had found was his motor falling silent and the rain spattering and a house where only strangers would open the door to him.

Getting out, he trotted into the yard, shin deep in dense weeds. Raindrops dabbed his tweed jacket, stroked his thick, dark hair. A tree stood almost at the doorway with branches flung out like shrouded arms. The house, he saw at once, was massively built of rough stones plastered together. Its roof was of flakelike slabs of shale. An ancient door of weathered planks stood between vacantly staring windows. He stepped up on the porch and knocked.

No answer. Only the quickening patter of the rain.

"Hello!" he called. "May I come in? My name's Dale Parr. My car's broken down. It's wet out here."

He listened again. Hushed, foggy silence inside.

He pushed at the door. It groaned inward. He stepped into dusty gloom. Blinking, he made out a chamber with several broken chairs, a ruinous sofa beneath a window, a dust-furred table. A sooty fireplace centered the rear wall.

"Hello!" Dale Parr raised his voice again. And no sound.

Then the place must be deserted. Probably no one had been here for years. He hurried through the rain to fetch from his car his suitcase and the paper bag with what was left of his lunch. Back inside, he examined the old fireplace. He hoped that the chimney would draw. He broke up two chairs that were already past mending. Some of the broad old floor planks had begun to crumble from joists beneath, and he ripped chunks from them. Carefully he heaped splinters on a wadded envelope and felt triumph as his match caught and kindled them. He put on larger frag-ments. The glow and crackle gave some cheer. Outside, the gray light grew slatily murky.

Unlucky about the car but lucky about this shelter, Parr comforted himself. He even had something for supper. There was half a bottle of wine, most of a box of crackers, a slab of good cheese. If he wanted water, it fell briskly outside just now. He could manage here tonight.

Despite the fire, the room seemed curtained in darkness. He squatted at the hearth to eat and drink. The crackers were crisp, the cheese had a grateful tang. He drank from the bottle, but left some to wake up on in the morning. The rain lulled him as he mused. At last he went back to the sofa. It smelled dank, it seemed caked with the dirt and de-cay of years, but he stretched out on it and closed his eyes. He thought how tired he was, how good it felt to relax. Without trying to, he slept.

And wakened to a glow of light, pale yellow as fresh but-ter. A voice spoke, the cheerful voice of a young woman:

"Excuse me, sir, but are you quite all right?"

Parr sat up quickly. She stood there smiling. One hand lifted a lamp, beautifully made of polished, cherry-red stone. A glass chimney supported the parchment shade. The light showed her to him.

Her round face tapered to a firm little chin. Curls of hair, tawny brown as syrup, tumbled to either side. She had a straight nose and wide blue eyes and smiled with the fullest and reddest of lips. He got to his feet.

"I'm sorry," he attempted. "I thought this house was deserted. My car broke down and I—"

"Oh, think nothing of that," she smiled. "As a matter of fact, the first time I came here, I thought the house was deserted, too."

She set the lamp on the table. Cluttering shadows fell back on all sides of the room.

Then he saw her as she was, tall and proud of figure. She wore dark blue, a long skirt and a snug jacket over a white blouse with a black bow at the throat. On one slim hand gleamed a ring, with a stone that flashed sparks. She smiled. Her teeth were small, white. She's beautiful, Parr thought. He felt glad to see her, there in the lamplight, with the rain throbbing outside.

And the room wasn't the crumbled, wasted room he had thought. The table gleamed richly, it was draped with a fringed white cloth. The fire danced on neat andirons. The sofa—not decaying, it had brocaded upholstery, with two black velvet cushions. Hadn't he burned the chairs? But there they were, good chairs, comfortable chairs. A picture hung above the fireplace; he hadn't noticed it before. It was a rich oil portrait of someone with a sternly dignified face and a white shirt front and a black coat with a rolled collar.

She knew he was confused. "We've tidied things up for you," she said, "while you slept so soundly."

"I do sleep soundly," he apologized. "I learned to lie down and sleep anywhere, when I was in the army in Korea."

"Korea?" she repeated the name as though she barely knew it. "Is there a war there?"

"The war's over, I was just there for the occupation." Parr felt glad, talking to her. He wanted to know her better, much better. He wondered if they were true, those stories he had always laughed at, about love at first sight. "My name's Dale Parr," he said. "I came to visit these mountains because my grandfather was born here."

"My name's Tolie," she said in her turn. "Just call me Tolie, because we're going to be friends." She half turned toward a rear door. "The others want to meet you, too."

"The others?"

He heard the disappointment in his own voice that there weren't just the two of them, himself and this girl Tolie who said they were going to be friends.

"Good evening, sir," boomed someone else.

In walked a tall, broad man, in a long black coat like an old-fashioned preacher. His white wing collar pedestaled a heavy, wise face with deepset dark eyes and a blade of nose and strong lines running from nostrils to corners of the firm mouth. He was the man whose picture hung above the fireplace. His hair and his long sideburns were thick and evenly cut. In their blackness glowed tags of gray, like steel-headed pins in cushions. Behind him entered a thinner, younger man, bearing a silver tray with a bottle and four glasses.

"This is Dale Parr," said Tolie to them. "Dale Parr, this is Mr. Addis. He owns this house. And this is Fenton."

The one with the tray bobbed his head shyly. His clothes were neat and snug on his gaunt body, a bobtailed dark jacket and checked trousers. His face, thought Parr, was furtive, under dull red hair parted in the middle.

"How do you do, Mr. Dale Parr," said Mr. Addis. His broad hand gripped Parr's tightly for just a moment, then let go. "We're glad for the accident that brought you here. Let us offer you some slight refreshment."

He waved for Fenton to set the tray on the table beside the lamp.

"I don't want to impose on you, sir," said Parr.

"No imposition at all," shrugged Mr. Addis.

"If I could telephone for somebody to come and fix my car—"

"Telephone?" echoed Mr. Addis. "We don't have that, Mr. Dale Parr. Sit down, sir. We're going to have a drink, and we make something of a ceremony of that."

Parr took a chair at the table. Tolie came and sat beside him. She gave him the sort of smile that meant for him to feel that they were all alone, he and she, after all; that the others were somewhere else, out of sight.

Again Mr. Addis motioned at Fenton, who poured from the bottle into each glass in turn. Parr took up his drink. It seemed to be little more than a spoonful. Again Tolie seemed to know what he was thinking.

"It's best to have just a sip at a time," she whispered.

"Yes, indeed," seconded the ringing voice of Mr. Addis. "We'll have more later, Mr. Dale Parr." He lifted his own glass. "The first drink is number one, which stands for unity." He looked around at them. "Sitrael," he toasted.

"Unity," said Tolie. "And Sitrael."

"Unity and Sitrael," repeated Fenton.

"Well, unity of course," said Parr, "and the other, though I don't know it."

"Sitrael," prompted Tolie.

"All right, and Sitrael," said Parr.

They drank. The sharp liquor warmed his throat all the way down. He felt grateful for it.

"If you don't mind," said Parr, "I want to wonder out loud about all this. Do I happen to be dreaming?"

"How would you be dreaming?" asked Tolie, almost at his ear.

"Well, but I came in and things were—deserted, abandoned. And I slept and woke up, or I think I woke up—"

"You're not dreaming," said Fenton, his first words.

His voice was timid, it half trembled. Parr wondered if he always sounded like that.

"Let's put it simply," said Mr. Addis, the lamplight winking on the silver points in his hair. "I've spent long years in planning things to suit myself here. I achieved that, and I find that it suits Tolie and Fenton, who are a sort of family to me. We're in the habit of being happy by night. It's always pleasant then. I have my studies and my books. I do what I hope is important research."

Parr smiled, the liquor warm within him. "And do Tolie and Fenton help you in your research?"

"They divert themselves and thrive on it," said Mr. Addis. "I daresay you'd like to see where I do my work."

Parr had not thought about that, but he had been politely brought up. "If you'd like to show me, sir."

103

He followed Mr. Addis through the rear door into a sort of hall. Several more doors stood open, one into what seemed a well-appointed kitchen, another into a bedroom. Mr. Addis conducted him into a room with shelved books all the way around, up to where dark beams ran across. The rain assailed a window. A black bearskin lay on the broad floor planks. The only furniture was an armchair and a table loaded with books. A hooded lamp hung from a rafter.

Parr went to the shelves, for he loved books. Here was a leather-bound set of Shakespeare, Cotton Mather's *Wonders of the Invisible World,* Burton's *Anatomy of Melancholy,* something with a title in Arabic characters that might not have been the Koran. Others, many others.

"For research, those volumes, and for recreation between spells of work," Mr. Addis said. "Here's my present direction of study."

Parr joined him beside the table. The top book of the stack lay open. Its cover looked shaggy, as though it had been bound in some of the bearskin rug. The page was not printed, but beautifully written in a black script that Parr could not read, with the initials of the paragraphs in red.

"Very rare and curious," said Mr. Addis. "The notebook of a German scientist named Kolber. The passage here refers to a friend he knew, Dr. Johannes Faustus."

"Faustus," echoed Parr. "The one in Marlowe's play, in Goethe's play, in Gounod's opera."

"Educated, are you?" said Mr. Addis. His big forefinger touched a line halfway down the page.

"Here's the sort of wisdom that's obvious the moment you hear it," he said. " 'All things are possible. If a thing is possible, it can become probable. If it is probable, it can be made actual.' "

"A process of logic," nodded Parr.

Mr. Addis took up another book, in stained blue cloth. "This is by John Dee, Queen Elizabeth's sorcerer."

Parr knew the name. "He hoped to raise spirits."

"And succeeded. Johannes Faustus also experimented along that line."

Parr looked at the table top. It was painted a glossy gray. Upon its surface showed a diagram, sketched in white. It looked like a star, the five rays jutting from the sides of an inner pentagon. Inside the triangular tracings of the rays showed words in strange letters. All around the outer points was drawn a circle.

"I put that pentacle there," said Mr. Addis. "To help in my work."

"I don't know the words on it," confessed Parr. "Some of the S's and N's look reversed."

"They're five names out of one of my books." Mr. Addis smiled with closed lips. "But all this must be tedious to a healthy young man. I think we need another small drink to relax."

"We won't quarrel about that, sir."

In the front room, Tolie and Fenton sat talking on the sofa. They rose as Parr and Mr. Addis came back. Tolie smiled as though in delight. Fenton gazed plaintively.

"Let's try another thimbleful," Mr. Addis said heartily. "Will you do the honors again, Fenton?"

Fenton made obedient haste to pour the drinks. They all sat down. Mr. Addis smiled above his glass.

"Two drinks for companionship, the closeness of two dear friends," he proclaimed.

"Companionship," said Tolie, so close to Parr that their elbows touched. Her look was like a touch.

"Companionship," droned Fenton.

"Companionship," Parr joined in.

"To Palanthan," said Mr. Addis, and drank. They all drank. Again, the liquor was delightfully fiery in Parr's throat.

"I hope you feel companionable, Dale Parr," said Tolie to him. "We're grateful for the storm that brought you to us tonight. Were you interested in what Mr. Addis is doing?"

"He seems to be a very special scholar," he replied, hoping that was tactful. "Of course, I don't have his advantages."

"You have your own advantages," she assured him. "Many advantages. Since you visited his sanctum, would you like to visit mine?"

He looked at the moving lights in her eyes and knew he would like it very much. Fenton watched dolefully as she slid her hand inside Parr's elbow and drew him along to the inner door and to a room beyond.

He had thought it a bedroom, but perhaps it was more than that. The bed itself, with a rainswept window beside it, was both sturdy and elegant, of what looked like black walnut. Its quilt, he recognized, was what his grandmother had called Melody Chain, variously colored squares with smaller squares inside them, assembled into a soft richness. At the bed's foot, a table with a mirror above it. A wardrobe cupboard for clothes. Two stools that, Parr guessed, would interest an antique dealer. And a stand littered with brushes and tubes of paint, and an easel with a canvas of a half-finished night landscape.

"You paint," he said.

"I try to," she told him. "I did the portrait of Mr. Addis over the fireplace. Do you like it?"

She was so close that she only had to whisper.

"Very much, Tolie."

"I'd like to paint you. Maybe I'll do that. Let's sit down."

They sat on the bed. Her hip and shoulder touched him, her eyes drank his.

"It's nice here of a night," she said, "but usually so quiet, so much like all nights. I'm glad of somebody new to talk to." Close at hand, she looked at him. "And to talk to me. Now, tell me about yourself."

That, Parr realized, was the most flattering thing a woman could say to a man. Readily he talked about the town he lived in, the college he had attended, the football he had played there, the poems he had tried to write. He explained that a legacy from his grandfather was enough to be idle on, and spoke of his impulse to look at the country where Parrs had lived and worked before he was born.

"And what about you?" he said at last. "And what about all this place I've come to, and what's going on in it?"

"You and I are going on in it, just now. It's hard to explain in a few words, but just accept it, as you accept the inevitable."

"Is this a dream of some kind?" he asked again.

"No, Dale Parr, it's not a dream of some kind," and she moved against him like a nestling cat. "Not a dream of any kind."

"Mr. Addis wants us," said the diffident voice of Fenton.

"We'll come in a moment," said Tolie.

106

"He's waiting."

A tiny frown creased her forehead. "Well, all right." She got to her feet and smiled sidelong at Parr. "We'll come."

They followed Fenton to the main room. Mr. Addis sat at the table. He smiled his greeting.

"Another drink, a step more in our little ceremony of fellowship," he said. "Sit down, Dale Parr. Sit down, all."

Fenton was trickling bright portions into the glasses.

"Our third drink," said Mr. Addis. "Three is the number of—"

"The Holy Trinity?" suggested Parr.

"Never mind that," said Mr. Addis, almost sharply. Then he smiled and creased his eyes. "To Thamaar," he pronounced.

Tolie and Fenton repeated the name. All drank, and the drink went down warmly. Parr smiled across the table at Fenton, who only looked at Tolie, who looked at Parr.

"Why don't we go back to our room and take up our discussion?" she said.

"I want to show him my quarters," Fenton mumbled. "Show him my work."

Parr felt sorry for this fellow, who had none of Mr. Addis's assurance, none of Tolie's sparkle. "All right," he said, rising. "Let's go, Fenton. I'll be interested."

Fenton's room was at the far end of the hall, past the kitchen. It appeared to be a sort of lean-to addition, built at the rear of the house. Rain drummed its shed roof. Light came from three fat, green candles burning in a sconce of dim brass on the round marble top of a table. Fenton's bed was a cot against a wall. There was a sort of bench of weathered wood. It was cluttered with tools. A set of rough shelves held bottles, racked test tubes, a Bunsen burner. Beside the sconce on the table lay sheets of scribbled paper.

"Then you're a scientist," said Parr. "A practicing scientist. I wish I knew more about things like that."

"Maybe I could teach you." Fenton stared at the table. "I'm trying some rather specialized matters. Mr. Addis has showed me things in his books, worth developing." He seemed more cheerful for a moment. "For instance, the universal alkahest."

"The alkahest?" repeated Parr. "The complete solvent, to turn base metal into gold, cure all diseases, give eternal life? Scientists have looked for that in every age. Nobody ever found it."

"Somebody's got to find it," said Fenton. "Somebody will. If I turn out to be the somebody, then I'll do so many things. Have so many things."

"Have what?"

"Perhaps love." Fenton tramped to the workbench and gazed out at the rainy night. "If it was nice out there, with a moon, I'd show you my garden, the herbs I grow. Potent, some of them."

He picked up a small metal case, set with levers and a lens.

"But lately," he said, "I've been working on a special camera. When I finish it, I'll make beautiful photographs of Tolie."

"Any photograph of Tolie would be beautiful," said Parr, and Fenton glanced up quickly, as though he had been stuck with a pin.

Tolie was at the door. "I don't want to butt in," she said, "but Mr. Addis insists he won't drink alone."

Parr nodded, to show that he would come at once. "Love," he said to Fenton, "is what everyone wants. What everyone needs."

"Do you want it and need it?"

"Naturally," smiled Parr. "Come on, let's go with Tolie."

They went, Fenton lagging at the rear. Mr. Addis sat in his chair. Probably he had not moved. Again Fenton measured out liquor into the glasses.

"Four drinks represent the four corners of a strong house, proof against storms and shelter for friends," said Mr. Addis. "Falaur."

They drank.

"Tell me, sir, what are the names you say in those toasts?" asked Parr.

"The names of the Kings of the North," replied Mr. Addis. "Names of mighty command and force."

"May I say something?" Parr ventured. "My first reaction here was just gratitude for your hospitality and entertainment." He could feel Tolie's smile. "But I still don't understand what you do here, who you are. I hope I'm not being too inquisitive."

"Not at all," said Mr. Addis, while Tolie and Fenton listened. "We owe you an explanation. As I said, we've been here for a number of years. I give myself over to my studies, Fenton follows his, Tolie brightens both our lives and relieves our tedium. Your coming, if I may say so, has been a welcome event. You'll like it here better and better as time goes on."

Parr set down his glass. "I think this will sound stupid, but I'll ask it, anyway. Do you happen to be haunting this house?"

Mr. Addis chuckled. Tolie's laugh was like silver. Fenton only swallowed. "Naturally we haunt it," said Mr. Addis. "It's our house."

"I mean," said Parr, feeling highly ridiculous, "are you— all right, are you dead?"

Louder laughter at that, even from Fenton this time.

"Some might think so, but I assure you we feel very much alive," said Mr. Addis cheerfully. "You seem uneasy, my young friend."

"I said it was stupid," said Parr. "After all, how could a house be haunted by even the ghosts of old furniture?"

"Maybe if the furniture died and dusted away," said Tolie. "Is that logic, Dale Parr?"

"Let's think about it while we have one more drink," said Mr. Addis. "The fifth."

Fenton busied himself with the bottle.

"The fifth drink, five," Mr. Addis half chanted. "The five points of the star. Of the pentacle, symbol of wonder and mastery." He raised his glass high. "Sitrami," he said.

"Sitrami," said Tolie after him, leaning toward Parr.

"No!" screamed Fenton wildly.

He leaped up from his chair, striking across the table. Parr's glass flew from his hand and shattered on the floor.

"You, so sure of yourself," Fenton yammered at Parr, "are you too blind to see? Five drinks, all five Kings of the North called up—five drinks, and you'll be here forever, too!"

Mr. Addis had surged to his feet in a flutter of coattails. "Are you out of your mind, Fenton?" he demanded.

"You'd claim him, bring his spirit here, too," Fenton quavered. "Bring him here forever—and Tolie wants him here!"

"Don't be any more of a fool than you can help," snapped out Tolie, also rising.

Fenton reached for her with both hands. "You know I love you," he wailed. "I'd hoped and hoped the time would come when—"

His face twisted.

"But now he's here, and I see how you look at him, hear how you talk to him—you want him, and I—I—"

She slapped Fenton's face. It was like the crack of a shot. He reeled back from it. Mr. Addis advanced on him.

"Run!" Fenton howled at Parr. "Get out of here, or you'll be like us, you'll be here forever, too!"

Parr ran, without waiting to wonder why he ran. He heard Tolie call his name, heard the feet of Mr. Addis on the floor as though in pursuit. Then he was tearing the door open, hurrying out and away, with the rain beating down upon him.

Later, he could never say which way he ran along the road, or through what drenching, clinging thickets when he stumbled out of it, or when the rain stopped and the stars and the moon glared down at him. But the sun was rising brightly when he staggered, all soggy and muddy and exhausted, into a little town called Sky Notch.

The people at the store there gave him coffee but only gazed at him until he panted out that his name was Dale Parr. Then big Duffy Parr came across from his service station and said they must be third or maybe fourth cousins. Someone brought more coffee and they heard his story and talked it over.

They believed him. They knew something about that house. It had stood empty for something like ninety years. The man of the house was Alexander Addis, who claimed all sorts of knowledge and special power, who once had stood out in a storm and dared God to strike him with lightning. After he'd died strangely and been buried without a funeral, there had been rumors about a haunting. Then a bright, wilful girl named Tolie Crummitt had visited there after dark on a dare and had been found stone-dead afterward. A limp young admirer, Fenton Cash, had sorrowed over her and vowed he'd go to her dying place and try to call her ghost to him. He, too, was found dead next morning. After that, folks decided to stay away.

The storekeeper allowed that, sure enough, maybe even the dead furniture could come to life with the human ghosts. Others nodded, to show they found good logic in that. But neither Duffy Parr nor anybody else would agree to go back and start the stalled car, even in the broad open light of the day. Finally Preacher Frank Ricks, in town to hold church service tomorrow, spoke up.

Preacher Ricks was old and leanly sinewy, with spectacles on his long nose. It appeared that he'd read about the Five Kings of the North in Reginald Scot's *Discouverie of Witchcraft,* which told about them in order to deny the wickedness credited to them. He refused to say the five names out loud, or permit Dale Parr to speak them. But he declared that he was protected by the Helmet of Salvation, and all right, he'd carry Dale Parr back there, in his shabby old sedan.

They used up most of an hour along those roads that were scarcely roads at all, and Parr wondered how many miles he'd fled in the stormy night to get to Sky Notch. At last they found his stalled car. Preacher Ricks hoisted the hood and tinkered expertly until the motor started again. When they were satisfied there would be no more trouble, they went, side by side, into the weedy yard. The tree with the armlike branches watched them, with puddles of water caught among its roots. The air was murky, just as it had been last evening.

"Let's go in, brother," said Preacher Ricks, and Parr followed him up on the rotten porch and in through the open doorway.

Nothing whatever in that shadowed front room, except dust and rot and tumbledown furniture and, of course, Parr's suitcase and the wine bottle and the scraps of his lunch in the paper sack. Preacher Ricks went through the rear door, and Parr forcing himself to walk just behind. In Tolie's room showed the bed, a grimy ruin. In Mr. Addis's study, the shelves hung shattered from the wall, and there were no books anywhere. Fenton's lean-to quarters were

111

another shambles. Finally, the two returned to the front room.

"This place should be exorcised," said Parr, remembering a film about such things. "Do you know how to do that?"

"No," frowned Preacher Ricks, shaking his head. "The faith I follow doesn't hold much with exorcism. The holy rituals I know are baptism, communion, burial of the dead, and so on. I know them by spirit anyway, if not word for word by heart. Do you think those might do?"

He did not wait for any answer but drew himself up stiffly and began to repeat the baptismal service. In the midst of it he paced outside and came back with a palmful of water dipped from the puddle at the tree's root. He nodded at Parr, who knelt. Preacher Ricks put his big wet hand on Parr's head. "Sanctify this water to the mystical washing away of sin," he intoned, and Parr wondered if he didn't hear, somewhere in the room, the catch of a breath and then the painful sigh of its being let out.

Then Preacher Ricks took up Parr's wine bottle and from the bag fetched out a broken cracker. He recited the rite of communion. Again Parr knelt. When Preacher Ricks put a bit of the cracker on his tongue and said to him, "Feed on it in your heart and be thankful," Parr again heard the catch of breath and the sigh.

Finally they both stood and Preacher Ricks repeated the service for the burial of the dead. The gloom seemed to thicken itself around them. But at last the hushed voice came to, "Come, ye blessed children of my Father, receive the kingdom prepared for you." Then light suddenly stole into the room. Parr, looking sidelong at the open door, saw sunshine in the yard that had been so shadowed.

Preacher Ricks cleared his throat. "Do you think it looks sort of different in here?" he asked Parr. "Like as if it had somehow cleared up?"

"In here and outside both," replied Parr. "Maybe you've truly put those spirits to rest."

"Let's devoutly hope so."

They walked out. No haze, no shadows.

"Bring your car along behind mine, back to Sky Notch," said Preacher Ricks. "We'll see if some kind soul there won't let us have some breakfast."

A major writer of the supernatural, Manly Wade Wellman was born in Portugese West Africa in 1903 where his father was a medical mission-ary. Brought to the United States at the age of six, he was educated at Wichita University and Columbia University and worked as a reporter until 1930, when he quit to become a full-time professional writer. In two decades more than three hundred thousand of his words were pub-lished in Weird Tales. *In 1946 Wellman's story, "A Star for a Warrior," won first prize in the first* Ellergy Queen's Mystery Magazine Annual Contest *(William Faulkner came in second); the prize money permitted him to move to North Carolina, where he lived the rest of his life. Well-man published many full-length works, including two large collections of his supernatural stories—grim and convincing—*Worse Things Wait-ing *(1973) and* Lonesome Vigils *(1982). He died in 1986.*

When the dead gather to remember those who have been forgotten, even forgotten burial grounds come to life. . . .

TEN

The Remember Service
John Bennett

Once every year, preferably at Eastertide, the dead gather at a convenient place to hold a remembrance service for the dead who have been forgotten.

It is a right pitiful thing to be forgotten. The grave sinks; the headboard rots and falls; the tall grass springs up; the wild vines and briers mat the grave like basketwork; no one comes any more; and the things which affection once left with the dead are scattered and lost beneath the accumulated leaves.

But, though the living have forgotten, the dead do not forget, and each year hold a remembrance service.

Mary Simmons lived for many years across Cooper River, beyond Mount Pleasant, in a neighborhood where are many little, old, forgotten burying grounds where the poor were buried long ago.

One Sunday afternoon, as she sat by her window dozing, she heard a sound of song somewhere. She listened. They were singing the old, old spiritual song which is chanted over the coffin on its way to the sea islands for burial:

No more rain gwine to wet you . . . no more!
No more sun gwine to hot you . . . no more!
No more cold gwine to cold you . . . no more!
  Oh, Lord, I want to go home . . . want to go home!

Mary was a great singer, and loved to let her deep voice go in chanting over the dead; so she rose and went out of the house through a thin falling rain to the place where the funeral service was holding.

There was a large crowd gathered in the little graveyard which she had not before noticed among the trees and broom-grass thickets, and the singing was very great.

Long before she reached the place she had begun herself to sing, and her strong voice rose at its loudest and richest as she joined the throng of mourners among the graves.

The light rain fell fitfully; at times but a warm, thin, inconsequential mist; again a sharp fall, spattering through the trees and pattering on the grass. It now began to rain harder, a real, downfalling shower; but no one seemed to care, and the singing went on loud and strong through the falling rain.

Mary put up her hands to remove her head covering, her best; when a tall, dark man standing beside her said, "No, sister; a song like yours shall have a better cover," and with that put his umbrella into her hands. Thus protected from the rain, and loving to sing her soul away, Mary sang with all her heart.

At last the service ended. The chanting ceased; and over the heads of the crowd she heard the powerful voice of the preacher asking benediction upon the throng:

"Brothers, sisters, fathers, mothers, husbands, wives, children: may the Lord of Abraham, Isaac and Jacob watch over us and guard between us while we are absent the one from the other! And may the blessing of God Almighty, the Father, the Son, and the Holy Ghost, be with you and abide with you all, forever. Amen!"

The last amen rose in a great shout which went up through the trees like fire through the roof . . . "Amen, amen, amen!"

And, suddenly, Mary realized that she was standing there alone in a little, overgrown, abandoned burying ground of a century ago, where no burials had been for generations, a place neglected and forgotten, the uncared graves all fallen in, the headboards broken down and rotted away to dust, and all the symbols of affectionate remembrance which had been placed there for comfort of the dead buried under the drift of old dead leaves which rose above her shoetop.

Frightened, and with fear increasing at every step, she ran from that place, and hastened home. As she reached her doorstep and paused to catch her breath, she suddenly recollected, and was aware that she still carried the umbrella which had been put into her hand by the dark man who stood by her side in the burying ground.

In perplexity she turned to look back. But as far as her eye could reach there was not a human being anywhere to be seen; not a living creature . . . nothing but the gray rain and the evening mist rising thin from the wet ground and drifting through the trees in the twilight.

She made the best of her way to her own room, frightened and wondering, expecting every instant to have the strangely acquired umbrella snatched outright from her hands or vanish in thin air.

But, instead, it remained in her grasp, substantial and material, an extraordinary thing to possess, without a doubt the free and friendly gift of a ghost.

What was more extraordinary, she retained the umbrella for years, until, worn with long usage and weakened by time, it fell apart and became useless.

Aware of its supernatural origin and character she never either lent it to a friend or permitted it to pass from her possession. Not that lent umbrellas never return, but convinced that, once the umbrella passed from the hands to which it had been confided, it would vanish like the throng from that strange remembrance service in the little abandoned burying ground beyond the village of Mount Pleasant.

As told by Mary Simmons.

Born in 1865, John Bennett was a successful illustrator, cartographer, guitarist, and advertising man. Educated at the University of South Carolina (Phi Beta Kappa), with Hervey Allen and Dubose Heyward he founded the Poetry Society of South Carolina. He is best known for his books Master Skylark *(1897) and* The Doctor to the Dead *(1946), a delightful collection of supernatural tales of blacks set in Charleston. He died in 1956.*

Eventually someone would have to find out why the plantation had gained the reputation as the "evil-speritist place in dis wull". . . .

ELEVEN

"No Haid Pawn"
Thomas Nelson Page

It was a ghostly place in broad daylight, if the glimmer that stole in through the dense forest that surrounded it when the sun was directly overhead deserved this delusive name. At any other time it was—why, we were afraid even to talk about it! and as to venturing within its gloomy borders, it was currently believed among us that to do so was to bring upon the intruder certain death. I knew every foot of ground, wet and dry, within five miles of my father's house, except this plantation, for I had hunted by day and night every field, forest, and marsh within that radius; but the swamp and "ma'shes" that surrounded this place I had never invaded. The boldest hunter on the plantation would call off his dogs and go home if they struck a trail that crossed the sobby boundary-line of No Haid Pawn.

"Jack 'my lanterns" and "evil sperits" only infested those woods, and the earnest advice of those whom we children acknowledged to know most about them was, "Don't you never go nigh dyah, honey; hit's de evil-speritest place in dis wull."

Had not Big William and Cephas and Poliam followed their dogs in there one night, and cut down a tree in which they had with their own eyes seen the coon, and lo! when it fell "de warn no mo' coon dyah 'n a dog!" and the next tree they had "treed in" not only had no coon in it, but when it was cut down it had fallen on Poliam and broken his leg. So the very woods were haunted. From this time they were abandoned to the "jack 'my lanterns" and ghosts, and another shadow was added to No Haid Pawn.

The place was as much cut off from the rest of the country as if a sea had divided it. The river, with marshy banks, swept around it in a wide horseshoe on three sides, and when the hammocks dammed it up, washed its way straight across and scoured out a new bed for itself, completely isolating the whole plantation.

The owners of it, if there were any, which was doubtful, were aliens, and in my time it had not been occupied for forty years. The Negroes declared that it was "gin up" to the "ha'nts an' evil sperits," and that no living being could live there. It had grown up in forest and had wholly reverted to original marsh. The road that once ran through the swamp had long since been choked up, and the trees were as thick and the jungle as dense now, in its track, as in the adjacent "ma'sh." Only one path remained. That, it was currently believed by the entire portion of the population who speculated on the subject, was kept open by the evil spirits. Certain it was that no human foot ever trod the narrow, tortuous line that ran through the brakes as deviously as the noiseless, stagnant ditches that curved through the jungle, where the musk-rats played and the moccasin slept unmolested. Yet there it lay, plain and well-defined, month after month and year after year, as No Haid Pawn itself stood, amid its surrounding swamps, all undisturbed and unchanging.

Even the runaway slaves who occasionally left their homes and took to the swamps and woods impelled by the cruelty of their overseers, or by a desire for personal freedom, never tried this swamp, but preferred to be caught and returned home to invading its awful shades.

We were brought up to believe in ghosts. Our fathers and mothers laughed at us, and endeavored to reason us out of such a superstition—the fathers with much of ridicule and satire, the mothers giving sweet religious reasons for their argument—but what could they avail against the actual testimony and the blood-curdling experiences of a score of witnesses, who recounted their personal observations with a degree of thrilling realism and a vividness that overbore any arguments our childish reason could grasp! The old mammies and uncles who were our companions and comrades believed in the existence of evil spirits as truly as in the exis-

tence of hell or heaven, as to which at that time no question
had ever been raised, so far as was known, in that slum-
berous world. [The Bible was the standard, and all disputes
were resolved into an appeal to that authority, the single
question as to any point being simply, "Is it in the Bible?"]
Had not Lazarus, and Mam' Celia, and William, and Twis'-
foot-Bob, and Aunt Sukie Brown, and others *seen* with their
own eyes the evil spirits, again and again, in the bodily
shape of cats, headless dogs, white cows, and other less
palpable forms! And was not their experience, who lived in
remote cabins, or wandered night after night through the
loneliest woods, stronger evidence than the cold reasoning
of those who hardly ever stirred abroad except in daylight?
It certainly was more conclusive to us; for no one could
have listened to those narrators without being impressed
with the fact that they were recounting what they had actually seen with their bodily eyes. The result of it all was, so far
as we were concerned, the triumph of faith over reason, and
the fixed belief, on our part, in the actual visible existence of
the departed, in the sinister form of apparition known as
"evil sperits." Every graveyard was tenanted by them; every
old house and every peculiarly desolate spot was known to
be their rendezvous; but all spots and places sank into insig-
nificance compared with No Haid Pawn.

The very name was uncanny. Originally it had designated
a long, stagnant pool of water lying in the centre of the tract,
which marked the spot from which the soil had been dug to
raise the elevation on which to set the house. More mod-
ernly the place, by reason of the filling up of ditches and the
sinking of dikes, had become again simple swamp and
jungle, or, to use the local expression, "had turned to
ma'sh," and the name applied to the whole plantation.

The origin of the name? The pond had no source; but
there was a better explanation than that. Anyhow, the very
name inspired dread, and the place was our terror.

The house had been built many generations before by a
stranger in this section, and the owners never made it their
permanent home. Thus, no ties either of blood or friendship
were formed with their neighbors, who were certainly open-
hearted and open-doored enough to overcome anything
but the most persistent unneighborliness. Why this spot was

selected for a mansion was always a mystery, unless it was that the new-comer desired to isolate himself completely. Instead of following the custom of those who were native and to the manner born, who always chose some eminence for their seats, he had selected for his a spot in the middle of the wide flat which lay in the horseshoe of the river. The low ground, probably owing to the abundance of land in that country, had never been "taken up" and up to the time of his occupation was in a condition of primeval swamp. He had to begin by making an artificial mound for his mansion. Even then, it was said, he dug so deep that he laid the corner-stone in water. The foundation was of stone, which was brought from a distance. Fabulous stories were told of it. The Negroes declared that under the old house were solid rock chambers, which had been built for dungeons, and had served for purposes which were none the less awful because they were vague and indefinite. The huge structure itself was of wood, and was alleged to contain many mysterious rooms and underground passages. One of the latter was said to connect with the No Haid Pawn itself, whose dark waters, according to the Negroes' traditions, were some day, by some process not wholly consistent with the laws of physics, to overwhelm the fated pile. An evil destiny had seemed to overshadow the place from the very beginning. One of the Negro builders had been caught and decapitated between two of the immense foundation stones. The tradition was handed down that he was sacrificed in some awful and occult rite connected with the laying of the corner-stone. The scaffolding had given way and had precipitated several men to the ground, most of whom had been fatally hurt. This also was alleged to be by hideous design. Then the plantation, in the process of being reclaimed, had proved unhealthy beyond all experience, and the Negroes employed in the work of diking and reclaiming the great swamp had sickened and died by dozens. The extension of the dangerous fever to the adjoining plantations had left a reputation for typhus malaria from which the whole section suffered for a time. But this did not prevent the colored population from recounting year after year the horrors of the pestilence of No Haid Pawn as a peculiar visitation, nor from relating with blood-curdling details the burial by scores, in a thicket just beside the pond, of the stricken "befo' dee *daid*, honey, befo' dee *daid!*" The bodies, it was said, used to float about in the guts of the swamp and on the haunted pond; and at night they might be seen if any one were so hardy as to venture there, rowing about in their coffins as if they were boats.

Thus the place from the beginning had an evil name, and when, year after year, the river rose and washed the levees away, or the musk-rats burrowed through and let the water in, and the strange masters cursed not only the elements but Heaven itself, the continued mortality of their Negroes was not wholly unexpected nor unaccounted for by certain classes of their neighbors.

At length the property had fallen to one more gloom, more strange, and more sinister than any who had gone before him—a man whose personal characteristics and habits were unique in that country. He was of gigantic stature and superhuman strength, and possessed appetites and vices in proportion to his size. He could fell an ox with a blow of his fist, or in a fit of anger could tear down the branch of a tree, or bend a bar of iron like a reed. He, either from caprice or ignorance, spoke only a *patois* not unlike the Creole French of the Louisiana parishes. But he was a West Indian. His brutal temper and habits cut him off from even the small measure of intercourse which had existed between his predecessors and their neighbors, and he lived at No Haid Pawn completely isolated. All the stories and traditions of the place at once centred on him, and fabulous tales were told of his prowess and of his life. It was said, among other things, that he preserved his wonderful strength by drinking human blood, a tale which in a certain sense I have never seen reason to question. Making all allowances, his life was a blot upon civilization. At length it culminated. A brutal temper inflamed by unbridled passions, after a long period of license and debauchery came to a climax in a final orgy of ferocity and fury, in which he was guilty of an act whose fiendishness surpassed belief, and he was brought to judgment.

In modern times the very inhumanity of the crime would probably have proved his security, and as he had destroyed his own property while he was perpetrating a crime of appalling and unparalleled horror, he might have found a defence in that standing refuge of extraordinary scoundrelism—insanity. This defence, indeed, was put in, and was pressed with much ability by his counsel, one of whom was my father, who had just then been admitted to the bar; but, fortunately for the cause of justice, neither courts nor juries were then so sentimental as they have become of late years, and the last occupant of No Haid Pawn paid under the law the full penalty of his hideous crime. It was one of the curious incidents of the trial that his Negroes all lamented his death, and declared that he was a good master when he was not drunk. He was hanged just at the rear of his own house, within sight of the spot where his awful crime was committed.

At his execution, which, according to the custom of the country, was public, a horrible coincidence occurred which furnished the text of many a sermon on retributive justice among the Negroes.

The body was interred near the pond, close by the thicket where the Negroes were buried; but the Negroes declared that it preferred one of the stone chambers under the mansion, where it made its home, and that it might be seen at any time of the day or night stalking headless about the place. They used to dwell with peculiar zest on the most agonizing details of this wretch's dreadful crime, the whole culminating in the final act of maniacal fury, when the gigantic monster dragged the hacked and headless corpse of his victim up the staircase and stood it up before the open window in his hall, in the full view of the terrified slaves. After these narrations, the continued reappearance of the murderer and his headless victim was as natural to us as it was to the Negroes themselves; and, as night after night we would hurry up to the great house through the darkness, we were ever on the watch lest he should appear to our frighted vision from the shades of the shrubbery-filled yard.

Thus it was that of all ghostly places No Haid Pawn had the distinction of being invested, to us, with unparalleled horror; and thus to us, no less than because the dikes had given way and the overflowed flats had turned again to swamp and jungle, it was explicable that No Haid Pawn was abandoned, and was now untrodden by any foot but that of its ghostly tenants.

The time of my story was 1855. The spring previous continuous rains had kept the river full, and had flooded the low grounds, and this had been followed by an exceptionally dense growth in the summer. Then, public feeling was greatly excited at the time of which I write, over the discovery in the neighborhood of several emissaries of the underground railway, or—as they were universally considered in that country—of the devil. They had been run off or had disappeared suddenly, but had left behind them some little excitement on the part of the slaves, and a great deal on the part of their masters, and more than the usual number of Negroes had run away. All, however, had been caught, or had returned home after a sufficient interval of freedom, except one who was supposed to have accompanied his instigators on their flight.

This man was a well-known character. He belonged to one of our neighbors, and had been bought and brought there from an estate on the Lower Mississippi. He was of immense size and possessed the features and expression of a bandit desperado. In character he was without amiability, fearless, brutal, and devoid of either superstition or reverence. The rest of the slaves in that section were dreadfully afraid of him, and were always in terror that he would harm them, to which awful power he laid well-known claim. His curses in strange dialect terrified them beyond measure, and they would do anything to conciliate him. He had been a continual source of trouble and an object of suspicion in the neighborhood from the time of his first appearance; and more than one hog that the Negroes declared had wandered into the marshes of No Haid Pawn had been suspected of finding its way to this man's cabin. His master had often been urged to get rid of him, but he was kept, I think, probably because he was valuable on the plantation. He was a fine butcher, a good work-hand, and a first-class boatman. Moreover, ours was a conservative population, in which every man minded his own business and let his neighbor's alone.

At the time of the visits of those secret agents to which I have referred, this Negro was discovered to be the leader in the secret meetings held under their auspices, and he would doubtless have been taken up and shipped off at once; but when the intruders fled, as I have related, their convert disappeared also. It was a subject of general felicitation in the neighborhood that he was gotten rid of, and his master, instead of being commiserated on the loss of his slave, was congratulated that he had not cut his throat.

No idea can be given at this date of the excitement occasioned in a quiet neighborhood in old times by the discovery of the mere presence of such characters as Abolitionists. It was as if the foundations of the whole social fabric were undermined. It was the sudden darkening of a shadow that always hung on the horizon. The slaves were in a large majority, and had they risen, though the final issue could not be doubted, the lives of every white on the plantations must have paid the forfeit. Whatever the right and wrong of slavery might have been, its existence demanded that no outside interference with it should be tolerated. So much was certain; self-preservation required this.

I was, at the time of which I speak, a well-grown lad, and had been for two sessions to a boarding school, where I had gotten rid of some portion—I will not say of all—of the superstition of my boyhood. The spirit of adventure was beginning to assert itself in me, and I had begun to feel a sense of enjoyment in overcoming the fears which once mastered me, though, I must confess, I had not entirely shaken off my belief in the existence of ghosts—that is, I did not believe in them at all in the day-time, but when night came I was not so certain about it.

Duck-hunting was my favorite sport, and the marshes on the river were fine ground for them usually, but this season the weather had been so singularly warm that the sport had been poor, and though I had scoured every canal in the marsh and every bend in the river as far as No Haid Pawn Hammock, as the stretch of drifted timber and treacherous marsh was called that marked the boundary-line of that plantation, I had had bad luck. Beyond that point I had never penetrated, partly, no doubt, because of the training of my earlier years, and partly because the marsh on either side of the hammock would have mired a cat. Often, as I watched with envious eyes the wild duck rise up over the dense trees that surrounded the place and cut straight for the deserted marshes in the horseshoe, I had had a longing to invade the mysterious domain, and crawl to the edge of No Haid Pawn and get a shot at the fowl that floated on its black surface; but something had always deterred me, and the long reaches of No Haid Pawn were left to the wild-fowl and the ghostly rowers. Finally, however, after a spell whose high temperature was rather suited to August than April, in desperation at my ill-luck I determined to gratify my curiosity and try No Haid Pawn. So one afternoon, without telling any one of my intention, I crossed the mysterious boundary and struck through the swamp for the unknown land.

The marsh was far worse than I had anticipated, and no one but a duck-hunter as experienced and zealous as myself, and as indifferent to ditches, briers, mire, and all that make a swamp, could have penetrated it at all. Even I could never have gotten on if I had not followed the one path that led into the marsh, the reputed "parf" of the evil spirits, and, as it was, my progress was both tedious and dangerous.

The track was a mysterious one, for though I knew it had not been trodden by a human foot in many years, yet there, a veritable "parf," it lay. In some places it was almost completely lost, and I would fear I should have to turn back, but an overhanging branch or a vine swinging from one tree to another would furnish a way to some spot where the narrow trail began again. In other spots old logs thrown across the miry canals gave me an uncomfortable feeling as I reflected what feet had last crossed on them. On both sides of this trail the marsh was either an impenetrable jungle or a mire apparently bottomless.

I shall never forget my sensations as I finally emerged from the woods into the clearing, if that desolate waste of willows, cane, and swamp growth could be so termed. About me stretched the jungle, over which a greenish lurid atmosphere brooded, and straight ahead towered the gaunt mansion, a rambling pile of sombre white, with numberless vacant windows staring at me from the leafless trees about it. Only one other clump of trees appeared above the canes and brush, and that I knew by intuition was the graveyard.

I think I should have turned back had not shame impelled me forward.

My progress from this point was even more difficult than it had been hitherto, for the trail at the end of the wood terminated abruptly in a gut of the swamp; however, I managed to keep on by walking on hammocks, pushing through clumps of bushes, and wading as best I could. It was slow and hot work, though.

It never once struck me that it must be getting late. I had become so accustomed to the gloom of the woods that the more open ground appeared quite light to me, and I had not paid any attention to the black cloud that had been for some time gathering overhead, or to the darkening atmosphere.

I suddenly became sensible that it was going to rain. However, I was so much engrossed in the endeavor to get on that even then I took little note of it. The nearer I came to the house the more it arrested my attention, and the more weird and uncanny it looked. Canes and bushes grew up to the very door; the window-shutters hung from the hinges; the broken windows glared like eyeless sockets; the portico had fallen away from the wall, while the wide door stood slightly ajar, giving to the place a singularly ghastly appearance, somewhat akin to the color which sometimes lingers on the face of a corpse. In my progress wading through the swamp I had gone around rather to the side of the house toward where I supposed the "pawn" itself to lie.

I was now quite near to it, and striking a little less miry ground, as I pushed my way through the bushes and canes, which were higher than my head, I became aware that I was very near the thicket that marked the graveyard, just beyond which I knew the pond itself lay. I was somewhat startled, for the cloud made it quite dusky, and, stepping on a long piece of rotten timber lying on the ground, I parted the bushes to look down the pond. As I did so the rattle of a chain grated on me, and, glancing up through the cane, before me appeared a heavy upright timber with an arm or crossbeam stretching from it, from which dangled a long chain, almost rusted away. I knew by instinct that I stood under the gallows where the murderer of No Haid Pawn had expiated his dreadful crime. His corpse must have fallen just where I stood. I started back appalled.

Just then the black cloud above me was parted by a vivid flame, and a peal of thunder seemed to rive the earth.

I turned in terror, but before I had gone fifty yards the storm was upon me, and instinctively I made for the only refuge that was at hand. It was a dreadful alternative, but I did not hesitate. Outside I was not even sure that my life was safe. And with extraordinary swiftness I had made my way through the broken iron fence that lay rusting in the swamp, had traversed the yard, all grown up as it was to the very threshold, had ascended the sunken steps, crossed the rotted portico, and entered the open door.

A long dark hall stretched before me, extending, as well as I could judge in the gloom, entirely across the house. A number of doors, some shut, some ajar, opened on the hall on one side; and a broad, dark stairway ascended on the other to the upper story. The walls were black with mould. At the far end a large bow-window, with all the glass gone, looked out on the waste of swamp, unbroken save by the clump of trees in the graveyard, and just beside this window was a break where the dark staircase descended to the apartments below. The whole place was in a state of advanced decay; almost the entire plastering had fallen with the damp, and the hall presented a scene of desolation that beggars description.

I was at last in the haunted house!

The rain, driven by the wind, poured in at the broken windows in such a deluge that I was forced in self-defence to seek shelter in one of the rooms. I tried several, but the doors were swollen or fastened; I found one, however, on the leeward side of the house, and, pushing the door, which opened easily, I entered. Inside I found something like an old bed; and the great open fireplace had evidently been used at some earlier time, for the ashes were still banked up in the cavernous hearth, and the charred ends of the logs of wood were lying in the chimney corners. To see, still as fresh and natural as though the fire had but just died out, these remnants of domestic life that had survived all else of a similar period struck me as unspeakably ghastly. The bedstead, however, though rude, was convenient as a seat, and I utilized it accordingly, propping myself up against one of the rough posts. From my position I commanded through the open door the entire length of the vacant hall, and could look straight out of the great bow-window at the head of the stairs, through which appeared, against the dull sky, the black mass of the graveyard trees, and a stretch of one of the canals or guts of the swamp curving around it, which gleamed white in the glare of the lightning.

I had expected that the storm would, like most thunderstorms in the latitude, shortly exhaust itself, or, as we say, "blow over;" but I was mistaken, and as the time passed, its violence, instead of diminishing, increased. It grew darker and darker, and presently the startling truth dawned on me that the gloom which I had supposed simply the effect of the overshadowing cloud had been really nightfall. I was shut up alone in No Haid Pawn for the night!

I hastened to the door with the intention of braving the storm and getting away; but I was almost blown off my feet. A glance without showed me that the guts with which the swamp was traversed in every direction were now full to the brim, and to attempt to find my way home in the darkness would be sheer madness; so, after a wistful survey, I returned to my wretched perch. I thought I would try and light a fire, but to my consternation I had not a match, and I finally abandoned myself to my fate. It was a desolate, if not despairing, feeling that I experienced. My mind was filled, not only with my own unhappiness, but with the thought of the distress my absence would occasion them at home; and for a little while I had a fleeting hope that a party would be sent out to search for me. This, however, was untenable, for they would not know where I was. The last place in which they would ever think of looking for me was No Haid Pawn, and even if they knew I was there they could no more get to me in the darkness and storm than I could escape from it.

I accordingly propped myself up on my bed and gave myself up to my reflections. I said my prayers very fervently. I thought I would try and get to sleep, but sleep was far from my eyes.

My surroundings were too vivid to my apprehension. The awful traditions of the place, do what I might to banish

130

them, would come to mind. The original building of the house, and its blood-stained foundation stones; the dead who had died of the pestilence that had raged afterward; the bodies carted by scores and buried in the sobby earth of the graveyard, whose trees loomed up through the broken window; the dreadful story of the dead paddling about the swamp in their coffins; and above all, the gigantic maniac whose ferocity even murder could not satiate, and who had added to murder awful mutilation: he had dragged the mangled corpse of his victim up those very steps and flung it out of the very window which gaped just beyond me in the glare of lightning. It all passed through my mind as I sat there in the darkness, and no effort of my will could keep my thoughts from dwelling on it. The terrific thunder, out-crashing a thousand batteries, at times engrossed my attention; but it always reverted to that scene of horror; and if I dozed, the slamming of the loose blinds, or the terrific fury of the storm, would suddenly startle me. Once, as the sounds subsided for a moment, or else I having become familiar with them, as I was sinking into a sleepy state, a door at the other end of the hall creaked and then slammed with violence, bringing me bolt upright on the bed, clutching my gun. I could have sworn that I heard footsteps; but the wind was blowing a hurricane, and, after another period of wakefulness and dreadful recollection, nature succumbed, and I fell asleep.

I do not know that I can be said to have lost consciousness even then, for my mind was still enchained by the horrors of my situation, and went on clinging to them and dwelling upon them even in my slumber.

I was, however, certainly asleep; for the storm must have died temporarily away about this hour without my knowing it, and I subsequently heard that it did.

I must have slept several hours, for I was quite stiff from my constrained posture when I became fully aroused.

I was awakened by a very peculiar sound; it was like a distant call or halloo. Although I had been fast asleep a moment before, it startled me into a state of the highest attention. In a second I was wide awake. There was not a sound except the rumble and roll of the thunder, as the storm once more began to renew itself, and in the segment of the circle that I could see along the hall through my door, and, indeed, out through the yawning window at the end, as far as the black clump of trees in the graveyard just at the bend of the canal, which I commanded from my seat whenever there was a flash of lightning, there was only the swaying of the bushes in the swamp and of the trees in the graveyard. Yet there I sat bolt upright on my bed, in the darkness, with every nerve strained to its utmost tension, and that unearthly cry still sounding in my ears. I was endeavoring to reason myself into the belief that I had dreamed it, when a flash of lightning lit up the whole field of my vision as if it had been in the focus of a sun-glass, and out on the canal, where it curved around the graveyard was a boat—a something—small, black, with square ends, and with a man in it, standing upright, and something lying in a lump or mass at the bow.

I knew I could not be mistaken, for the lightning by a process of its own, photographs everything on the retina in minutest detail, and I had a vivid impression of everything from the foot of the bed, on which I crouched, to the gaunt arms of those black trees in the graveyard just over that ghostly boatman and his dreadful freight. I was wide awake.

The story of the dead rowing in their coffins was verified!

I am unable to state what passed in the next few minutes.

The storm had burst again with renewed violence and was once more expending itself on the house; the thunder was again rolling overhead; the broken blinds were swinging and slamming madly; and the dreadful memories of the place were once more besetting me.

I shifted my position to relieve the cramp it had occasioned, still keeping my face toward that fatal window. As I did so, I heard above, or perhaps I should say under, the storm a sound more terrible to me—the repetition of that weird halloo, this time almost under the great window. Immediately succeeding this was the sound of something scraping under the wall, and I was sensible when a door on the ground-floor was struck with a heavy thud. It was pitch-dark, but I heard the door pushed wide open, and as a string of fierce oaths, part English and part Creole French, floated up the dark stairway, muffled as if sworn through clinched teeth, I held my breath. I recalled the unknown tongue the ghostly murderer employed; and I knew that the murderer of No Haid Pawn had left his grave, and that his ghost was coming up that stair. I heard his step as it fell on the first stair heavily yet almost noiselessly. It was an unearthly sound—dull, like the tread of a bared foot, accompanied by the scraping sound of a body dragging. Step by step he came up the black stairway in the pitch darkness as steadily as if it were daytime, and he knew every step, accompanied by that sickening sound of dragging. There was a final pull up the last step, and a dull, heavy thud, as, with a strange, wild laugh, he flung his burden on the floor.

For a moment there was not a sound, and then the awful silence and blackness were broken by a crash of thunder that seemed to tear the foundations asunder like a mighty earthquake, and the whole house, and the great swamp outside, were filled with a glare of vivid, blinding light. Directly in front of me, clutching in his upraised hand a long, keen, glittering knife, on whose blade a ball of fire seemed to play, stood a gigantic figure in the very flame of the lightning and stretched at his feet lay, ghastly and bloody, a black and headless trunk.

I staggered to the door and, tripping, fell prostrate over the sill.

When we could get there, nothing was left but the foundation. The haunted house, when struck, had literally burned to the water's edge. The changed current had washed its way close to the place, and in strange verification of the Negroes' traditions, No Haid Pawn had reclaimed its own, and the spot with all its secrets lay buried under its dark waters.

A gentleman of the Old South, Thomas Nelson Page was born in Virginia in 1858 and educated at Washington and Lee University and the University of Virginia. Typical of the South's aristocracy, Page tried his hand at many professions, practicing law in Richmond from 1875 to 1893 and serving as United States Ambassador to Italy in 1913, while becoming a noted novelist, historian, biographer, and lecturer. Most of his books are centered in the Old South, including In Old Virginia *(1887),* The Burial of the Guns *(1894), and* Robert E. Lee: Man and Soldier *(1926).*

When Uncle Jim and Crystal stopped for gas near Chattanooga, they unwittingly became guests of the station master. . . .

TWELVE

See the Station Master
George Florance-Guthridge

Indian Summer, Indianapolis. Humidity is high, tempers flaring, rapes and murders and larcenies up, my mill down for two-week inventory; I decide to take Crystal to Florida to see her mother. My darling Crystal, child of the modern age, born with a plastic spoon in her mouth. Too soon will she know too much about too much, without senselessly being exposed to a city in heat.

I pick her up after school, saving her a hot busride home and further needless mingling with strangers in a world grown feverish. She resists my suggestion concerning Florida—such a stubborn girl!—then starts to run away. I grab her shoulders and hold her neck so gently, oh so gently. Then we drive south, not speaking, down I-65. The '55 T-Bird, opera windows and four-on-the-floor, is air-conditioned, Crystal reclines with her cheek against the passenger window, her head awkwardly crook'd, a slight moisture clinging to her neck as if to hide the fingermarks.

The world seems to bow as we push through shimmering heat, colorful trees standing against smog-dulled sky. "I know you might not want to see your mother, but this will be a long, long trip if you won't talk to me," I say as we near Edinburg. A smile appears to touch her lips, though she doesn't look my way. Dusk is coming on; passing fields reflect darkly in her eyes and along the windshield's interior. "You're a good girl, Crystal," patting her knee. "The very best." I straighten a pleat on her skirt, and smile. One of the few saving graces of a world gone mad: the starched, white blouses and blue skirts of parochial schools. Crystal thinks so too. I can tell by the glazed happiness in her eyes. I lean Crystal against my shoulder, her weight heavy and her right arm dangling, and I stroke her long soft hair as we drive past stables and white fences enclosing horses I might someday be able to afford for her. We are lovers of thoroughbreds, she and I. She of white stallions and carefree afternoons. Me of blond, ponytailed girls on white stallions. So much I wish to give her!

We swing onto I-64, stream past Lexington, bypass Knoxville, then leave the freeway at Chattanooga; the in-city wending and the brooding dawnlit presence of Lookout Mountain might bring on another of my migraines. Signs bloom along the two-lane. Collegeville, Graysville, Ringgold. Wreathed in fog, we stop at a roadside picnic table. I climb out and stretch; Crystal slumps down across the bucket seats, not awakening.

A passing headlight lances out and is gone, momentarily searing my soul, and in that moment, the skipbeat tableau, I see the fingermarks on Crystal's neck have darkened to blue-black weals. People won't understand if they discover us! I sit her up and slide back into the car.

Then another surprise, more terrible than those headlights.

The Bird is nearly empty.

I should have known! Should have thought things through, and filled extra gas cans. Now we've got to chance stopping where people will see, and not understand.

Hands sweaty on the leather-enwrapped steering wheel, I roar back onto the road, spewing gravel. We pass through dawnmists and beneath sycamores heavy with shadow and Spanish moss. Finally—a populated area. BLAZE MOTEL: ROOMS BY NIGHT OR MONTH, says a sign resembling an uptilted carpenter's square; and in smaller cursive lettering. No. A hundred yards further, hunkered before a drive-in theatre and a row of boxy tract houses, is a service station. A winged red horse rides a teardrop sign atop a downward-tapering pole. Three old-fashioned bubble-headed gas pumps squat beneath a canopy that leans slightly sideways, like someone tipping a hat. I gear down. The T-Bird's muffler pops and rumbles. AC Sparkplugs, a sign informs me from a window streaked with dirt. A blue square clock above the office door says 5:15 and that Farmer's has Auto-Boat-Homeowner.

A blue-worksuited station attendant is standing in front of the pumps, waterhose in hand, washing oil and gasoline off the concrete pad. Not spraying the area, thumb against the hose end, but rather standing slumped, shoulders so thin they look pinched, the water arcing out feebly and splashing without pressure.

He doesn't move as I ease toward him.

I drum my fingers against the steering wheel. Then, impatient, I beep the horn.

The water continues to arc. He watched it solemnly through heavy-hooded eyes, his face pasty-white, cadaverous-looking except for deeply redded lips. Straight hair sticking from beneath his blue cap is slicked across his forehead. The Bird inches forward until the grill nearly touches him. Water cascades onto the hood; a hollow, metallic sound. I roll down the window. A blast of humid air hits me. "Hey!" I shout, again honk, really laying into it this time. Fear seizes me; I glance toward Crystal, then toward the row of tract houses.

No lights come on.

The attendant doesn't move.

Rock-and-roll suddenly jangles. I swivel, and am staring into the grinning, sallow-cheeked face of an attendant holding a transistor radio against his ear. Why is it that gas stations seem to hire zombies? His eyes are protruding slightly, as if his thickly veined lids have to stretch to keep the eyeballs from falling out. "Fill it," I tell him. My hand finds Crystal's. The attendant nods more to the music than in answer and bop-stepping, heads for the pumps, snapping his fingers, his thick red lips going *ooh-wa-wa,* hitch of the shoulders, then again *ooh-wa-wa.* "It takes regular, not premium!" I yell as he lifts a hose.

He raises his index finger, points it down as if to acknowledge, *one for your side, buddy.*

> *I got my thr-ell,*
> *on Blueberry he-ll,*
> *on Blueberry he-ll*
> *where ah-a met you.*

Fats Domino tells me from twenty-five years ago as the attendant pulls the gas hose to its maxiumum length, the black cord straining, and rams the nozzle scraping into the tank.

"Hey. Take it easy!"

Again the acknowleding forefinger.

A grinding. The garage door lifts. What looks like tiny yellow and blue flames dance in the inner darkness, at floor level. Someone welding? A burly T-shirted man, belly wobbling, ducks beneath the door and ambles toward the car, wiping his hands on a red rag. The door cranks down *whumping* against the concrete. The man bends and peers in, one hand on the cartop. Startled, I shift to block his view of Crystal. His eyes are cold. The fat beneath his chin appears to harden. "You ain't got call to go honking like that," he says, combing thinning hair back with his fingers. "It's enough to wake the dead."

"But he was blocking my way!" I point toward the attendant with the water hose.

Water suddenly splashes against my windshield.

"And now look!" I start to open the door and climb out. Spray mists against the side of my face and into the car.

"Now don't go getting your bowels in an uproar," the man says, holding the door so I can't climb out. "He's just a-washing the windows. Ain't no harm done." And then, gesturing, "Aaron, you stop with that hoo-raw!"

The spashing halts. The runoff comes down the windshield in droopy veils. I turn the key to ACC and work the wipers. The attendant stands facing the car, head down, staring at the ground, holding the hose straight up at his side, the water emerging and doubling back on itself, soaking his sleeve. His shoulders jerk and his chest heaves. He seems to be crying.

"You, Clarence. Git on up front there. Take a look-see at this man's earl."

The other attendant be-bops forward, transistor blaring as he passes, sets the radio on the fender, opens the hood, checks the oil by wiping the dipstick with his fingers, lifts the radio, slams the hood down.

Shoulders hitching, fingers snapping, Clarence starts back toward the hose. The T-shirted man grabs his arm. "You treat a car like this with respect," he says in a ugly low voice, his face darkening and his index finger sticking in front of Clarence's nose. "You hearing me?" Clarence's grin momentarily broadens, then fear enters his eyes and his face appears to collapse. Taking the transistor from his ear and lowering his head, he peers up, a dog expecting a beating, from the top of watery eyes.

The T-shirted man turns aside and, gripping the top of the window frame, leans back to inspect the Bird. Clarence carefully sidesteps around him. Radio against leg, the sound muffled, he makes for the hose. "Yep. Real collector's item," the T-shirted man says, grinning, showing crooked teeth. He moves around the car, stroking the fender, tapping the hood, admiring a headlight. "Just a bright little lady." Pausing by the passenger door, he raps a knuckle against the glass where I've placed Crystal with a pillow against the window, and then saunters on around back. "You ought to be real proud," he says, coming around again. His enormous head thrusts into the window and, folded arms against the door, he surveys the interior. I lean away from his stench. "Mint *con*-dition," he says. A pack of Camels—I can see the label through the cloth—is rolled up in his sleeve. "Yer little gal's just as asleep as she can be," he says, nodding. "Cuter'n a bug's ear." He winks.

"She's had a hard day. We're on our way to Florida." I force a smile, but my hands are trembling. I clutch the wheel.

"Tourist, huh?"

"Not really." Something in his voice troubles me. "Her mother—Phyllis—lives in Orlando." Immediately I'm angry with myself; where we're headed, and why, is no one else's business.

"Going to Disneyworld, I'll bet."

"Oh yes. Disneyworld." I manage a slight laugh. "But mainly to see her mother. Her mother lives in Orlando."

"Yes," he says. "Orlando. That's where she lives, all right." He stands upright, again wiping his hands on the rag. "I'll tend to you later," he says to Clarence, then, whistling "Blueberry Hill," wanders toward the garage, the fat along

139

the sides of his back shifting beneath his T-shirt. The door cranks open. Tiny blue flames flutter and leap inside the garage. I stick my head out the window for a better look. No flames. He enters shadows. The door comes down.

"Three-fifty."

I roll my hip up, reaching for my wallet. And then, *"What?"*

"Three-fifty," Clarence says. His hand is out, but he's not looking at me. He's staring toward the garage door. A nervous tic twitches beneath his left eye. He keeps the radio pressed against his side.

35.9 says the price gauge.

"Pumps so old they can't show dollars?" I laugh. "Haven't you people heard of the gas crunch?"

"Gas war?"—still looking toward the garage.

"You couldn't have filled this car for three-fifty!" I glance at the fuel gauge. It's at F.

"Make it 'five, then." His fingers make a crablike, impatient motion.

I smile triumphantly as I stuff a bill into his hand. "I should come here more often."

"Sure, man. Whatever you say." Water suddenly drums against my hood, the other attendant standing slump-shouldered, the hose cascading. But I don't let myself get angry; not at these prices! I back up before Clarence can change his mind.

"Hah!" I slap Crystal's leg with delight as we swing onto the two lane. "Five bucks!" I put my arm around her shoulders and pull her close, her flesh cold and clammy, and for the next few miles I drive one-handed, humming. What a glorious morning! A blue interstate sign comes up, an arrow pointing south down a gravel road. I steer around a dead cat, the car sliding slightly as if restless for the freeway. Sunlight, breaking through the trees, is so brilliant it's almost spangling. Slatty shadows race past. "Next stop, Orlando!" I tell Crystal, giving her another hug.

Half a mile later I see the figures.

Blue-worksuited and blue-capped, two lanky men are hunched over something alongside the road. They gaze up as I roar by, their eyes fear-strickened, the sunlight slanting like tape across pallid faces. Red-splashed mouths leer. One of the men flicks his hand, sloughing off what looks like soggy sausage, and quickly licks his fingers. Then both men sprint for the woods, eyeing me over their shoulders. I gear down. Too fast. The Bird shudders and slides. A guardrail flashes along my right like an undulating ribbon.

Crystal falls forward as I'm pulling the Bird out of the skid. I grab for her to keep her from hurting herself. Her head hits my arm. A thud jolts the car, then metal screeches against metal, and a guardpost lurches toward me. I wrench the wheel to the left, my brakes squealing. Metal crunches. The steering wheel leaps backward, slamming against my chest, then a soft fuzzy darkness pulls down and I hear the crying of metal and the hissing of a radiator as if in a dream.

"Crystal?"

My voice enters my consciousness even before I open my eyes. I blink. Sunlight swims within my vision, and I wince. I lean back in the seat, trying to suck in air. My chest feels like some great weight is pressing upon me. There's a cottony, hung-over taste in my mouth. I touch my forehead, feel wet warmth.

"Darling?" I probe my scalp. A small cut along my forehead; very little blood.

Crystal doesn't answer. I jerk upright, anger and dread clenching my stomach. She's lying sideways, face up, arms around the gearshift. Her cheeks are ashen, her eyes rolled back. I slap her temples. "Speak to me!"

I'm all right, Uncle Jim.

"Thank Goodness!" I hug her and we rock to and fro, my eyes filled with tears and my pulse pounding. "Oh, baby, baby." I pull her onto my lap.

I've ruined your beautiful car, she whispers; *if only I hadn't hit your arm!*

"Just so you're all right. That's all that matters."

I climb out. The right fender is crumpled, the grill and radiator askew, the headlight hanging like an eyeball dangling by threads. I glance about the woods for the two figures, but the men aren't in sight. Squinting against the sunlight, my head throbbing, I walk across the road.

There in the dust is an opossum, eyes open and mouth closed and tiny claws curled down. Gouts of flesh have been ripped from its side. Pink and black entrails shine wetly. I retch and stagger back, hand over my mouth. Because I remember what I saw, or thought I'd seen; what made me gear down so suddenly. *Eating. The men had been eating.* I double over, again retching dryly, bile drooling between my fingers.

Uncle Jim?

I run, shaking my head.

She's lying across the seat, knees up, eyes rolled back, smiling. Struggling for air I lean with one hand against the wheel, the other clutching the seatback. My breaths come in shallow gasps. I shift position, blocking her line of vision from that terrible thing across the road, and touch her knee to calm her, assure her. Nothing evil or ugly will reach her, nothing will harm her, she'll know only good things, as long as I'm alive and we're together. Her legs are long, lovely, spindly; colt's legs. Babysoft down on her calves. *It's wonderful being with you,* she says. Sunlight is touching her face, her cheeks tawny and sleek. *I don't mind that you killed me. Really. It's about what I should have expected from you.*

"I didn't . . . You're just sleeping, that's all!" I angrily sit her upright and ease into the car, then sit gripping the wheel and glaring across the hood.

I remember you watching me from outside the school playground, clutching the wire as if you'd tear the fence down, and I'd be with my girlfriends, talking about boys and schoolwork and junk like that, but really I'd be watching you from the corner of my eye, and worrying, knowing how you are . . . A lech.

"Don't say that."

At home, when you and Mother made the bed squeak, I'd lie in my room, pretending to be asleep, and not knowing how to tell Mother that, you know, that you were constantly looking at me . . .

"Well, I *was* looking at you. But not the way you think. You and your dirty little mind! The whole time your mother and I would be together I'd be wanting you, not anything, well, anything *sexual,* just wanting to be near you, and feeling guilty for it. But I've never touched you, and never will. Our love is pure. You know that." I shake my finger at her.

There's more than one name for rape.

I glower and again grip the wheel. I'm not going to listen to any more of her asinine brattishness! I glance toward the opossum and, feeling nauseated, crank the key. The Bird spits, but starts—wheezing and jerking and the right wheel grinding against the inside of the crumpled fender as, jamming the gearshift forward, I send the Bird squealing in a circle. The two men were just looking at the thing, I tell myself, or maybe were highway department men or something, responsible for clearing the road. "Your mother shouldn't have gone away and left us!" I tell her. "There we were—your mother run off to Florida, you and your father suddenly thrown together, and me on the outside. The three of us, in that sweltering Indiana heat. She shouldn't have done that. Now shut up and buckle up. We're going back to that station." We'll get the Bird fixed, then we're headed to Florida as fast as speed limits allow. I wonder what Phyllis will say when I tell her how I feel about Crystal. Well, that's down the road.

Crystal doesn't touch her seatbelt. Just sits with her head forward, chin against chest, pouting. I shake my head in despair. Usually she's so mature, so very much older than her twelve years. Then other times . . .

The front and back garage doors are open when we return. A slight breeze has come up, and a cool feeling bangs amid the humidity. Wrench in hand and cigarette in mouth, Clarence is working beneath a dented-up Impala on the rack.

I find the T-shirted man in the office, leaning back in a swivel chair and smoking, his feet on a desk strewn with papers as he watches a Chicano couple at the pay phone, the wife jabbering and, cigarette in hand, pushing her hair back, the husband, also smoking, staring sullenly at the floor.

"They're trying to get a-holt of someone who's sposed to get a-holt of someone else, someone with money, who's sposed to get a-holt of Western Union, who's sposed to wire money, so's they can pay me and get that goddamn hunk of tin off'n my rack," the T-shirted man says.

"And if they can't pay?" I ask.

"We keep the car till they do." He shrugs. "That don't work, we scrap the mother." Then, "So what can I do for you this time?" He cranes to see over the desk, apparently assuring himself the T-Bird has returned and he's speaking to the right person.

"Had an accident. Hit gravel and slammed into a guard-rail."

"Oh?" Again craning.

"Right side. It'll need some body work." Then I quickly add, "Nothing special. Just pound it out and I'll be on my way; I'll get it fixed when we reach Florida. And something's wrong with the engine. Carburetor, maybe. I thought I might have cracked the radiator, but it seems to be all right. At least, the car didn't overheat on the way back."

He nods absently, then his face suddenly goes white and he swings his legs down. "*She's* all right, ain't she?"

After a moment. "Oh, you mean Crystal. She's fine. Fine. Sleeping now."

"Sure do sleep a lot, that little gal." His eyes twinkle, and his broken-tooth grin hints of lechery.

"Well, what with the accident and all," my voice hard.

"Hey, Clarence?" the T-shirted man asks through the door adjoining office and garage. One eye closed, Clarence is squinting up toward the Impala through the little square hole in the back of a socket wrench. "Clarence!" The attendant doesn't turn. The T-shirted man's face clouds, and he glances around the desk. He grabs a small crescent wrench, pitches it into the garage. It hits ringing on the concrete, bounces, swacks the attendant on the calf. Clarence glances downward stupidly, eyes bulged. "See to that car yonder?" the T-shirted man asks, pointing toward the pumps. "Fella here had hisself an ac-ce-dent." Clarence points with the socket wrench handle toward the underside of the Impala. "That pile of shit ain't going nowhere," the T-shirted man says. "You get on out there." Then, to the Chicano couple, "And you grease-heads hurry and get off'n my telephone, you hearing me?"

The husband smiles and nods, obviously not understanding. I ignore him, follow Clarence to the car. I've left the engine running, and for a few moments Clarence stands beside the broken headlight, apparently listening, gazing at the grill and rubbing his hand on the fender. Finally there's a *screeek* as he opens the hood. The sputtering sounds worse. His eyes are heavy-lidded and glistening as he removes the top of the air filter. He wipes grime from the engine block, licks his fingers as if wetting them to turn a page, and peers into the carburetor. He takes a screwdriver from his back pocket and prods the carburetor's butterfly. Then he steps back, blows his nose in an oil-stained red rag. "Try gunning 'er," he says, a rag-covered finger exploring a nostril.

I climb inside. "What do you think it is?" I yell, my head out the window. Clarence doesn't answer. He's leaning over the engine, tinkering. Something pops, then there's a hiss as if I've blown a tire. Sparks fly. I lurch open the door and start to climb out, but Clarence waves me back. He eyes the engine grimly. Steam rises in lazy billows. He motions: *turn the key.*

The engine doesn't turn over. Dead.

I jump out, slam the door and push him aside. He doesn't protest—just looks downcast, screwdriver and crescent wrench in hand. "Look here!" I hold up the battery cable. My blood's up, my face burning. "You bumped the thing off the goddamn terminal!" Immediately my words haunt me. *Bumped* the cable off? But I say nothing else; he looks pitiful, and God knows where another station might be. He doesn't resist when I grab his tools. I replace and tighten the cable mount, climb back in the Bird. The other attendant— Aaron—appears in the shadows alongside the garage, holding a gas nozzle disconnected from its hose. The thing seems to be dripping . . . dripping flame, tiny blue and yellow firestars splashing against the pavement. I stick my head out the window for a better look. Aaron turns and walks away.

Get hold of yourself, Jim. For Crystal's sake. You'll have another migraine.

I turn the key.

The engine grinds, and grinds, and grinds down, a dying growl.

"Goddamn it!" I beat my fist against the dash. Again and again I try the key. The grinding grows lower. I sit cursing, my face aflame and temples pulsing, all the anger I've al-

ways felt for things that won't work, things that won't do as
they're told, as they're asked, as they're pleaded with, cars
and bad faucets and corroded screw heads that won't
budge, girls who won't go to Florida and only laughing and
insisting I'm a jerk when I tell her I'll get her drugs if she
wants some, her goddamn schoolmates carrying coke vials
in their training bras and snorting powder up their nostrils
and throwing their heads back and laughing about a mid-
dle-aged man stupid enough to buy it for them just so they
won't tell about him on the playground, *an accountant no
less,* stupid enough to fall in love with tinkly laughter and
spindly legs, and she not a user and not willing to go to
Florida with you even if you were the last man in the world,
or the wealthiest, or the most handsome, all of which you're
not, just a creep Mother had *sense* enough to dump—that
anger welling up, boiling, percolating my brain.

The key bends.

"No." I put my head against my hands, on the wheel.
The word sounds distant. "Please, Crystal; no."

"Starter's out," Clarence says, standing beside the door.
His voice is low and sympathetic, like that of a physician
telling you you have cancer or clap.

"The hell." I don't look up. The damn pasty-faced clown!
No wonder they're called grease monkeys! "It wouldn't just
grind if it were the starter. It would make cranking noises, or
something." I speak softly, questioningly, for I'm not sure he
isn't right. I never did understand engines, friends back in
high school talking about cams and gear ratios and synch,
and me smiling, nodding, wondering about trig and book-
keeping III, wondering if my friends knew my head was
what they with their cutdown, blocked-out, souped-up smit-
tied '57 Chevs called "empty-engined."

"Starter," Clarence insists. But those half-hooded eyes
are pulled down further, betraying disbelief.

"The hell"—this time the words coming from behind me.
The T-shirted man is standing with his forearm against the
car roof, his other hand fisted against his hip. With his
tongue he moves a toothpick to the other side of his mouth.
"Just 'cause you got buzzard brains don't mean you can go
telling a pack of lies," he says to Clarence, holding up the

146

toothpick as if examining it. "Fuel pump, is what it is. Anyone can see that."

"Fuel pump?" I ask.

"Yep." He flicks the toothpick at Clarence and strides toward the office. Then suddenly turns. "Going to be a while
'fore we can get to it though. Wetbacks in here just got a-
holt of some money." He pokes his thumb over his shoulder. "Two, maybe three hours, iff'n we can find a pump.
Couple other helpers coming in 'round noon; I'll put them
on it. Things'll start hopping here pretty soon, this being
Saturday and all."

Saturday. And I picked up Crystal only yesterday, waiting
for the weekend so the number of schooldays she'd miss
would be minimized. It seemed so long ago!

Then he says, "Cafe 'round the corner from that movie
house there." He points toward the drive-in. ROXY, the
marquee says; Horror At Carnival Beach. I lift my hand in
acknowledgement, and he goes in the office, plops in the
chair, puts his feet up. Clarence, beside the pumps, takes a
radio from his breast pocket and looks at it curiously as he
works the circular on/off control. The plastic front's smashed
and the back's missing, wires and battery hanging jumbled.
No music's playing. He smiles sheepishly, slams down the
hood and, snapping his fingers, ambles toward the garage,
the radio against his ear.

For several moments I sit gripping the wheel, staring vacantly, fighting anger. My headache's a jackhammer. Need
some sleep. In my rear-view I can see the motel's no-va-
cancy sign is off. I take my shaving kit and a blanket from
the trunk and, wrapping up Crystal, steal away when the T-
shirted man has his back turned, talking to the Chicanos.
Crystal's sleeping soundly. I lie her amid tall bunchgrass
growing among the wooden buttresses behind the drive-in
screen. "Be right back," I whisper, and kiss her cheek.

The motel clerk, a blowsy redhead with sagging jowls and
too much rouge, is putting on lipstick when I enter. She
smacks her lips and drops the lipstick tube and her compact
into her purse, snaps it shut and sticks it under the counter.
"Help you?" She folds a curl behind her ear. I explain that

147

my car's broken down and I need a room for a few hours. "Oh?" her voice lilting.

"For my daughter and I. She's at the station."

"Oh," her voice lower.

The room proves perfect—shielded from the motel office, yet with a view of the car. Two double beds: green bedspreads, the kind with little tufts arranged in chevrons. Some of the tufts have pulled out, and a yellow blanket peeks through the holes when I bring Crystal in. A black and white TV on a rickety Danish-modern bureau mirrors us. I kick the door shut with my heel and, kneeling awkwardly, pull back the covers. Then I help Crystal out of her skirt. She lies quietly, elbow akimbo, her left hand behind her head, on the pillow. Her right knee is turned against her left, legs together. Her smile is slight, but sweet, as I close her eyelids. I go into the bathroom. For Your Sanitary Convenience, the toilet tells me. I remove the label carefully and wipe the seat with toilet paper before using.

After a shave and shower I walk to Bea's Honeypot: Good Food, Good Conversation. The cafe specializes in pecan pie and blather about how bad business is, what with them fastfood places down on Elvira. I return with two paper plates folded like taco shells around charred T-bones, two styrofoam cups of greasy coffee, plastic knives and forks, a silver packet of ketchup with a dotted line along one corner. In Florida we'll eat better, I promise myself. No more of that junk food Crystal thinks she likes.

I eat hunched over on the bedside, the covers and sheet pulled up to Crystal's chin. I offer her forkfuls of steak, but even when I whisper her name she refuses to open her eyes or mouth. The playful pup! My heart is thudding with delight and desire. I can hardly eat, I'm trembling so. Finally I can't control myself any longer. I wash off my paper plate, put it in the bathroom trashcan, remove and hang up my sports jacket and shirt. The hangers are wire instead of broad-shouldered wood; I try hanging up my undershirt, but the straps keep sliding off. I fold and place the undershirt in the bureau. Leave my trousers on. I am not large-genitaled—when my marriage was crumbling, Jonaca, my ex, used to mock me—but the bulge might show if I strip to my boxer shorts, and there's no sense shocking her. I kneel beside her, draw the blanket back to uncover her feet. "Crystal," I whisper. Her flesh feels like ice. Poor thing must have gotten her toesies cold in the car. I make a mental note not to keep the Bird's air conditioning turned up so high. I put her toes in my mouth, to warm them. Dust-moted sunlight, filtered by the yellow chiffon curtains, touches her cheek. After a moment she seems to smile, and I again cover her legs.

"At the office," I tell her, "were page after page of accounting sheets. Sometimes it felt like the grids were trying to put me into boxes. And the columns forever coming out wrong! Then I'd enter a 12, and think of you." 12: woman and swan; goddess and kneeling, bowing slave. How beautiful my Crystal! As pure as my own daughter. When I'd sleep with Phyllis—the first and only woman I was brave and foolish enough to bed with after my divorce—I'd awaken in a sweat, apulse with heat flashes, remembering how Jonaca and that squinty-eyed judge had taken Temple. Not even allowed visitation rights! Then I'd dream of Crystal in the next room, all innocence and intrigue, and calm would come. Crystal, my soothing drug.

"I worship you, my darling."

I know, Uncle Jim. Her eyes don't open. *But I'm afraid.*

Afraid to be alone, to sleep alone. I can understand that. Happiness washes over me. I slip under the covers beside her, and close my eyes. Her presence fills my spirit. My migraine stops throbbing. My heart quietens. Then I sleep, my dreams no longer only of her but of us together, our hands together and lives together, intertwined and pure.

Darkness has fallen when I awaken. Crystal continues to sleep; careful not to bother her, I slip from bed and quietly dress. Over at the station the two attendants are only now pushing the T-bird into the garage. Strangely, I only feel joy at their sloth. Whistling, I walk toward the office for a paper. Rounding the corner I can see the drive-in screen. A bikinied girl with blond hair styled in a bubble, her back to the screen, is holding a beachball and running awkwardly after a dark-haired boy with a deep tan. In the background is a man-shaped shadow: hint of ominous portents. I shake my head in wonderment. Such mindlessness down into which our world's been funneled!

The news proves bad, as usual. Race riots in Houston, a longshoreman strike in New York now affecting L.A., a torture cult discovered outside Omaha, interest rates up another point, nothing about girls smart enough to turn up missing in order to get out of Indianapolis. I read the paper while sitting in the lobby. Then I'll put the paper in the trash, where it belongs. No sense Crystal knowing of such things. Girls her age need to be protected.

"Car still ain't fixed?" Chanking gum, the motel clerk comes through the paisley curtain separating the lobby from what I assume are her quarters.

"Apparently not," and shrug.

"That ain't the swiftest bunch," she says, checking keys and sticking mail in the pigeon-holed boxes behind the counter. "Not by any sense of the word. There's goings-on over there that just don't set right, if you ask me. I swear he beats them boys."

"Oh, I'm sure he doesn't."

Her brow lifts, a confiding look. "I seen that Clarence kid once, with his shirt off. Had welts on his back the size of egg yolks. And them boys don't seem to have no homes, the way the four of them are always over there. So who else could have gave him them welts?"

Again I shrug. I turn back to the paper.

"Well, I'd keep a lookout of my car, if I was you. I wouldn't trust that bunch to turn off the water if the house was flooding, if you catch my drift. Fellow was there once, I bet there weren't nothing wrong with his car more'n needing gas or maybe something tightened. Took the rotor out of his distributor, them boys did, and told him it was the fuel pump. He found out about it and went to Deputy Cady."

I jerk the paper together so quickly it rumples to a wad. The blood has drained from my face.

"There was hell to pay around here when that happened," she says. And then, as I rush out the door, "Hey, ain't you going to take your paper?"

As I near my room I forget all about the car. The motel door's wide open. But the place was locked when I left! I know it was. Crystal? Crystal?

Gone. Went looking for me at the car, perhaps? I run down the alley, heels clocking against the blacktop, dread and despair and terror knotted in the pit of my stomach.

Halfway to the station I stop cold, seized by the image on the drive-in screen, and feel my soul shrivel. I stand whimpering, shaking my head in disbelief, wanting to beat my fists against my chest in anguish. On the screen the lanky blondhaired girl is lying on a pink coverlet, staring up in open-mouthed terror as a shadow slowly spreads over the beach, now over the blanket, now across her face. I can see clearly now, see it's Crystal up there as she raises her arms to fend off some offscreen, oncoming menace. Beyond the theater, past the bright-yellow fence, people are emerging from the tract houses, mothers and fathers and pigtailed girls and boys with Falcons sweatshirts, bringing out checkered green-and-white lawnchairs and chaise lounges printed with hyacinths and daffodils, setting up cedar tables, opening tassel-fringed umbrellas and boxes of Colonel Sanders' and Arby's double-deluxe with horseradish and Bea's oh-so-delicious pecan pie with her own special topping, relaxing now, laughing, delighting as on the screen long-fingered hands matted with dark fur find the girl's throat. Crystal's throat. And I run.

The garage doors yawn open, and the Bird slowly rises on the rack. The T-shirted man is in the driver's seat, his arm around Crystal in a fatherly embrace, she with her head tilted back, giggling and stuffing popcorn into her mouth, he leaning over to make some silly commentary on the show, both of them all innocence and intrigue, a scene out of the frontrow of a 1950's drive-in. "Crystal!" I shriek. "Please!"

Greenish fire erupts around the base of the rising pedestal, forcing me back, my arms upraised against the heat. Four attendants, blue-worksuited and blue-capped, emerge from the shadows of the office, carrying gas nozzles. White faces lifted, mouths bloodsplashed, eyes gleaming, they stand on opposite sides of the circle, watching the station master, their nozzles dripping blue and yellow flames. I can hear Crystal's bright laughter from above as on the screen a werewolf, eyes wild and froth dripping from his fangs, carries the limp girl towards the ferris wheel, a crowd of swimsuited spectators parting in a panic and then a close-up of the dark-haired youth inserting a silver bullet in the chamber of a rifle. He raises the weapon; camera angle of the werewolf seen through the crosshairs of a rifle scope. The trigger is squeezed, and above me Crystal's laughter suddenly rings louder, more cheerful, and somehow says *forever.* The laughter of the dead. I lower my arms and face the fire, my selfhood and hope crumpling like a bit of burning tissue. Is this, I wonder, some hell to which I'm to be relegated, forever to wear a blue cap and a blue worksuit, eternally youthful and beaten-down and crying as I watch the master accept a young girl's love, something I have never had and never will, while I must face what men fear most— a loved one enjoying another's embrace? Am I, like the other attendants, to rise each day to be run over by nightmare death, my eternity one of service and of cats and opossums on country roads?

If so, to be near Crystal, I shall endure the travail.

Probably the only writer of science and fantasy fiction living in an Eskimo village, George Florance-Guthridge was born in Vancouver, British Columbia, in 1948. Educated at Portland State University and the University of Iowa, he wrote stories for literary and children's magazines before specializing in science fiction. He has taught at Loras College in Iowa and the University of Montana and is currently teaching courses in non-fiction, advertising, and science fiction on St. Lawrence Island, Alaska.

While Margy Emmons could not live with the guilt of her husband's death, she did learn to live with his ghost. . . .

THIRTEEN

Ghost and Flesh, Water and Dirt

William Goyen

Was somebody here while ago acallin for you. . . .

O don't say that, don't tell me who . . . was he fair and had a wrinkle in his chin? I wonder was he the one . . . describe me his look, whether the eyes were pale light-colored and swimmin and wild and shifty; did he bend a little at the shoulders was his face agrievin what did he say where did he go, whichaway, hush don't tell me; wish I could keep him but I cain't, so go, go (but come back).

Cause you know honey there's a time to go roun and tell and there's a time to set still (and let a ghost grieve ya); so listen to me while I tell, cause I'm in my time a tellin and you better run fast if you don wanna hear what I tell, cause I'm goin ta tell . . .

Dreamt last night again I saw pore Raymon Emmons, all last night seen im plain as day. There uz tears in iz glassy eyes and iz face uz all meltin away. O I was broken of my sleep and of my night disturbed, for I dreamt of pore Raymon Emmons live as ever.

He came on the sleepin porch where I was sleepin (and he's there to stay) ridin a purple horse (like King was), and then he got off and tied im to the bedstead and come and stood over me and commenced iz talkin. All night long he uz talkin and talkin, his speech (whatever he uz sayin) uz like steam streamin outa the mouth of a kettle, streamin and streamin and streamin. At first I said in my dream, "Will you

153

do me the favor of tellin me just who in the world you can be, will you please show the kindness to tell me who you can be, breakin my sleep and disturbin my rest?" "I'm Raymon Emmons," the steamin voice said, "and I'm here to stay; putt out my things that you've putt away, putt out my oatmeal bowl and putt hot oatmeal in it, get out my rubberboots when it rains, iron my clothes and fix my supper . . . I never died and I'm here to stay."

(Oh go way ole ghost of Raymon Emmons, whisperin in my ear on the pilla at night; go way ole ghost and lemme be! Quit standin over me like that, all night standin there sayin somethin to me . . . behave ghost of Raymon Emmons, behave yoself and lemme be! Lemme get out and go roun, lemme put on those big ole rubberboots and go clompin. . . .)

Now you shoulda known that Raymon Emmons. *There* was *somebody*, I'm tellin you. Oh he uz a bright thang, quick'n fair, tall, about six feet, real lean and a devlish face full of snappin eyes, he had eyes all over his face, didn't miss a thang, that man, saw everthang; and a clean brow. He was a rayroad man, worked for the Guff Coast Lines all iz life, our house always smelt like a train.

When I first knew of him he was livin at the Boardinhouse acrost from the depot (oh that uz years and years ago), and I uz in town and wearin my first pumps when he stopped me on the corner and ast me to do him the favor of tellin him the size a my foot. I was not afraid atall to look at him and say the size a my foot uz my own affair and would he show the kindness to not be so fresh. But when he said I only want to know because there's somebody livin up in New Waverley about your size and age and I want to send a birthday present of some houseshoes to, I said that's different; and we went into Richardson's store, to the back where the shoes were, and tried on shoes till he found the kind and size to fit me and this person in New Waverley. I didn't tell im that the pumps I'uz wearin were Sistah's and not my size (when I got home and Mama said why'd it take you so long? I said it uz because I had to walk so slow in Sistah's pumps).

Next time I saw im in town (and I made it a point to look for im, was why I come to town), I went up to im and said do you want to measure my foot again Raymon Emmons, ha! And he said any day in the week I'd measure that pretty foot; and we went into Richardson's and he bought *me* a pair of white summer pumps with a pink tie (and I gave Sistah's pumps back to her). Miz Richardson said my lands Margy you buyin lotsa shoes lately, are you goin to take a trip (O I took a trip, and one I come back from, too).

We had other meetins and was plainly in love; and when we married, runnin off to Groveton to do it, everbody in town said things about the marriage because he uz thirty and I uz seventeen.

We moved to this house owned by the Picketts, with a good big clothesyard and a swing on the porch, and I made it real nice for me and Raymon Emmons, made curtains with fringe, putt jardinears on the front bannisters and painted the fern buckets. We furnished those unfurnished rooms with our brand new lives, and started goin along.

Between those years and this one I'm tellin about them in, there seems a space as wide and vacant and silent as the Neches River, with my life *then* standin on one bank and my life *now* standin on the other, lookin acrost at each other like two diffrent people wonderin who the other can really be.

How did Raymon Emmons die? Walked right through a winda and tore hisself all to smithereens. Walked right through a second-story winda at the depot and fell broken on the tracks—nothin much left a Raymon Emmons after he walked through that winda—broken his crown, hon, broken his crown. But he lingered for three days in Victry Hospital and then passed, sayin just before he passed away, turning towards me, "I hope you're satisfied. . . ."

Why did he die? From grievin over his daughter and mine, Chitta was her name, that fell off a horse they uz both ridin on the Emmonses' farm. Horse's name was King and we had im shot.

Buried im next to Chitta's grave with iz insurance, two funerals in as many weeks, then set aroun blue in our house, cryin all day and cryin half the night, sleep all broken and disturbed of my rest, thinkin oh if he'd come knockin at

that door right now I'd let him in, oh I'd let Raymon Emmons in! After he died, I set aroun sayin "who's gonna meet
all the hours in a day with me, whatever is in each one—*all
those hours*—who's gonna be with me in the mornin, in the
ashy afternoons that we always have here, in the nights of
lightnin who's goan be lyin there, seen in the flashes and
makin me feel as safe as if he uz a lightnin rod (and honey
he *wuz*); who's gonna be like a light turned on in a dark
room when I go in, who's gonna be at the door when I open
it, who's goin to be there when I wake up or when I go to
sleep, who's goin to call my name? I cain't stand a life of just
me and our furniture in a room, who's gonna *be* with me?"
Honey it's true that you never miss water till the well runs
dry, tiz truly true.

Went to talk to the preacher, but he uz no earthly help,
regalin me with iz pretty talk, he's got a tongue that will trill
out a story pretty as a bird on a bobwire fence—but meanin
what?—sayin "the wicked walk on every hand when the
vilest men are exalted"—now what uz that mean?—; went
to set and talk with Fursta Evans in her Millinary Shop
(who's had her share of tumult in her sad life, but never
shows it) but she uz no good, sayin "Girl pick up the pieces
and go on . . . here try on this real cute hat" (that woman
had nothin but hats on her mind—even though she taught
me *my* life, grant cha *that*—for brains she's got hats). Went
to the graves on Sundays carryin potplants and crying over
the mounds, one long wide one and one little un—how sad
are the little graves a childrun, childrun ought not to have to
die it's not right to bring death to childrun, they're just little
toys grownups play with or neglect (thas how some of em
die, too, honey, but won't say no more bout that); but all
childrun go to Heaven so guess it's best—the grasshoppers
flying all roun me (they say graveyard grasshoppers spit tobacco juice and if it gets in your eye it'll putt your eye out)
and an armadilla diggin in the crepemyrtle bushes—sayin
"dirt lay light on Raymon Emmons and iz child," and
thinkin "all my life is dirt I've got a family of dirt." And then I
come back to set and scratch aroun like an armadilla myself
in these rooms, alone; but honey that uz no good either.

And then one day, I guess it uz a year after my family
died, there uz a knock on my door and it uz Fursta Evans

knockin when I opened it to see. And she said "honey now listen I've come to visit with you and to try to tell you somethin: why are you so glued to Raymon Emmonses memry when you never cared a hoot bout him while he was on earth, you despised all the Emmonses, said they was just trash, wouldn't go to the farm on Christmas or Thanksgivin, wouldn't set next to em in church, broke pore Raymon Emmons's heart because you'd never let Chitta stay with her grandparents and when you finely did the Lord purnished you for bein so hateful by takin Chitta. Then you blamed it on Raymon Emmons, hounded im night and day, said he killed Chitta, drove im stark ravin mad. While Raymon Emmons was live you'd never even give him the time a day, wouldn't lift a hand for im, you never would cross the street for im, to you he uz just a dog in the yard, and you know it, and now that he's dead you grieve yo life away and suddenly fall in love with im." Oh she tole me good and proper—said, "you never loved im till you lost im, till it uz too late, said now set up and listen to me and get some brains in yo head, chile." Said, "cause listen honey, I've had four husbands in my time, two of em died and two of em quit me, but each one of em I thought was goin to be the *only* one, and I took each one for that, then let im go when he uz gone, kept goin roun, kept ready, we got to honey, left the gate wide open for anybody to come through, friend or stranger, ran with the hare and hunted with the hound, honey we got to *greet* life not grieve life," is what she said.

"Well," I said, "I guess that's the way life is, you don't know what you have till you don't have it any longer, till you've lost it, till it's too late."

"Anyway," Fursta said, "little cattle little care—you're beginnin again now, fresh and empty handed, it's later and it's shorter, yo life, but go on from *here* not *there*," she said. "You've had one kind of a life, had a husband, put im in iz grave (now leave im there!), had a child and putt her away, too; start over, hon, the world don't know it, the world's fresh as ever—it's a new day, putt some powder on yo face and start goin roun. Get you a job, and try that; or take you a trip. . . ."

"But I got to stay in this house," I said. "Feel like I cain't budge. Raymon Emmons is here, live as ever, and I cain't get away from im. He keeps me fastened to this house."

"Oh poot," Fursta said, lightin a cigarette. "Honey you're losin ya mine. Now listen here, put on those big ole rubber-boots and go clompin, go steppin high and wide—cause listen here, if ya don't they'll have ya up in the Asylum at Rusk sure's as shootin, specially if you go on talkin about this ghost of Raymon Emmons the way you do."

"But if I started goin roun, what would people say?"

"You can tell em its none of their beeswax. Cause listen honey, the years uv passed and are passin and you in ever one of em, passin too, and not gettin any younger—yo hair's getting bunchy and the lines clawed roun yo mouth and eyes by the glassy claws of crying sharp tears. We got to paint ourselves up and go on, young *outside,* anyway—cause listen honey the sun comes up and the sun crosses over and *goes down*—and while the sun's up we got to get on that fence and crow. Cause night muss fall—and then thas all. Come on, les go roun; have us a Sataday night weddin ever Sataday night; forget this ole patched-faced ghost I hear you talkin about. . . ."

"In this town?" I said. "I hate this ole town, always rain fallin—'cept this ain't rain it's rainin, Fursta, it's rainin mildew. . . ."

"O deliver me!" Fursta shouted out, and putt out her cigarette, "you won't do. Are you afraid you'll *melt?*"

"I wish I'd melt—and run down the drains. Wish I uz rain, fallin on the dirt of certain graves I know and seepin down into the dirt, could lie in the dirt with Raymon Emmons on one side and Chitta on the other. Wish I uz dirt. . . ."

"I wish you are just crazy," Fursta said. "Come on, you're gonna take a trip. You're gonna get on a train and take a nonstop trip and get off at the end a the line and start all over again new as a New Year's Baby, baby. I'm gonna see to that."

"Not on no train, all the king's men couldn't get me to ride a train again, no siree. . . ."

"Oh no train my foot," said Fursta.

"But what'll I use for money please tell me," I said.

"With Raymon Emmons's insurance of course—it didn't take all of it to bury im, I know. Put some acreage tween you and yo past life, and maybe some new friends and scenery too, and pull down the shade on all the water that's gone

under the bridge; and come back here a new woman. Then
if ya want tew you can come into my millinary shop with
me."

"Oh," I said, "is the world still there? Since Raymon Emmons walked through that winda seems the whole world's
gone, the whole world went out through that winda when
he walked through it."

Closed the house, sayin "goodbye ghost of Raymon Emmons," bought my ticket at the depot, deafenin my ears to
the sound of the tickin telegraph machine, got on a train and
headed west to California. Day and night the trainwheels on
the traintracks said *Raymon Emmons Raymon Emmons
Raymon Emmons,* and I looked through the winda at dirt
and desert, miles and miles of dirt, thinking I wish I uz dirt I
wish I uz dirt. O I uz vile with grief.

In California the sun was out, wide, and everbody and
everthing lighted up; and oh honey the world *was* still there.
I decided to stay awhile. I started my new life with Raymon
Emmons's insurance money. It uz in San Diego, by the
ocean and with mountains of dirt standin gold in the blue
waters. A war had come. I was alone for awhile, but not for
long. Got me a job in an airplane factory, met a lotta girls,
met a lotta men. I worked in fusilodges.

There uz this Nick Natowski, a brown clean Pollock from
Chicargo, real wile, real Satanish. What kind of a life did he
start me into? I don't know how it started, but it did, and in a
flash we uz everwhere together, dancin and swimmin and
everything. He uz in the war and in the U.S. Navy, but we
didn't think of the war or of water. I just liked him tight as a
glove in iz uniform, I just liked him laughin, honey, I just
liked him *ever* way he was, and that uz all I knew. And then
one night he said, "Margy I'm goin to tell you somethin,
goin on a boat, be gone a long long time, goin in a week."
Oh I cried and had a nervous fit and said, "Why do you
have to go when there's these thousands of others all aroun
San Diego that could go?" and he said, "We're goin away to
Coronada for that week, you and me, and what happens
there will be enough to keep and save for the whole time
we're apart." We went, honey, Nick and me, to Coronada, I
mean we really *went.* Lived like a king and queen—where
uz my life behind me that I thought of onct and a while like a

story somebody was whisperin to me?—laughed and loved and I cried; and after that week at Coronada, Nick left for sea on his boat, to the war, sayin I want you to know baby I'm leavin you my allotment.

I was blue, so blue, all over again, but this time it uz diffrent someway, guess cause I uz blue for somethin live this time and not dead under dirt, I don't know; anyway I kept goin roun, kept my job in fusilodges and kept goin roun. There was this friend of Nick Natowski's called George, and we went together some. "But why doesn't Nick Natowski write me, George?" I said. "Because he cain't yet," George said, "but just wait and he'll write." I kept waitin but no letter ever came, and the reason he didn't write when he could of, finely, was because his boat was sunk and Nick Natowski in it.

Oh what have I ever done in this world, I said, to send my soul to torment? Lost one to dirt and one to water, makes my life a life of mud, why was I ever put to such a test as this O Lord, I said. I'm goin back home to where I started, gonna get on that train and backtrack to where I started from, want to look at dirt awhile, can't stand to look at water. I rode the train back. Somethin drew me back like I'd been pastured on a rope in California.

Come back to this house, opened it up and aired it all out, and when I got back you know who was there in that house? That ole faithful ghost of Raymon Emmons. He'd been there, waitin, while I went aroun, in my goin roun time, and was there to have me back. While I uz gone he'd covered everthing in our house with the breath a ghosts, fine ghost dust over the tables and chairs and a curtain of ghost lace over my bed on the sleepinporch.

Took me this job in Richardson's Shoe Shop (this town's big now and got money in it, the war 'n oil made it rich, ud never know it as the same if you hadn't known it before; and Fursta Evans married to a rich widower), set there fittin shoes on measured feet all day—it all started in a shoestore measurin feet and it ended that way—can you feature that? Went home at night to my you-know-what.

Comes ridin onto the sleepinporch ever night regular as clockwork, ties iz horse to the bedstead and I say hello

Raymon Emmons and we start our conversation. Don't ask me what he says or what I say, but ever night is a night full of talkin, and it lasts the whole night through. Oh onct in a while I get real blue and want to hide away and just set with Raymon Emmons in my house, cain't budge, don't see daylight nor dark, putt away my wearin clothes, couldn't walk outa that door if my life depended on it. But I set real still and let it all be, claimed by that ghost until he unclaims me—and then I get up and go roun, free, and that's why I'm here, settin with you here in the Pass Time Club, drinkin this beer and tellin you all I've told.

Honey, why am I tellin all this? Oh all our lives! So many things to tell. And I keep em to myself a long long time, tight as a drum, won't open my mouth, just set in my blue house with that ole ghost agrievin me, until there comes a time of tellin, a time to tell, a time to putt on those big ole rubber-boots.

Now I believe in *tellin,* while we're live and goin roun; when the tellin time comes I say spew it out, we just got to tell things, things in our lives, things that've happened, things we've fancied and things we dream about or are haunted by. Cause you know honey the time to shut yo mouth and set moultin and mildewed in yo room, grieved by a ghost and fastened to a chair, comes back roun again, don't worry honey, it comes roun again. There's a time ta tell and a time ta set still ta let a ghost grieve ya. So listen to me while I tell, cause I'm in my time a tellin, and you better run fast if you don wanna hear what I tell, cause I'm goin ta tell. . . .

The world is changed, let's drink ower beer and have us a time, tell and tell and tell, let's get that hot bird in a cole bottle tonight. Cause next time you think you'll see me and hear me tell, you won't: I'll be flat where I cain't budge again, like I wuz all that year, settin and hidin way . . . until the time comes roun again when I can say oh go way ole ghost of Raymon Emmons, go way ole ghost and lemme be!

Cause I've learned this and I'm gonna tell ya: there's a time for live things and a time for dead, for ghosts and for flesh 'n bones: all life is just a sharin of ghosts and flesh. Us

161

humans are part ghost and part flesh—part fire and part ash—but I think maybe the ghost part is the longest lastin, the fire blazes but the ashes last forever. I had fire in California (and water putt it out) and ash in Texis (and it went to dirt); but I say now, while I'm tellin you, there's a world both places, a world where there's ghosts and a world where there's flesh, and I believe the real right way is to take our worlds, of ghosts or of flesh, take each one as they come and take what comes in em: take a ghost and grieve with im, settin still; and take the flesh 'n bones and go roun; and even run out to meet what worlds come in to our lives, strangers (like you), and ghosts (like Raymon Emmons) and lovers (like Nick Natowski) . . . and be what each world wants us to be.

And I think that ghosts, if you set still with em long enough, can give you over to flesh 'n bones; and that flesh 'n bones, if you go roun when it's time, can send you back to a faithful ghost. One provides the other.

Saw pore Raymon Emmons all last night, all last night seen im plain as day.

Born in Texas in 1915, William Goyen was an avant-garde writer whose prize-winning work has been praised for its purity of prose and damned for its doomed characters—drifting lost souls who cannot communicate with anyone. Educated at Rice University, Goyen became a teacher of drama and novel at the New School of Social Research (1955–60) and later at Columbia University. An editor at McGraw-Hill Book Company, he received the McMurray Bookshop Award for his novel, The House of Breath, *and Guggenheim Fellowships in 1952 and 1954, and a Ford Foundation grant (1963–64). The shorter fiction of his dark vision is collected in* Ghosts and Flesh *(1952); he died in 1983.*

When the friends left behind the boat they loved, they wanted it to bring them back together some day. . . .

FOURTEEN

Bond of Reunion
Carl Carmer

Six good companions vowed one end-of-summer night that they would sometime come back to Pascagoula. They had parted in many another September knowing that in June they would be together again beside Mississippi's gulf waters. Now they were possessed by the youthful mood of "perhaps never again" as their driftwood fire lighted the weathered pillars of the house behind them and the line of shore ahead where dark ripples winked on white sand.

The four girls had been childhood neighbors and close friends in New Orleans. Two of them would be graduating from college in the spring and there would be no more long, sun-drenched vacations at the rambling seaside house of Jane's mother. The two boys were brothers—Bud and Jimmie—and they had grown up in Pascagoula, helping the widowed mother with her pecan orchards and running wild in the moss-hung woods and along the gulf-coast bayous.

"It won't take," said Jimmie, youngest of the party, "unless each one of us leaves something he likes behind him. Then we can be sure there'll be a time when we can all be back to tell each other all that's happened to us since we went away."

"What do you like most of all?" said Bud, laughing, knowing what his brother's answer would be.

"The *Sparrow*," said Jimmie promptly, and all looked for the black outline of his catboat rocking at her mooring just offshore.

"It's funny," said Elizabeth thoughtfully, "but I never think of the *Sparrow* as belonging to anybody. She's more like

163

one of us—the seventh one. We've sailed her over every inch of water in miles and miles. She's taken us swimming every summer day since we were infants. We all love her so much—well, almost as much as Jimmie does."

"I reckon if we leave her here," said Jimmie, "each one of us will be leaving the one thing in Pascagoula he loves most—and she'll make sure we'll be back—all of us—whenever the time comes."

The five who still live say their vow was all but forgotten six years later. They were scattered—as they had known they would be—and the idea of reunion had become impracticable and remote. Elizabeth had married a Yankee and lived in faraway New York. Of the rest of the girls, one was a social worker in Virginia, one was a housewife in Baton Rouge, and Jane, whose mother now lived the year round in Pascagoula, was teaching in a New Orleans grammar school.

Then a letter brought each one of them an almost unbearable sorrow.

"Jimmie has been murdered," wrote Jane's mother. "He took a load of pecans into New Orleans and had to leave the truck in town for repairs. On his way to the railroad station he was hit over the head and robbed by someone who must have seen him receive payment for the load. He lay in the gutter, his skull crushed, for an hour or so before he was picked up. He died, unidentified, in Charity Hospital the next day."

The girls say they were so overcome with grief on reading the letter that the postscript made little impression on their minds, though they all remembered it later:

"The *Sparrow* has gone. On the day Jimmie died, when no one was looking she slipped her moorings and drifted away. Of course Bud has had no time yet to look for her. I notified our friends the Coast Guard and they tell me they have made a thorough search of all bayous but have found no trace of her."

The end of the story came three years later—and not so long ago. Elizabeth went to New Orleans to have the family doctor remove her tonsils. After the operation the social worker came home on her vacation and the Baton Rouge housewife could not resist the opportunity of being with her old friends. Though they had seen each other separately, it was the first time that all four girls had been together since the night on the beach when they had made their vow. On the first day of the week-end they were motoring to Pascagoula.

"It won't be the same without Jimmie," said Elizabeth. "I don't know whether I can stand it."

"You get used to his not being there," said Jane.

Their automobile crossed the bridge over the Pascagoula River into the town at four o'clock. They knew this because they looked at their watches when Elizabeth exclaimed that the new roads had made the trip hours shorter than it used to be. They stopped at a drugstore for a few minutes to buy cigarettes, then drove the two miles out to the old beach house. Jane's mother stood in the doorway and Elizabeth jumped from the car and ran to greet her. She stopped short when she saw that the older woman was pale and wild-eyed, shaking with emotion.

"The *Sparrow* came home," she said. "At four o'clock she drifted in. She's down there bumping the sea-wall now."

As the eyes of the girls followed the direction of her pointing they saw the top of the little mast bobbing up and down. And suddenly Bud was with them, an older Bud whose eyes seemed to burn with grief.

"He told us that the *Sparrow* would see that we all came back," he said, "and now—"

"Don't say it," said Jane sharply, and they were all silent in the shock of their inescapable surmise.

Novelist, folklorist, teacher, and soldier, Carl Carmer is a regional novelist of two regions, Alabama and upstate New York. Born in New York in 1893, he was educated at Hamilton College, served as a 1st Lieutenant in the Field Artillery in World War I, taught English and history at Syracuse University, Rochester University, and the University of Alabama, and worked as a reporter and editor before becoming a full-time writer. Winner of the Children's Book Festival Award for Windfall Fiddle *(1950), he is best known for novels like* Genese Fever *(1941) and* Stars Fell on Alabama *(1934). His best supernatural works appeared in* The Screaming Ghost and Other Stories *(1956). He died in New York in 1976.*

Although Joe Indian believed he didn't believe the Indian religion he was brought up to respect, he had to prove it to himself. . . .

FIFTEEN

Ride the Thunder

Jack Cady

A lot of people who claim not to believe in ghosts will not drive 150 above Mount Vernon. They are wrong. There is nothing there. Nothing with eyes gleaming from the roadside, or flickering as it smoothly glides not quite discernible along the fence rows. I know. I pull it now, although the Lexington route is better with the new sections of interstate complete. I do it because it makes me feel good to know that the going-to-hell old road that carried so many billion tons of trucking is once more clean. The macabre presence that surrounded the road is gone, perhaps fleeing back into smoky valleys in some lost part of the Blue Ridge where haunted fires are said to gleam in great tribal circles and the forest is so thick that no man can make his way through.

Whatever, the road is clean. It can fall into respectable decay under the wheels of farmers bumbling along at 35 in their 53 Chevies.

Or have you driven Kentucky? Have you driven that land that was known as a dark and bloody ground. Because, otherwise you will not know about the mystery that sometimes surrounds those hills, where a mist edges the distant mountain ridges like a memory.

And, you will not know about Joe Indian who used to ride those hills like a curse, booming down out of Indiana or Southern Illinois and bound to Knoxville in an old B-61 that was probably only running because it was a Mack. You would see the rig first on 150 around Vincennes in Indiana. Or, below Louisville on 64, crying its stuttering wail into the wind and lightning of a river valley storm as it ran under the

167

darkness of electricity-charged air. A picture of desolation riding a road between battered fields, the exhaust shooting coal into the fluttering white load that looked like windswept rags. Joe hauled turkeys. Always turkeys and always white ones. When he was downgrade he rode them at seventy plus. Uphill he rode them at whatever speed the Mack would fetch.

That part was all right. Anyone who has pulled poultry will tell you that you have to ride them. They are packed so tight. You always lose a few. The job is to keep an airstream moving through the cages so they will not suffocate.

But the rest of what Joe Indian did was wrong. He was worse than trash. Men can get used to trash, but Joe bothered guys you would swear could not be bothered by anything in the world. Guys who had seen everything. Twenty years on the road, maybe. Twenty years of seeing people broken up by stupidness. Crazy people, torn-up people, drunks. But Joe Indian even bothered guys who had seen all of that. One of the reasons might be that he never drank or did anything. He never cared about anything. He just blew heavy black exhaust into load after load of white turkeys.

The rest of what he did was worse. He hated the load. Not the way any man might want to swear over some particular load. No. He hated every one of those turkeys on every load. Hated it personally the way one man might hate another man. He treated the load in a way that showed how much he despised the easy death that was coming to most of those turkeys—the quick needle thrust up the beak into the brain the way poultry is killed commercially. Fast. Painless. The night I saw him close was only a week before the trouble started.

He came into a stop in Harrodsburg. I was out of Tennessee loaded with a special order of upholstered furniture to way and gone up in Michigan and wondering how the factory had ever caught that order. The boss had looked sad when I left. That made me feel better. If I had to fight tourists all the way up to the lake instead of my usual Cincinnati run, at least he had to stay behind and build sick furniture. When I came into the stop I noticed a North Carolina job, one of those straight thirty or thirty-five footers with the attic. He was out of Hickory. Maybe one of the reasons I stopped was because there would be someone there who had about the same kind of trouble. He turned out to be a dark-haired and serious man, one who was very quiet. He had a load of couches on that were made to sell but never, never to use. We compared junk for a while, then looked through the window to see Joe Indian pull in with a truck that looked like a disease.

The Mack sounded sick, but from the appearance of the load it must have found seventy on the downgrades. The load looked terrible at close hand. Joe had cages that were homemade, built from siding of coal company houses when the mines closed down. They had horizontal slats instead of the vertical dowel rod. All you could say of them was that they were sturdy, because you can see the kind of trouble that sort of cage would cause. A bird would shift a little, get a wing-tip through the slat and the air stream would do the rest. The Mack came in with between seventy-five and a hundred broken wings fluttering along the sides of the crates. I figured that Joe must own the birds. No one was going to ship like that. When the rig stopped, the wings drooped like dead banners. It was hard to take.

"I know him," the driver who was sitting with me said.

"I know of him," I told the guy, "but, nothing good."

"There isn't any, any more," he said quietly and turned from the window. His face seemed tense. He shifted his chair so that he could see both the door and the restaurant counter. "My cousin," he told me.

I was surprised. The conversation kind of ran out of gas. We did not say anything because we seemed waiting for something. It did not happen.

All that happened was that Joe came in looking like his name.

"Is he really Indian?" I asked.

"Half," his cousin said. "The best half if there is any." Then he stopped talking and I watched Joe. He was dressed like anybody else and needed a haircut. His nose had been broken at one time. His knuckles were enlarged and beat-up. He was tall and rough-looking, but there was nothing that you could pin down as unusual in a tough guy except that he wore a hunting knife sheathed and hung on his belt.

The bottom of the sheath rode in his back pocket. The hilt was horn. The knife pushed away from his body when he sat at the counter.

He was quiet. The waitress must have known him from before. She just sat coffee in front of him and moved away. If Joe had seen the driver beside me he gave no indication. Instead he sat rigid, tensed like a man being chased by something. He looked all set to hit, or yell, or kill if anyone had been stupid enough to slap him on the back and say hello. Like an explosion on a hair-trigger. The restaurant was too quiet. I put a dime in the juke and pressed something just for the sound. Outside came the sound of another rig pulling in. Joe Indian finished his coffee, gulping it. Then he started out and stopped before us. He stared down at the guy beside me.

"Why?" the man said. Joe said nothing. "Because a man may come with thunder does not mean that he can ride the thunder," the driver told him. It made no sense. "A man is the thunder," Joe said. His voice sounded like the knife looked. He paused for a moment, then went out. His rig did not pull away for nearly ten minutes. About the time it was in the roadway another driver came in angry and half-scared. He headed for the counter. We waved him over. He came, glad for some attention.

"Jesus," he said.

"An old trick," the guy beside me told him.

"What?" I asked.

"Who is he?" The driver was shaking his head.

"Not a truck driver. Just a guy who happens to own a truck."

"But, how come he did that." The driver's voice sounded shaky.

"Did what?" I asked. They were talking around me.

The first guy, Joe's cousin, turned to me. "Didn't you ever see him trim a load?"

"What!"

"Truck's messy," the other driver said. "That's what he was saying. Messy. Messy." The man looked half sick.

I looked at them still wanting explanation. His cousin told me. "Claims he likes neat cages. Takes that knife and goes around the truck cutting the wings he can reach . . . just enough. Never cuts them off, just enough so they rip off in the air stream."

"Those are live," I said.

"Uh huh."

It made me mad. "One of these days he'll find somebody with about thirty-eight calibers of questions."

"Be shooting around that knife," his cousin told me. "He probably throws better than you could handle a rifle."

"But why . . ." It made no sense.

"A long story," his cousin said, "And I've got to be going." He stood up. "Raised in a coal camp," he told us. "That isn't his real name but his mother was full Indian. His daddy shot coal. Good money. So when Joe was a kid he was raised Indian, trees, plants, animals, mountains, flowers, men . . . all brothers. His ma was religious. When he became 16 he was raised coal miner white. Figure it out." He turned to go.

"Drive careful," I told him, but he was already on his way. Before the summer was out Joe Indian was dead. But by then all of the truck traffic was gone from 150. The guys were routing through Lexington. I did not know at first because of trouble on the Michigan run. Wheel bearings in Sault Ste. Marie to help out the worn compressor in Grand Rapids. Furniture manufacturers run their lousy equipment to death. They expect every cube to run on bicycle maintenance. I damned the rig, but the woods up there were nice with stands of birch that jumped up white and luminous in the headlights. The lake and straits were good. Above Traverse City there were not as many tourists. But, enough. In the end I was pushing hard to get back. When I hit 150 it took me about twenty minutes to realize that I was the only truck on the road. There were cars. I learned later that the thing did not seem to work on cars. By then it had worked on me well enough that I could not have cared less.

Because I started hitting animals. Lots of animals. Possum, cat, rabbit, coon, skunk, mice, even birds and snakes . . . at night . . . with the moon tacked up there behind a thin and swirling cloud cover. The animals started marching, looking up off the road into my lights and running right under the wheels.

Not one of them thumped!

I rode into pack after pack and there was no thump, no crunch, no feeling of the soft body being pressed and torn under the drive axle. They marched from the shoulder into the lights, disappeared under the wheels and it was like running through smoke. At the roadside, even crowding the shoulder, larger eyes gleamed from nebulous shapes that moved slowly back. Not frightened; just like they were letting you through. And you knew that none of them were real. And you knew that your eyes told you they were there. It *was* like running through smoke, but the smoke was in dozens of familiar and now horrible forms. I tried not to look. It did not work. Then I tried looking hard. That worked too well, especially when I cut on the spot to cover the shoulder and saw forms that were not men and were not animals but seemed something of both. Alien. Alien. I was afraid to slow. Things flew at the windshields and bounced off without a splat. It lasted for ten miles. Ordinarily it takes about seventeen minutes to do those ten miles. I did it in eleven or twelve. It seemed like a year. The stop was closed in Harrodsburg. I found an all night diner, played the juke, drank coffee, talked to a waitress who acted like I was trying to pick her up, which would have been a compliment . . . just anything to feel normal. When I went back to the truck I locked the doors and climbed into the sleeper. The truth is I was afraid to go back on that road.

So I tried to sleep instead and lay there seeing that road stretching out like an avenue to nowhere, flanked on each side by trees so that a man thought of a high speed tunnel. Then somewhere between dream and imagination I began to wonder if that road really did end at night. For me. For anybody. I could see in my mind how a man might drive that road and finally come into something like a tunnel, high beams rocketing along walls that first were smooth then changed like the pillared walls of a mine with timber shoring on the sides. But not in the middle. I could see a man driving down, down at sixty or seventy, driving deep towards the center of the earth and knowing that it was a mine. Knowing that there was a rock face at the end of the road but the man unable to get his foot off the pedal. And then the thoughts connected and I knew that Joe Indian was the trouble with the road, but I did not know why or how. I was shaking and cold. In the morning it was not all bad. The movement was still there but it was dimmed out in daylight. You caught it in flashes. I barely made Mount Vernon, where I connected with 25. The trouble stopped there. When I got home I told some lies and took a week off. My place is out beyond LaFollette, where you can live with a little air and woods around you. For awhile I was nearly afraid to go into those woods.

When I returned to the road it was the Cincinnati run all over with an occasional turn to Indianapolis. I used the Lexington route and watched the other guys. They were all keeping quiet. The only people who were talking were the police who were trying to figure out the sudden shift in traffic. Everybody who had been the route figured if they talked about it, everyone else would think they were crazy. You would see a driver you knew and say hello. Then the two of you would sit and talk about the weather. When truckers stop talking about trucks and the road something is wrong.

I saw Joe once below Livingston on 25. His rig looked the same as always. He was driving full out like he was asking to be pulled over. You could run at speed on 150. Not on 25. Maybe he *was* asking for it, kind of hoping it would happen so that he would be pulled off the road for a while. Because a week after that and a month after the trouble started I heard on the grapevine that Joe was dead.

Killed, the word had it, by ramming over a bank on 150 into a stream. Half of his load had drowned. The other half suffocated. Cars had driven past the scene for two or three days, the drivers staring straight down the road like always. No one paid enough attention to see wheel marks that left the road and over the bank.

What else the story said was not good and maybe not true. I tried to dismiss it and kept running 25. The summer was dwindling away into fall, the oak and maple on those hills were beginning to change. I was up from Knoxville one night and saw the North Carolina job sitting in front of a stop. No schedule would have kept me from pulling over. I climbed down and went inside.

For a moment I did not see anyone I recognized, then I looked a second time and saw Joe's cousin. He was changed. He sat at a booth. Alone. He was slumped like an old man. When I walked up he looked at me with eyes that seemed to see past or through me. He motioned me to the other side of the booth. I saw that his hands were shaking.

"What?" I asked him, figuring that he was sick or had just had a close one.

"Do you remember that night?" He asked me. No lead up. Talking like a man who had only one thing on his mind. Like a man who could only talk about one thing.

"Yes," I told him, "and I've heard about Joe." I tried to lie. I could not really say that I was sorry.

"Came With Thunder," his cousin told me. "That was his other name, the one his mother had for him. He was born during an August storm."

I looked at the guy to see if he was kidding. Then I remembered that Joe was killed in August. It made me uneasy.

"I found him," Joe's cousin told me. "Took my car and went looking after he was three days overdue. Because . . . I knew he was driving that road . . . trying to prove something in spite of Hell."

"What? Prove what?"

"Hard to say. I found him hidden half by water, half by trees and the brush that grows up around here. He might have stayed on into the winter if someone hadn't looked." The man's hands were shaking. I told him to wait, walked over and brought back two coffees. When I sat back down he continued.

"It's what I told you. But, it has to be more than that. I've been studying and studying. Something like this . . . always is." He paused and drank the coffee, holding the mug in both hands.

"When we were kids," the driver said, "we practically lived at each other's house. I liked his best. The place was a shack. Hell, my place was a shack. Miners made money then, but it was all scrip. They spent it for everything but what they needed." He paused, thoughtful. Now that he was telling the story he did not seem so nervous.

"Because of his mother," he continued. "She was Indian. Creek maybe but west of Creek country. Or maybe from a northern tribe that drifted down. Not Cherokee because their clans haven't any turkeys for totems or names that I know of . . ."

I was startled. I started to say something.

"Kids don't think to ask about stuff like that," he said. His voice was an apology as if he were wrong for not knowing the name of a tribe.

"Makes no difference anyway," he said. "She was Indian religious and she brought Joe up that way because his old man was either working or drinking. We all three spent a lot of time in the hills talking to the animals, talking to flowers . . ."

"What?"

"They do that. Indians do. They think that life is round like a flower. They think animals are not just animals. They are brothers. Eveything is separate like people."

I still could not believe that he was serious. He saw my look and seemed discouraged, like he had tried to get through to people before and had not had any luck.

"You don't understand," he said. "I mean that dogs are not people, they are dogs. But each dog is important because he has a dog personality as same as a man has a man personality."

"That makes sense," I told him. "I've owned dogs. Some silly. Some serious. Some good. Some bad."

"Yes," he said. "But, most important. When he dies a dog has a dog spirit the same way a man would have a man spirit. That's what Joe was brought up to believe."

"But they kill animals for food," I told him.

"That's true. It's one of the reasons for being an animal . . . or maybe, even a man. When you kill an animal you are supposed to apologize to the animal's spirit and explain you needed meat."

"Oh."

"You don't get it," he said. "I'm not sure I do either but there was a time . . . anyway, it's not such a bad way to think if you look at it close. But the point is Joe believed it all his life. When he got out on his own and saw the world he couldn't believe it any more. You know? A guy acting like that. People cause a lot of trouble being stupid and mean."

"I know."

"But he couldn't quite not believe it either. He had been trained every day since he was born, and I do mean every day."

"Are they that religious?"

"More than any white man I ever knew. Because they live it instead of just believe it. You can see what could happen to a man?"

"Not quite."

"Sure you can. He couldn't live in the camp anymore because the camp was dead when the mines died through this whole region. He had to live outside so he had to change, but a part of him couldn't change . . . Then his mother died. Tuberculosis. She tried Indian remedies and died. But I think she would have anyway."

"And that turned him against it." I could see what the guy was driving at.

"He was proving something," the man told me. "Started buying and hauling the birds. Living hand to mouth. But, I guess everytime he tore one up it was just a little more hate working out of his system."

"A hell of a way to do it."

"That's the worst part. He turned his back on the whole thing, getting revenge. But always, down underneath, he was afraid."

"Why be afraid?" I checked the clock. Then I looked at the man. There was a fine tremble returning to his hands.

"Don't you see," he told me. "He still halfway believed. And if a man could take revenge, animals could take revenge. He was afraid of the animals helping out their brothers." The guy was sweating. He looked at me and there was fear in his eyes. "They do, you know. I'm honest-to-God afraid that they do."

"Why?"

"When he checked out missing I called the seller, then called the process outfit where he sold. He was three days out on a one day run. So I went looking and found him." He watched me. "The guys aren't driving that road."

"Neither am I," I told him. "For that matter, neither are you."

"It's all right now," he said. "There's nothing left on that road. Right outside of Harrodsburg, down that little grade

176

and then take a hook left up the hill, and right after you top it . . ."

"I've driven it."

"Then you begin to meet the start of the hill country. Down around the creek I found him. Fifty feet of truck laid over in the creek and not an ounce of metal showing to the road. Water washing through the cab. Load tipped but a lot of it still tied down. All dead of course."

"A mess."

"Poultry rots quick," was all he said.

"How did it happen?"

"Big animal," he told me. "Big like a cow or a bull or a bear . . . There wasn't any animal around. You know what a front end looks like. Metal to metal doesn't make that kind of dent. Flesh."

"The stream washed it away."

"I doubt. It eddies further down. There hasn't been that much rain. But he hit something . . ."

I was feeling funny. "Listen, I'll tell you the truth. On that road I hit everything. If a cow had shown up I'd have run through it, I guess. Afraid to stop. There wouldn't have been a bump."

"I know," he told me. "But Joe bumped. That's the truth. Hard enough to take him off the road. I've been scared. Wondering. Because what he could not believe I can't believe either. It does not make sense, it does not . . ." He looked at me. His hands were trembling hard.

"I waded to the cab," he said. "Waded out there. Careful of sinks. The smell of the load was terrible. Waded out to the cab hoping it was empty and knowing damned well that it wasn't. And I found him."

"How?"

"Sitting up in the cab sideways with the water swirling around about shoulder height and . . . Listen, maybe you'd better not hear. Maybe you don't want to."

"I didn't wait this long not to hear," I told him.

"Sitting there with the bone handle of the knife tacked to his front where he had found his heart . . . or something, and put it in. Not ain time though. Not in time."

"You mean he was hurt and afraid of drowning?"

"Not a mark on his body except for the knife. Not a break anywhere, but his face . . . sitting there, leaning into that knife and hair all gone, chewed away. Face mostly gone, lips, ears, eyelids all gone. Chewed away, scratched away. I looked, and in the opening that had been his mouth something moved like disappearing down a hole . . . but, in the part of the cab that wasn't submerged there was a thousand footprints, maybe a thousand different animals . . ."

His voice broke. I reached over and steadied him by the shoulder. "What was he stabbing?" the man asked. "I can't figure. Himself, or . . ."

I went to get more coffee for us and tried to make up something that would help him out. One thing I agreed with that he had said. I agreed that I wished he had not told me.

Ohio-born Jack Cady has enjoyed a wide and varied literary career. Newspaper editor and owner, university teacher and visiting professor of English are among his accomplishments. He has won such writing awards as a "First" from the Atlantic Monthly *for his short story, "The Burning" (which also received the Governor's Award and the Iowa Award in 1972) and the National Literary Award for his short story "The Shark" (1971). Much of his work has supernatural themes, such as the ghost novel* The Jonah Watch *(1982) and* The Man Who Could Make Things Vanish *(1983).*

Until Robert Trask realized whose face he had seen, it looked as if he never would learn. . . .

SIXTEEN

Night Court
Mary Elizabeth Counselman

Bob waited, humming to himself in the stifling telephone booth, his collar and tie loosened for comfort in the late August heat, his Panama tilted rakishly over one ear to make room for the instrument. Through it he could hear a succession of female voices: "Garyville calling Oak Grove thuh-ree, tew, niyun, six . . . collect . . ." "Oak Grove. What was that number . . . ?" "Thuh-ree, tew . . ."

He stiffened as a low, sweetly familiar voice joined the chorus:

"Yes, yes! I—I accept the charges . . . Hello? Bob . . . ?"

Instinctively he pressed the phone closer to his mouth, the touch of it conjuring up the feel of cool lips, soft blond hair, and eyes that could melt a steel girder.

"Marian? Sure it's me! . . . Jail? No! No, honey, that's all over. I'm free! Free as a bird, yeah! The judge said it was unavoidable. Told you, didn't I?" He mugged into the phone as though somehow, in this age of speed, she could see as well as hear him across the twenty-odd miles that separated them. "It was the postponement that did it. Then they got this new judge—and guess what? He used to go to school with Dad and Uncle Harry! It was a cinch after that . . . Huh?"

He frowned slightly, listening to the soft voice coming over the wire; the voice he could not wait to hear congratulating him. Only, she wasn't. She was talking to him—he grinned sheepishly—the way Mom talked to Dad sometimes, when he came swooping into the driveway. One drink too many at the country club after his Saturday golf . . .

179

"Say!" he snorted. "Aren't you *glad* I don't have to serve ten to twenty years for manslaughter . . . ?"

"Oh, Bob." There was a sadness in his fiancee's voice, a troubled note. "I . . . I'm glad. Of course I'm glad about it. But . . . it's just that you sound so smug, so . . . That poor old Negro . . ."

"Smug!" He stiffened, holding the phone away slightly as if it had stung him. "Honey . . . how can you say a thing like that! Why, I've done everything I could for his family. Paid his mortgage on that little farm! Carted one of his kids to the hospital *every* week for two months, like . . ." His voice wavered, laden with a genuine regret. "Like the old guy would do himself, I guess, if he was still . . . *Marian!* You think I'm not *sorry* enough; is that it?" he demanded.

There was a little silence over the wire. He could picture her, sitting there quietly in the Marshalls' cheery-chintz living room. Maybe she had her hair pinned back in one of those ridiculous, but oddly attractive, "horse-tails" the teen-agers were wearing this year. Her little cat-face would be tilted up to the lamp, eyes closed, the long fringe of lashes curling up over shadowy lids. Bob fidgeted, wanting miserably to see her expression at that moment.

"Well? Say something!"

The silence was broken by a faint sigh.

"Darling . . . What is there to say? You're so thoughtless! Not callous; I don't mean that. Just . . . *careless!* Bob, you've got to unlearn what they taught you in Korea. You're . . . you're home again, and this is what you've been fighting for, isn't it? For . . . for the people around us to be safe? For life not to be cheap, something to be thrown away just to save a little *time* . . ."

"Say, listen!" He was scowling now, anger hardening his mouth into ugly lines. "I've had enough lectures these past two months—from Dad, from the sheriff, from Uncle Harry. You'd think a guy twenty-two years old, in combat three years and got his feet almost frozen off, didn't know the score! What's the matter with everybody?" Bob's anger was mounting. "Listen! I got a medal last year for killing fourteen North Koreans. For gunning 'em down! Deliberately!

But now, just because I'm driving a little too fast and some old creep can't get his wagon across the highway . . ."

"Bob!"

". . . now, all at once, I'm not a hero, I'm a murderer! I don't know the value of human life! I don't give a hoot how many people I . . ."

"Darling!"

A strangled sob came over the long miles. That stopped him. He gripped the phone, uncertainty in his oddly tip-tilted eyes that had earned him, in service, the nickname of "Gook."

"Darling, you're all mixed up. Bob . . . ? Bob dear, are you listening? If I could just *talk* to you tonight . . . ! What time is it? Oh, it's after *six!* I . . . I don't suppose you could drive over here tonight . . . "

The hard line of his mouth wavered, broke. He grinned.

"No? Who says I can't?" His laughter, young, winged and exultant, floated up. "Baby, I'll burn the road . . . Oops! I mean . . . " He broke off, sheepishly. "No, no; I'll keep 'er under fifty. Honest!" Laughing, he crossed his heart—knowing Marian so well that he knew she would sense the gesture left over from their school days. "There's so much to talk over now," he added eagerly. "Uncle Harry's taking me into the firm. I start peddling real estate for him next week. No kiddin'! And . . . and that little house we looked at . . . It's for sale, all right! Nine hundred down, and . . . ."

"Bob . . . Hurry! Please!" The voice over the wire held, again, the tone he loved, laughing and tender. "But drive carefully. Promise!"

"Sure, sure! Twenty miles, twenty minutes!"

He hung up, chuckling, and strode out into the street. Dusk was falling, the slow Southern dusk that takes its time about folding its dark quilt over the Blue Ridge foothills. With a light, springy step Bob walked to where his blue convertible was parked outside the drugstore, sandwiched between a pickup truck and a sedan full of people. As he climbed under the steering wheel, he heard a boy's piping voice, followed by the shushing monotone of an elder:

"Look! That's Bob Trask! He killed that old Negro last Fourth-o-July . . . "

"Danny, hush! Don't talk so loud! He can hear . . ."

"Benny Olsen told me it's his second bad wreck . . ."

"Danny!"

". . . and that's the third car he's tore up in two years. Boy, you oughta seen that roadster he had! Sideswiped a truck and tore off the whole . . ."

"Hmph! License was never revoked, either! Politics! If his uncle wasn't city commissioner . . ."

Bob's scowl returned, cloudy with anger. People! They made up their own version of how an accident happened. That business with the truck, for instance. Swinging out into the highway just as he had tried to pass! Who could blame him for *that*? Or the fact that, weeks later, the burly driver had happened to die? From a ruptured appendix! The damage suit had been thrown out of court, because nobody could prove the collision had been what caused it to burst.

Backing out of the parking space in a bitter rush, Bob drove the convertible south, out of Gareyville on 31, headed for Oak Grove. Accidents! Anybody could be involved in an accident! Was a guy supposed to be lucky all the time? Or a mind-reader, always clairvoyant about the other driver?

As the white ribbon of the highway unreeled before him, Bob's anger cooled. He smiled a little, settling behind the steering wheel and switching on the radio. Music poured out softly. He leaned back, soothed by its sound and the rush of wind tousling his dark hair.

The law had cleared him of reckless driving; and that was all that counted. The landscape blurred as the sun sank. Bob switched on his headlights, dimmed. There was, at this hour, not much traffic on the Chattanooga Road.

Glancing at his watch, Bob pressed his foot more heavily on the accelerator. Six-fifteen already? Better get to Marian's before that parent of hers insisted on dragging her off to a movie. He chuckled. His only real problem now was to win over Marian's mother, who made no bones of her disapproval of him, ever since his second wreck. *Show me the way a man drives a car, and I'll tell you what he's like inside . . .* " Bob had laughed when Marian had repeated those words. A man could drive, he had pointed out, like an old-maid schoolteacher and still be involved in an accident that was not legally his fault. All right, *two* accidents! A guy could have lousy luck twice, couldn't he? Look at the statistics! Fatal accidents happened every day . . .

Yawning, at peace with himself and the lazy countryside sliding past his car window, Bob let the speedometer climb another ten miles an hour. Sixty-five? He smiled, amused. Marian was such an old grandma about driving fast! After they were married, he would have to teach her, show her. Why, he had had this old boat up to ninety on this same tree-shaded stretch of highway! A driver like himself, a good driver with a good car, had perfect control over his vehicle at any . . .

The child seemed to appear out of nowhere, standing in the center of the road. A little girl in a frilly pink dress, her white face turned up in sudden horror, picked out by the headlights' glare.

Bob's cry was instinctive as he stamped on the brakes, and wrenched at the steering wheel. The car careened wildly, skidding sidewise and striking the child broadside. Then, in a tangle of wheels and canvas top, it rolled into a shallow ditch, miraculously rightside up. Bob felt his head strike something hard—the windshield. It starred out with tiny shimmering cracks, but did not shatter. Darkness rushed over him; the sick black darkness of the unconscious; but through it, sharp as a knifethrust, bringing him back to hazy awareness, was the sound of a child screaming.

"Oh, no ohmygodohgod . . ." Someone was sobbing, whimpering the words aloud. Himself.

Shaking his head blurrily, Bob stumbled from the tilted vehicle and looked about. Blood was running from a cut in his forehead, and his head throbbed with a surging nausea. But, ignoring the pain, he sank to his knee and peered under the car.

She was there. A little girl perhaps five years old. Ditch water matted the soft blond hair and trickled into the half-closed eyes, tiptilted at a pixie-like angle and fringed with long silky lashes. Bob groaned aloud, cramming his knuckles into his squared mouth to check the sob that burst out of him like a gust of desperate wind. She was pinned under a front wheel. Such a lovely little girl, appearing out here, miles from town, dressed as for a party. A sudden thought struck him that he knew this child, that he had seen her somewhere, sometime. On a bus? In a movie lobby . . . ? Where?

He crawled under the car afraid to touch her, afraid not to. She did not stir. Was she dead? Weren't those frilly little organdy ruffles on her small chest moving, ever so faintly . . . ? If he could only get her out from under that wheel! Get the car moving, rush her to a hospital . . . ! Surely, surely there was some spark of life left in that small body . . . !

Bob stood up, reeling, rubbing his eyes furiously as unconsciousness threatened to engulf him again. It was at that moment that he heard the muffled roar of a motorcycle. He whirled. Half in eagerness, half in dread, he saw a shadowy figure approaching down the twilight-misted highway.

The figure on the motorcycle, goggled and uniformed as a state highway patrolman, braked slowly a few feet away. With maddening deliberateness of movement, he dismounted, flipped out a small report-pad, and peered at the convertible, jotting down its license number. Bob beckoned frantically, pointing at the child pinned under the car. But the officer made no move to help him free her; took no notice of her beyond a cursory glance and a curt nod.

Instead, tipping back his cap from an oddly pale face, he rested one booted foot on the rear bumper and beckoned Bob to his side.

"All right, buddy . . ." His voice, Bob noted crazily, was so low that he could scarcely hear it; a whisper, a lip-movement pronouncing sounds that might have been part of the wind soughing in the roadside trees. "Name: Robert Trask? I had orders to be on the lookout for you . . ."

"Orders?" Bob bristled abruptly, caught between anxiety for the child under his car and an instinct for self-preservation. "Now, wait! I've got no record of reckless driving. I . . . I was involved in a couple of accidents; but the charges were dropped . . . Look!" he burst out. "While you're standing here yapping, this child may be . . . Get on that scooter of yours and go phone an ambulance, you! I'll report you for dereliction of duty! . . . Say!" he yelled, as the officer did not move, but went on scribbling in his book. "What kind of man *are* you, anyway? Wasting time booking me, when there still may be time to save this . . . this poor little . . . !"

The white, goggle-obscured face lifted briefly, expressionless as a mask. Bob squirmed under the scrutiny of eyes hidden behind the green glass; saw the lips move . . . and noticed, for the first time, how queerly the traffic officer held his head. His pointed chin was twisted sidewise, meeting the left shoulder. When he looked up, his whole body turned, like a man with a crick in his neck . . .

"What kind of man are *you?*" said the whispering lips. "That's what we have to find out . . . And that's why I got orders to bring you in. *Now!*"

"Bring me in . . . ?" Bob nodded dully. "Oh, you mean I'm under arrest? Sure, sure . . . But the little girl!" He glared, suddenly enraged by the officer's stolid indifference to the crushed form under the car. "Listen, if you don't get on that motorbike and go for help, I . . . I'll knock you out and go myself! Resisting arrest; leaving the scene of an accident . . . Charge me with anything you like! But if there's still time to save her . . ."

The goggled eyes regarded him steadily for a moment. Then, nodding, the officer scribbled something else in his book.

"Time?" the windy whisper said, edged with irony. "Don't waste time, eh? . . . Why don't you speed-demons think about other people *before* you kill them off? Why? *Why?* That's what we want to find out, what we *have* to find out . . . *Come on!*" The whisper lashed out, sibilant as a striking snake. "Let's go, buddy! *Walk!*"

Bob blinked, swayed. The highway patrolman, completely ignoring the small body pinned under the convertible, had strode across the paved road with a peremptory beckoning gesture. He seemed headed for a little byroad that branched off the highway, losing itself among a thick grove of pine trees. It must, Bob decided eagerly, lead to some farmhouse where the officer meant to phone for an ambulance. Staggering, he followed, with a last anxious glance at the tiny form spread-eagled under his car wheel. Where had he seen that little face? *Where* . . . ? Some neighbor's child, visiting out here in the country . . . ?

185

"You . . . you think she's . . . dead?" he blurted, stumbling after the shadowy figure ahead of him. "Is it too late . . . ?"

The officer with the twisted neck half-turned, swiveling his whole body to look back at him.

"That," the whispering voice said, "all depends. Come on, you—snap it up! We got all night, but there's no sense wastin' time! Eh, buddy?" The thin lips curled ironically. "Time! That's the most important thing in the world . . . to them as still have it!"

Swaying dizzily, Bob hurried after him up the winding little byroad. It led, he saw with a growing sense of unease, through a country cemetery . . . Abruptly, he brought up short, peering ahead at a gray gleam through the pines. Why, there was no farmhouse ahead! A fieldstone chapel with a high peaked roof loomed against the dusk, its arched windows gleaming redly in the last glow of the sunset.

"Hey!" he snapped. "What *is* this? Where the hell are you taking me?"

The highway patrolman turned again, swiveling his body instead of his stiff, twisted neck.

"Night court," his whisper trailed back on a thread of wind.

"*Night* court!" Bob halted completely, anger stiffening his resolve not to be railroaded into anything, no matter what he had done to that lovely little girl back there in the ditch. "Say! Is this some kind of a gag? A kangaroo court, is it? You figure on lynching me after you've . . . ?"

He glanced about the lonely graveyard in swift panic, wondering if he could make a dash for it. This was no orderly minion of the law, this crazy deformed figure stalking ahead of him! A crank, maybe? Some joker dressed up as a highway patrolman . . . ? Bob backed away a few steps, glancing left and right. A crazy man, a crackpot . . . ?"

He froze. The officer held a gun leveled at his heart.

"Don't try it!" The whisper cracked like a whiplash. "Come on, bud. You'll get a fair trial in this court—fairer than the likes of you deserve!"

Bob moved forward, helpless to resist. The officer turned his back, almost insolently, and stalked on up the narrow road. At the steps of the chapel he stood aside, however, waving his gun for Bob to open the heavy doors. Swallow-ing on a dry throat, he obeyed—and started violently as the rusty hinges made a sound like a hollow groan.

Then, hesitantly, his heart beginning to hammer with ap-prehension, Bob stepped inside. Groping his way into the darker interior of the chapel, he paused for a moment to let his eyes become accustomed to the gloom. Row on row of hardwood benches faced a raised dais, on which was a pulpit. Here, Bob realized with a chill coursing down his spine, local funeral services were held for those to be buried in the churchyard outside. As he moved forward, his footsteps echoed eerily among the beamed rafters over-head . . .

Then he saw them. People in those long rows of benches! Why, there must be over a hundred of them, seated in silent bunches of twos and threes, facing the pulpit. In a little al-cove, set aside for the choir, Bob saw another, smaller group—and found himself suddenly counting them with a surge of panic. There were twelve in the choir box. Twelve, the number of a jury! Dimly he could see their white faces, with dark hollows for eyes, turning to follow his halting pro-gress down the aisle.

Then, like an echo of a voice, deep and reverberating, someone called his name.

"The defendant will please take the stand . . . !"

Bob stumbled forward, his scalp prickling at the ghostly resemblance of this mock-trial to the one in which he had been acquitted only that morning. As though propelled by unseen hands, he found himself hurrying to a seat beside the pulpit, obviously reserved for one of the elders, but now serving as a witness-stand. He sank into the big chair, peer-ing through the half-darkness in an effort to make out some of the faces around him . . .

Then, abruptly, as the "bailiff" stepped forward to "swear him in," he stifled a cry of horror.

The man had no face. Where his features had been there was a raw, reddish mass. From this horror, somehow, a nightmare slit of mouth formed the words: ". . . to tell the truth, the whole truth, and nothing but the truth, so help you God?"

"I . . . I do," Bob murmured; and compared to the whispered tones of the bailiff, his own voice shocked him with its loudness.

"State your name."

"R-robert Trask . . ."

"Your third offense, isn't it, Mr. Trask?" the judge whispered drily. "A habitual reckless-driver . . ."

Bob was shaking now, caught in the grip of a nameless terror. What was this? Who were all these people, and why had they had him brought here by a motorcycle cop with a twisted . . . ?

He caught his breath again sharply, stifling another cry as the figure of a dignified elderly man became visible behind the pulpit, where before he had been half-shrouded in shadow. Bob blinked at him, sure that his stern white face was familiar—very familiar, not in the haunting way in which that child had seemed known to him, lying there crushed under his car. This man . . .

His head reeled all at once. Of course! Judge Abernathy! Humorous, lenient old Judge Ab, his father's friend, who had served in the Gareyville circuit court . . . Bob gulped. In 1932! Why, he had been only a youngster then! Twenty years would make this man all of ninety-eight years old, if . . . And it was suddenly that *"if"* which made Bob's scalp prickle with uneasiness. *If he were alive.* Judge Ab was *dead!* Wasn't he? Hadn't he heard his mother and dad talking about the old man, years ago; talking in hushed, sorrowful tones about the way he had been killed by a hit-and-run driver who had never been caught?

Bob shook his head, fighting off the wave of dizziness and nausea that was creeping over him again. It was crazy, the way his imagination was running away with him! Either this was not Judge Ab, but some old fellow who vaguely resembled him in this half-light . . . Or it *was* Judge Ab, alive, looking no older than he had twenty-odd years ago, at which time he was supposed to have been killed.

Squinting out across the rows of onlookers, Bob felt a growing sense of unreality. He could just make out, dimly, the features of the people seated in the first two rows of benches. Other faces, pale blurs against the blackness, moved restlessly as he peered at them . . . Bob gasped. His eyes made out things in the semi-gloom that he wished he had not seen. Faces mashed and cut beyond the semblance of a face! Bodies without arms! One girl . . . He swayed in his chair sickly; her shapely form was without a head!

He got a grip on his nerves with a tremendous effort. Of course! It wasn't real; it was all a horrible, perverted sort of practical joke! All these people were tricked up like corpses in a Chamber-of-Commerce "horror" parade. He tried to laugh, but his lips jerked with the effort . . . Then they quivered, sucking in breath.

The "prosecuting attorney" had stepped forward to question him—as, hours ago, he had been questioned by the attorney for Limestone County. Only . . . Bob shut his eyes quickly. It couldn't be! They wouldn't, whoever these people in this lonely chapel might be, they *wouldn't* make up some old Negro to look like the one whose wagon he had . . . had . . .

The figure moved forward, soundlessly. Only someone who had seen him on the morgue slab, where they had taken him after the accident, could have dreamed up that wooly white wig, that wrinkled old black face, and . . . And that gash at his temple, on which now the blood seemed to have dried forever . . .

"Hidy, Cap'm," the figure said in a diffident whisper. "I got to ast you a few questions. Don't lie, now! Dat's de *wust* thing you could do—tell a lie in dis-*yeah* court! . . . 'Bout how fast you figger you was goin' when you run over de girl-baby?"

"I . . . Pretty fast," he blurted. "Sixty-five, maybe seventy an hour."

The man he had killed nodded, frowning. "Yassuh. Dat's about right, sixty-five accordin' to de officer here." He glanced at the patrolman with the twisted neck, who gave a brief, grotesque nod of agreement.

Bob waited sickly. The old Negro—or whoever was dressed up as a dead man—moving toward him, resting his hand on the ornate rail of the chapel pulpit.

"Cap'm . . ." His soft whisper seemed to come from everywhere, rather than from the moving lips in that black face. "Cap'm . . . *why?* How come you was drivin' fifteen miles over the speed limit on this-yeah road? Same road where you run into my wagon . . ."

The listeners in the tiers of pews began to sway all at once, like reeds in the wind. *"Why?"* someone in the rear took up the word, and then another echoed it, until a faint, rhythmic chant rose and fell over the crowded chapel:

"Why? Why? Why? . . . Why? Why? Why?"

"Order!" The "judge," the man who looked like a judge long dead, banged softly with his gavel; or it could have been a shutter banging at one of those arched chapel windows, Bob thought strangely.

The chanting died away. Bob swallowed nervously. For the old Negro was looking up at him expectantly, waiting for an answer to his simple question—the question echoed by those looking and listening from that eery "courtroom." *Why?* Why was he driving so fast? If he could only make up something, some good reason . . .

"I . . . I had a date with my girl," Bob heard his own voice, startling in its volume compared to the whispers around him.

"Yassuh?" The black prosecutor nodded gently. "She was gwine off someplace, so's you had to hurry to catch up wid her? Or else, was she bad-off sick and callin' for you . . . ?"

"I . . . No," Bob said, miserably honest. "No. There wasn't any hurry. I just . . . didn't want to . . ." He gestured futilely. "I wanted to be with her as quick as I could! Be-because I love her . . ." He paused, waiting to hear a titter of mirth ripple over the listeners.

There was no laughter. Only silence, sombre and accusing.

"Yassuh." Again the old Negro nodded his graying head, the head with the gashed temple. "All of us wants to be wid the ones we love. We don't want to waste no time doin' it . . . Only, you got to remember de Lawd give each of us a certain po'tion of time to use. And he don't aim for us to cut off de supply dat belong to somebody else. They got a right to live and love and be happy, too!"

The grave words hit Bob like a hammer blow—or like, he thought oddly, words he had been forming in his own mind, but holding off, not letting himself think because they might hurt. He fidgeted in the massive chair, twisting his hands together in sudden grim realization. Remorse had not, up to this moment, touched him deeply. But now it brought tears welling up, acid-like, to burn his eyes.

"Oh . . . please!" he burst out. "Can't we get this over with, this . . . this crazy mock-trial? I don't know who you are, all you people here. But I know you've . . . you've been incensed because my . . . my folks pulled some wires and got me out of two traffic-accidents that I . . . I should have been punished for! Now I've . . . I've run over a little girl, and you're afraid if I go to regular court-trial, my uncle will get me free again; is that it? That's it, isn't it . . . ?" he lashed out, half-rising. "All this . . . masquerade! Getting yourselves up like . . . like people who are dead . . . ! You're doing it to scare me!" He laughed harshly. "But it doesn't scare me, kid tricks like . . . like . . ."

He broke off, aware of another figure that had moved forward, rising from one of the forward benches. A burly man in overalls, wearing a trucker's cap . . . One big square hand was pressed to his side, and he walked as though in pain. Bob recognized those rugged features with a new shock.

"Kid . . . listen!" His rasping whisper sounded patient, tired. "We ain't here to scare anybody . . . Hell, that's for Hallowe'en parties! The reason we hold court here, night after night, tryin' some thick-skinned jerk who thinks he owns the road . . . Look, we just want t' know *why;* see? Why we had to be killed. Why some nice joe like you, with a girl and a happy future ahead of 'im, can't understand that . . . that *we* had a right to live, too! Me! Just a dumb-lug of a truck jockey, maybe . . . But I was doin' all right. I was gettin' by, raisin' my kids right . . ." The square hand moved from the man's side, gestured briefly and pressed back again.

"I figured to have my fool appendix out, soon as I made my run and got back home that Sunday. Only, you . . . Well, gee! Couldn't you have spared me ten seconds, mac?" the hoarse whisper accused. "Wouldn't you loan me that much of your . . . your precious time, instead of takin' away all of mine? Mine, and this ole darkey's? And to-night . . ."

An angry murmur swept over the onlookers, like a rising wind.

"*Order!*" The gavel banged again, like a muffled heart beat. "The accused is not on trial for previous offenses. Remarks of the defense attorney—who is distinctly out of order—will be stricken from the record. Does the prosecution wish to ask the defendant any more questions to determine the *reason* for the accident?"

The old Negro shook his head, shrugging. "Nawsuh, Jedge. Reckon not."

Bob glanced sidewise at the old man who looked so like Judge Ab. He sucked in a quick breath as the white head turned, revealing a hideously crushed skull matted with some dark brown substance. Hadn't his father said something, years ago, about that hit-and-run driver running a wheel over his old friend's head? Were those . . . were those tire-tread marks on this man's white collar . . . ? Bob ground his teeth. How far would these Hallowe'en mummers go to make their macabre little show realistic . . . ?

But now, to his amazement, the burly man in trucker's garb moved forward, shrugging.

"Okay, Your Honor," his hoarse whisper apologized. "I . . . I know it's too late for justice, not for us here. And if the court appoints me to defend this guy, I'll try . . . Look buddy," his whisper softened. "You have reason to believe your girl was steppin' out on you? That why you was hurryin', jumpin' the speed-limit, to get there before she . . . ? You were out of your head, crazy-jealous?"

Bob glared. "Say!" he snapped. "This is going too far, dragging my financée's name into this . . . this fake trial . . . Go ahead! I'm guilty of reckless driving—three times! I admit it! There was no reason on this earth for me to be speeding, no excuse for running over that . . . that poor little kid! It's . . . it's just that I . . ." His voice broke, "I didn't *see* her! Out here in the middle of nowhere—a child! How was I to know? The highway was clear, and then all at once, there she was right in front of my car . . . But . . . but I *was* going too fast. I deserve to be lynched! Nothing you do to me would be enough . . ."

He crumpled in the chair, stricken with dry sobs of remorse. But fear, terror of this weirdly-made-up congregation, left him slowly, as, looking from the judge to the highway patrolman, from the old Negro to the trucker, he saw only pity in their faces, and a kind of sad bewilderment.

"But—why? Why need it happen?" the elderly judge asked softly, in a stern voice Bob thought he could remember from childhood. "Why does it go on and on? This senseless slaughter! If we could only *understand* . . . ! If we could only make the living understand, and stop and think, before it's too late for . . . another such as we. There is no such thing as an accidental death! Accidents are murders— because someone could have prevented them!"

The white-haired man sighed, like a soft wind blowing through the chapel. The sigh was caught up by others, until it rose and fell like a wailing gust echoing among the rafters.

Bob shivered, hunched in his chair. The hollow eyes of the judge fixed themselves on him, stern but pitying. He hung his head, and buried his face in his hands, smearing blood from the cut on his forehead.

"I . . . I . . . Please! Please don't say any more!" he sobbed. "I guess I just didn't realize, I was too wrapped up in my own selfish . . ." His voice broke. "And now it's too late . . ."

As one, the shadowy figures of the old Negro and the burly truck driver moved together in a kind of grim comradeship. They looked at the judge mutely as though awaiting his decision. The gaunt figure with the crushed skull cleared his throat in a way Bob thought he remembered . . .

"Too late? Yes . . . for these two standing before you. But the dead," his sombre whisper rose like a gust of wind in the dark chapel, "the dead can not punish the living. They are part of the past, and have no control over the present . . . or the future."

"Yet, sometimes," the dark holes of eyes bored into Bob's head sternly, "the dead can guide the living, by giving them a glimpse into the future. The future as it will be . . . unless the living use their power to change it! Do you understand, Robert Trask? Do you understand that you are on trial in this night court, not for the past but for the future . . . ?"

Bob shook his head, bewildered. "The . . . future? I don't understand. I . . ." He glanced up eagerly. "The little girl!

You . . . you mean, she's all right? She isn't dead . . . ? he pressed, hardly daring to hope.

"She is not yet born," the old man whispered quietly. "But one day you will see her, just as you saw her tonight, lying crushed under your careless wheels . . . unless . . ." The whisper changed abruptly; became the dry official voice of a magistrate addressing his prisoner. "It is therefore the judgment of this court that, in view of the defendant's plea of guilty and in view of his extreme youth and of his war record, sentence shall be suspended pending new evidence of criminal behavior in the driver's seat of a motor vehicle. If such new evidence should be brought to the attention of this court, sentence shall be pronounced and the extreme penalty carried out . . . Do you understand, Mr. Trask?" the grave voice repeated. "*The extreme penalty!* . . . Case dismissed."

The gavel banged. Bob nodded dazedly, again burying his face in his hands and shaking with dry sobs. A wave of dizziness swept over him. He felt the big chair tilt, it seemed, and suddenly he was falling, falling forward into a great black vortex that swirled and eddied . . .

Light snatched him back to consciousness, a bright dazzling light that pierced his eyeballs and made him gag with nausea. Hands were pulling at him, lifting him. Then, slowly, he became aware of two figures bending over him: a gnome-like little man with a lantern, and a tall, sunburned young man in the uniform of a highway patrolman. It was not, Bob noted blurrily, the same one, the one with the twisted neck . . . He sat up, blinking.

"My, my, young feller!" The gnome with the lantern was trying to help him up from where he lay on the chapel floor in front of the pulpit. "Nasty lump on your head there! I'm the sexton: live up the road a piece. I heard your car hit the ditch a while ago, and called the highway Patrol. Figgered you was drunk . . ." He sniffed suspiciously, then shrugged. "Don't smell drunk. What happened? You fall asleep at the wheel?"

Bob shut his eyes, groaning. He let himself be helped to one of the front pews and leaned back against it heavily before answering. Better tell the truth now. Get it over with . . .

"The . . . little girl. Pinned under my car—you found her?" He forced out the words sickly. "I . . . didn't see her, but . . . It was my fault. I was . . . driving too fast. Too fast to stop when she stepped out right in front of my . . ."

He broke off, aware that the tall tanned officer was regarding him with marked suspicion.

"What little girl?" he snapped. "There's nobody pinned under your car, buddy! I looked. Your footprints were the only ones leading away from the accident . . . and I traced them here! Besides, you were dripping blood from that cut on you . . . Say! You trying to kid somebody?"

"No, no!" Bob gestured wildly. "Who'd kid about a thing like . . . ? Maybe the other highway patrolman took her away on his motorcycle! He . . . All of them . . . There didn't seem any doubt that she'd been killed instantly. But then, the judge said she . . . she wasn't even born yet! They made me come here, to . . . to try me! In . . . night court, they called it! All of them pretending to be . . . dead people, accident victims. Blood all over them! Mangled . . ." He checked himself, realizing how irrational he sounded. "I fainted," his voice trailed uncertainly. "I guess when they . . . they heard you coming, they all ran away . . ."

"*Night* court?" The officer arched one eyebrow, tipped back his cap, and eyed Bob dubiously. "Say, you *sure* you're sober, buddy? Or maybe you got a concussion . . . There's been nobody here. Not a soul; has there, Pop?"

"Nope." The sexton lifted his lamp positively, causing shadows to dance weirdly over the otherwise empty chapel. A film of dust covered the pews, undisturbed save where Bob himself now sat. "Ain't been nary a soul here since the Wilkins funeral; that was Monday three weeks ago. My, you never saw the like o' flowers . . ."

The highway patrolman gestured him to silence, peering at Bob once more. "What was that you said about another speed cop? There was no report tonight. What was his badge number? You happen to notice?"

Bob shook his head vaguely; then dimly recalled numbers he had seen on a tarnished shield pinned to that shadowy uniform.

"Eight something . . . 84! That was it! And . . . and he had a kind of twisted set to his head . . ."

The officers scowled suddenly, hands on hips. "Sa-ay!" he said in a cold voice. "What're you tryin' to pull? No-body's worn Badge No. 84 since Sam Lacy got killed two years ago. Chasin' a speed-crazy high school kid, who swerved and made him fall off his motor. Broke his neck!" He compressed his lips grimly. "You're tryin' to pull some kind of gag about *that?*"

"No! N-no . . . !" Bob rose shakily to his feet. "I . . . I . . . Maybe I just dreamed it all! That clonk on the head . . ." He laughed all at once, a wild sound, full of hysterical relief. "You're positive there was no little girl pinned under my wheel? No . . . no signs of . . . ?"

He started toward the wide-flung doors of the chapel, re-eling with laughter. But it had all seemed so real! Those nightmare faces, the whispering voices: that macabre trial for a traffic fatality that had never happened anywhere but in his own overwrought imagination . . . !

Still laughing, he climbed into his convertible; found it undamaged by its dive into the ditch, and backed out onto the road again. He waved. Shrugging, grinning, the high-way officer and the old sexton waved back, visible in a yellow-circle of lanternlight.

Bob gunned his motor and roared away. A lone tourist, rounding a curve, swung sharply off the pavement to give him room as he swooped over on the wrong side of the yellow line. Bob blew his horn mockingly, and trod impa-tiently on the accelerator. Marian must be tired of waiting! And the thought of holding her in his arms, laughing with her, telling her about that crazy, dream-trial . . . Dead men! Trying him, the living, for the traffic-death of a child yet to be born! "The extreme penalty!" If not lynching, what would that be? He smiled, amused. Was anything that could happen to a man really "a fate worse than death . . . ?"

Bob's smile froze.

Quite suddenly his foot eased up on the accelerator. His eyes widened, staring ahead at the dark highway illumi-nated by the twin glare of his headlights. Sweat popped out on his cool forehead all at once. Jerkily his hands yanked at the smooth plastic of the steering-wheel, pulling the con-vertible well over to the right side of the highway . . .

In that instant, Bob thought he knew where he had seen the hauntingly familiar features of that lovely little girl lying dead, crushed, under the wheel of his car. "The extreme penalty?" He shuddered, and slowed down, driving more carefully into the darkness ahead. The darkness of the future . . .

For, the child's blond hair and long lashes, he knew with a swift chill of dread, had been a tiny replica of Marian's . . . and the tip-tilted pixy eyes, closed in violent death, had borne a startling resemblance to his own.

A descendant of John Rolfe, who was among the original settlers of the Jamestown Colony in 1607, Mary Elizabeth Counselman was born in Georgia in 1911 and grew up on a honest-to-Scarlett-O'Hara plantation. Educated at the University of Alabama and Monterallo University, she began selling fiction and poetry to such diverse publications as the Saturday Evening Post *and* Jungle Stories. *Her "The Three Marked Pennies" became the most popular story ever to appear in* Weird Tales. *The best of her supernatural writing, including "Night Court," is collected in* Half in Shadow *(Arkham House, 1978).*

When the ghost of Julia Hetman appeared to her husband and son, the results were not what she had hoped. . . .

SEVENTEEN

The Moonlit Road
Ambrose Bierce

I

STATEMENT OF JOEL HETMAN, JR.

I am the most unfortunate of men. Rich, respected, fairly well educated and of sound health—with many other advantages usually valued by those having them and coveted by those who have them not—I sometimes think that I should be less unhappy if they had been denied me, for then the contrast between my outer and my inner life would not be continually demanding a painful attention. In the stress of privation and the need of effort I might sometimes forget the somber secret ever baffling the conjecture that it compels.

I am the only child of Joel and Julia Hetman. The one was a well-to-do country gentleman, the other a beautiful and accomplished woman to whom he was passionately attached with what I now know to have been a jealous and exacting devotion. The family home was a few miles from Nashville, Tennessee, a large, irregularly built dwelling of no particular order of architecture, a little way off the road, in a park of trees and shrubbery.

At the time of which I write I was nineteen years old, a student at Yale. One day I received a telegram from my father of such urgency that in compliance with its unexplained demand I left at once for home. At the railway station in Nashville a distant relative awaited me to apprise me of the reason for my recall: my mother had been bar-

barously murdered—why and by whom none could conjecture, but the circumstances were these:

My father had gone to Nashville, intending to return the next afternoon. Something prevented his accomplishing the business in hand, so he returned on the same night, arriving just before the dawn. In his testimony before the coroner he explained that having no latchkey and not caring to disturb the sleeping servants, he had, with no clearly defined intention, gone round to the rear of the house. As he turned an angle of the building, he heard a sound as of a door gently closed, and saw in the darkness, indistinctly, the figure of a man, which instantly disappeared among the trees of the lawn. A hasty pursuit and brief search of the grounds in the belief that the trespasser was someone secretly visiting a servant proving fruitless, he entered at the unlocked door and mounted the stairs to my mother's chamber. Its door was open, and stepping into black darkness he fell headlong over some heavy object on the floor. I may spare myself the details; it was my poor mother, dead of strangulation by human hands!

Nothing had been taken from the house, the servants had heard no sound, and excepting those terrible fingermarks upon the dead woman's throat—dear God! that I might forget them!—no trace of the assassin was ever found.

I gave up my studies and remained with my father, who, naturally, was greatly changed. Always of a sedate, taciturn disposition, he now fell into so deep a dejection that nothing could hold his attention, yet anything—a footfall, the sudden closing of a door—aroused in him a fitful interest; one might have called it an apprehension. At any small surprise of the senses he would start visibly and sometimes turn pale, then relapse into a melancholy apathy deeper than before. I suppose he was what is called a "nervous wreck." As to me, I was younger then than now—there is much in that. Youth is Gilead, in which is balm for every wound. Ah, that I might again dwell in that enchanted land! Unacquainted with grief, I knew not how to appraise my bereavement; I could not rightly estimate the strength of the stroke.

One night, a few months after the dreadful event, my father and I walked home from the city. The full moon was about three hours above the eastern horizon; the entire countryside had the solemn stillness of a summer night; our footfalls and the ceaseless song of the katydids were the only sound, aloof. Black shadows of bordering trees lay athwart the road, which, in the short reaches between, gleamed a ghostly white. As we approached the gate to our dwelling, whose front was in shadow, and in which no light shone, my father suddenly stopped and clutched my arm, saying, hardly above his breath:

"God! God! what is that?"

"I hear nothing," I replied.

"But see—see!" he said, pointing along the road, directly ahead.

I said: "Nothing is there. Come, Father, let us go in—you are ill."

He had released my arm and was standing rigid and motionless in the center of the illuminated roadway, staring like one bereft of sense. His face in the moonlight showed a pallor and fixity inexpressibly distressing. I pulled gently at his sleeve, but he had forgotten my existence. Presently he began to retire backward, step by step, never for an instant removing his eyes from what he saw, or thought he saw. I turned half round to follow, but stood irresolute. I do not recall any feeling of fear, unless a sudden chill was its physical manifestation. It seemed as if an icy wind had touched my face and enfolded my body from head to foot; I could feel the stir of it in my hair.

At that moment my attention was drawn to a light that suddenly streamed from an upper window of the house: one of the servants, awakened by what mysterious premonition of evil who can say, and in obedience to an impulse that she was never able to name, had lit a lamp. When I turned to look for my father he was gone, and in all the years that have passed no whisper of his fate has come across the borderland of conjecture from the realm of the unknown.

II

STATEMENT OF CASPAR GRATTAN

Today I am said to live; tomorrow, here in this room, will lie a senseless shape of clay that all too long was I. If anyone lift the cloth from the face of that unpleasant thing it will be in gratification of a mere morbid curiosity. Some, doubtless, will go further and inquire, "Who was he?" In this writing I supply the only answer that I am able to make—Caspar Grattan. Surely, that should be enough. The name has served my small need for more than twenty years of a life of unknown length. True, I gave it to myself, but lacking another I had the right. In this world one must have a name; it prevents confusion, even when it does not establish identity. Some, though, are known by numbers, which also seem inadequate distinctions.

One day, for illustration, I was passing along a street of a city, far from here, when I met two men in uniform, one of whom, half pausing and looking curiously into my face, said to his companion, "That man looks like 767." Something in the number seemed familiar and horrible. Moved by an uncontrollable impulse, I sprang into a side street and ran until I fell exhausted in a country lane.

I have never forgotten that number, and always it comes to memory attended by gibbering obscenity, peals of joyless laughter, the clang of iron doors. So I say a name, even if self-bestowed, is better than a number. In the register of the potter's field I shall soon have both. What wealth!

Of him who shall find this paper I must beg a little consideration. It is not the history of my life; the knowledge to write that is denied me. This is only a record of broken and apparently unrelated memories, some of them as distinct and sequent as brilliant beads upon a thread, others remote and strange, having the character of crimson dreams with interspaces blank and black—witch-fires glowing still and red in a great desolation.

Standing upon the shore of eternity, I turn for a last look landward over the course by which I came. There are twenty years of footprints fairly distinct, the impressions of bleeding feet. They lead through poverty and pain, devious and unsure, as of one staggering beneath a burden—

Remote, unfriended, melancholy, slow.

Ah, the poet's prophecy of Me—how admirable, how dreadfully admirable!

Backward beyond the beginning of this *via dolorosa*—this epic of suffering with episodes of sin—I see nothing clearly; it comes out of a cloud. I know that it spans only twenty years, yet I am an old man.

One does not remember one's birth—one has to be told. But with me it was different; life came to me full-handed and dowered me with all my faculties and powers. Of a previous existence I know no more than others, for all have stammering intimations that may be memories and may be dreams. I know only that my first consciousness was of maturity in body and mind—a consciousness accepted without surprise or conjecture. I merely found myself walking in a forest, half-clad, footsore, unutterably weary and hungry. Seeing a farmhouse, I approached and asked for food, which was given me by one who inquired my name. I did not know, yet knew that all had names. Greatly embarrassed, I retreated, and night coming on, lay down in the forest and slept.

The next day I entered a large town which I shall not name. Nor shall I recount further incidents of the life that is now to end—a life of wandering, always and everywhere haunted by an overmastering sense of crime in punishment of wrong and of terror in punishment of crime. Let me see if I can reduce it to narrative.

I seem once to have lived near a great city, a prosperous planter, married to a woman whom I loved and distrusted. We had, it sometimes seems, one child, a youth of brilliant parts and promise. He is at all times a vague figure, never clearly drawn, frequently altogether out of the picture.

One luckless evening it occurred to me to test my wife's fidelity in a vulgar, commonplace way familiar to everyone who has aquaintance with the literature of fact and fiction. I went to the city, telling my wife that I should be absent until the following afternoon. But I returned before daybreak and went to the rear of the house, purposing to enter by a door with which I had secretly so tampered that it would seem to lock, yet not actually fasten. As I approached it, I heard it gently open and close, and saw a man steal away into the darkness. With murder in my heart, I sprang after him, but he had vanished without even the bad luck of identification. Sometimes now I cannot even persuade myself that it was a human being.

Crazed with jealousy and rage, blind and bestial with all the elemental passions of insulted manhood, I entered the house and sprang up the stairs to the door of my wife's chamber. It was closed, but having tampered with its lock also, I easily entered and despite the black darkness soon stood by the side of her bed. My groping hands told me that although disarranged it was unoccupied.

"She is below," I thought, "and terrified by my entrance has evaded me in the darkness of the hall."

With the purpose of seeking her I turned to leave the room, but took a wrong direction—the right one! My foot struck her, cowering in a corner of the room. Instantly my hands were at her throat, stifling a shriek, my knees were upon her struggling body; and there in the darkness, without a word of accusation or reproach, I strangled her till she died!

There ends the dream. I have related it in the past tense, but the present would be the fitter form, for again and again the somber tragedy reenacts itself in my consciousness— over and over I lay the plan, I suffer the confirmation, I redress the wrong. Then all is blank; and afterward the rains beat against the grimy window-panes, or the snows fall upon my scant attire, the wheels rattle in the squalid streets where my life lies in poverty and mean employment. If there is ever sunshine I do not recall it; if there are birds they do not sing.

There is another dream, another vision of the night. I stand among the shadows in a moonlit road. I am aware of another presence, but whose I cannot rightly determine. In the shadow of a great dwelling I catch the gleam of white garments; then the figure of a woman confronts me in the road—my murdered wife! There is death in the face; there are marks upon the throat. The eyes are fixed on mine with an infinite gravity which is not reproach, nor hate, nor menace, nor anything less terrible than recognition. Before this awful apparition I retreat in terror—a terror that is upon me as I write. I can no longer rightly shape the words. See! they—

Now I am calm, but truly there is no more to tell: the incident ends where it began—in darkness and in doubt.

Yes, I am again in control of myself: "the captain of my soul." But that is not respite; it is another stage and phase of expiation. My penance, constant in degree, is mutable in kind: one of its variants is tranquillity. After all, it is only a life-sentence. "To Hell for life"—that is a foolish penalty: the culprit chooses the duration of his punishment. Today my term expires.

To each and all, the peace that was not mine.

III

STATEMENT OF THE LATE JULIA HETMAN, THROUGH THE MEDIUM BAYROLLES

I had retired early and fallen almost immediately into a peaceful sleep, from which I awoke with that indefinable sense of peril which is, I think, a common experience in that other, earlier life. Of its unmeaning character, too, I was entirely persuaded, yet that did not banish it. My husband, Joel Hetman, was away from home; the servants slept in another part of the house. But these were familiar conditions; they had never before distressed me. Nevertheless, the strange terror grew so insupportable that conquering my reluctance to move I sat up and lit the lamp at my bedside. Contrary to my expectation this gave me no relief; the light seemed rather an added danger, for I reflected that it would shine out under the door, disclosing my presence to whatever evil thing might lurk outside. You that are still in the flesh, subject to horrors of the imagination, think what a monstrous fear that must be which seeks in darkness security from malevolent existences of the night. That is to spring to close quarters with an unseen enemy—the strategy of despair!

Extinguishing the lamp I pulled the bedclothing about my head and lay trembling and silent, unable to shriek, forgetful to pray. In this pitiable state I must have lain for what you call hours—with us there are no hours, there is no time.

At last it came—a soft, irregular sound of footfalls on the stairs! They were slow, hesitant, uncertain, as of something that did not see its way; to my disordered reason all the more terrifying for that, as the approach of some blind and mindless malevolence to which is no appeal. I even thought that I must have left the hall lamp burning and the groping of this creature proved it a monster of the night. This was foolish and inconsistent with my previous dread of the light, but what would you have? Fear has no brains; it is an idiot. The dismal witness that it bears and the cowardly counsel that it whispers are unrelated. We know this well, we who have passed into the Realm of Terror, who skulk in eternal dusk among the scenes of our former lives, invisible even to ourselves and one another, yet hiding forlorn in lonely places; yearning for speech with our loved ones, yet dumb, and as fearful of them as they of us. Sometimes the disability is removed, the law suspended: by the deathless power of love or hate we break the spell—we are seen by those whom we would warn, console, or punish. What form we seem to them to bear we know not; we know only that we terrify even those whom we most wish to comfort, and from whom we most crave tenderness and sympathy.

Forgive, I pray you, this inconsequent digression by what was once a woman. You who consult us in this imperfect way—you do not understand. You ask foolish questions about things unknown and things forbidden. Much that we know and could impart in our speech is meaningless in yours. We must communicate with you through a stammering intelligence in that small fraction of our language that you yourselves can speak. You think that we are of another world. No, we have knowledge of no world but yours, though for us it holds no sunlight, no warmth, no music, no laughter, no song of birds, nor any companionship. O God! what a thing it is to be a ghost, cowering and shivering in an altered world, a prey to apprehension and despair!

No, I did not die of fright: the Thing turned and went away. I heard it go down the stairs, hurriedly, I thought, as if itself in sudden fear. Then I rose to call for help. Hardly had my shaking hand found the door-knob when—merciful heaven!—I heard it returning. Its footfalls as it remounted the stairs were rapid, heavy and loud; they shook the house. I fled to an angle of the wall and crouched upon the floor. I tried to pray. I tried to call the name of my dear husband. Then I heard the door thrown open. There was an interval of unconsciousness, and when I revived I felt a strangling clutch upon my throat—felt my arms feebly beating against something that bore me backward—felt my tongue thrusting itself from between my teeth! And then I passed into this life.

No, I have no knowledge of what it was. The sum of what we knew at death is the measure of what we know afterward of all that went before. Of this existence we know many things, but no new light falls upon any page of that; in memory is written all of it that we can read. Here are no heights of truth overlooking the confused landscape of that dubitable domain. We still dwell in the Valley of the Shadow, lurk in its desolate places, peering from brambles and thickets at its mad, malign inhabitants. How should we have new knowledge of that fading past?

What I am about to relate happened on a night. We know when it is night, for then you retire to your houses and we can venture from our places of concealment to move unafraid about our old homes, to look in at the windows, even to enter and gaze upon your faces as you sleep. I had lingered long near the dwelling where I had been so cruelly changed to what I am, as we do while any that we love or hate remain. Vainly I had sought some method of manifestation, some way to make my continued existence and my great love and poignant pity understood by my husband and son. Always if they slept they would wake, or if in my desperation I dared approach them when they were awake, would turn toward me the terrible eyes of the living, frightening me by the glances that I sought from the purpose that I held.

On this night I had searched for them without success, fearing to find them; they were nowhere in the house, nor about the moonlit lawn. For, although the sun is lost to us forever, the moon, full-orbed or slender, remains to us.

Sometimes it shines by night, sometimes by day, but always it rises and sets, as in that other life.

I left the lawn and moved in the white light and silence along the road, aimless and sorrowing. Suddenly I heard the voice of my poor husband in exclamations of astonishment, with that of my son in reassurance and dissuasion; and there by the shadow of a group of trees they stood— near, so near! Their faces were toward me, the eyes of the elder man fixed upon mine. He saw me—at last, at last, he saw me! In the consciousness of that, my terror fled as a cruel dream. The death-spell was broken: Love had conquered Law! Mad with exultation I shouted—I *must* have shouted, "He sees, he sees: he will understand!" Then, controlling myself, I moved forward, smiling and consciously beautiful, to offer myself to his arms, to comfort him with endearments, and, with my son's hand in mine, to speak words that should restore the broken bonds between the living and the dead.

Alas! alas! his face went white with fear, his eyes were as those of a hunted animal. He backed away from me, as I advanced, and at last turned and fled into the wood— whither, it is not given to me to know.

To my poor boy, left doubly desolate, I have never been able to impart a sense of my presence. Soon, he, too, must pass to this Life Invisible and be lost to me forever.

A writer of shadowy horror and mystery stories, Ambrose Bierce was born in Ohio in 1842. He served in the Union Army during the Civil War and worked as a United States Treasury agent during Reconstruction and as a railroad surveyor in the West before beginning his literary career in San Francisco. Bierce attracted national attention with his horrifying stories of the Civil War in Tales of Soldiers and Civilians *(1893) and his tales of the supernatural and early science fiction. He vanished in 1913 in Mexico while serving as a war correspondent during Pancho Villa's rebellion.*